THE #1 BEST

pulls you int
and fiction, sus
Thomas Greani
a tale with style

—NELSON DeMILLE

"RAISING ATLANTIS
is a wonderfully honed cliff-hanger—an outrageous
adventure with a wild dose of the supernatural."

—CLIVE CUSSLER

R A I S I N G
ATLANTIS

THOMAS GREANIAS

POCKET **STAR** BOOKS

New York   London   Toronto   Sydney

This book is a work of fiction. Names, characters, places and incidents are products of the author's imagination or are used fictitiously. Any resemblance to actual events or locales or persons, living or dead, is entirely coincidental.

An *Original* Publication of POCKET BOOKS

 A Pocket Star Book published by
POCKET BOOKS, a division of Simon & Schuster, Inc.
1230 Avenue of the Americas, New York, NY 10020

ISBN 13: 978-1-5011-0701-6
ISBN 10: 1-5011-0701-1

First Pocket Books printing August 2005

10 9 8 7 6 5 4 3 2 1

POCKET STAR BOOKS and colophon are registered trademarks of Simon & Schuster, Inc.

Cover design by Tom Hallman

Manufactured in the United States of America

For information regarding special discounts for bulk purchases, please contact Simon & Schuster Special Sales at 1-800-456-6798 or business@simonandschuster.com

For Laura

ACKNOWLEDGMENTS

For publishing this novel and getting it into the hands of more readers around the world than any first novel deserves, I'm forever grateful to my agent, Simon Lipskar, who believed in me from the beginning, and to my editor, Emily Bestler, who made it all possible.

For making the original eBook a number one best seller on Amazon, I thank the board of Atlantis Interactive, Inc., and the tens of thousands of subscribers to @lantisTV from all seven continents—including Antarctica.

For graciously lending me their ears and world-class expertise in the field of archaeology, I owe a great debt to Thomas R. Pickering, former under secretary of state for political affairs at the U.S. State Department and notable lay archaeologist; Dr. Zahi Hawass, director general of the Giza Pyramids for the Egyptian Supreme Council of Antiquities and the world's foremost authority on the Great Pyramid; and Dr. Kent Weeks, professor of Egyptology at the American University in Cairo and director of the Theban Mapping Project. Thank you, gentlemen, for your time and encouragement. All errors and embellishments in this fiction are mine and mine alone.

For expanding my perspective on the geopolitics of Antarctica, I must also thank the State Department's Bureau of Oceans and International Environmental and Scientific Affairs; the U.S. Center for Polar Archives,

Washington, D.C.; the U.S. Naval Support Force, Antarctica; the crew of the aircraft carrier U.S.S. *Constellation;* and members of various government agencies who have asked not to be named as sources of sensitive information.

For keeping my feet firmly planted on unstable ground, I am indebted to the research of Caltech seismologist Egill Hauksson, Paul Richards of Columbia University's Lamont-Doherty Earth Observatory, and UC Berkeley geophysicist Raymond Jeanloz.

For their imaginative investigations of the lost continent of Atlantis and the astronomical alignments of the Giza Pyramids and temples of South America, I must acknowledge the contributions of authors Rand and Rose Flem-Ath, Colin Wilson, Graham Hancock and Robert Bauval. For enlightenment into the international and spiritual ramifications of archaeology, I am grateful to William J. Fulco, S.J., Ph.D., at Loyola Marymount University in Los Angeles.

For the encouragement to write a damn good novel, I thank my friend and mentor, James N. Frey, the finest fiction coach in America. For telling it like it is, however awful, I thank überpollster and pal George Barna of the Barna Research Group. For all those lunches, I thank Doug Lagerstrom.

Finally, I would like to thank my wife, Laura Greanias, executive news editor of the *Los Angeles Times* and my unofficial editor. Though the earth give way and the mountains fall into the sea, I will always love you.

Nothing lasts long under the same form. I have seen what once was solid earth now changed into sea, and lands created out of what was ocean. Ancient anchors have been found on mountaintops.

—Pythagoras of Samos,
Greek mathematician (c.582–c.507 B.C.)

In a polar region there is continual disposition of ice, which is not symmetrically distributed about the pole. The earth's rotation acts on these unsymmetrically deposited masses, and produces centrifugal momentum that is transmitted to the rigid crust of the earth. The constantly increasing centrifugal momentum produced this way will, when it reaches a certain point, produce a movement of the earth's crust over the rest of the earth's body, and this will displace the polar regions toward the equator.

—Albert Einstein,
U.S. physicist (A.D. 1879–1955)

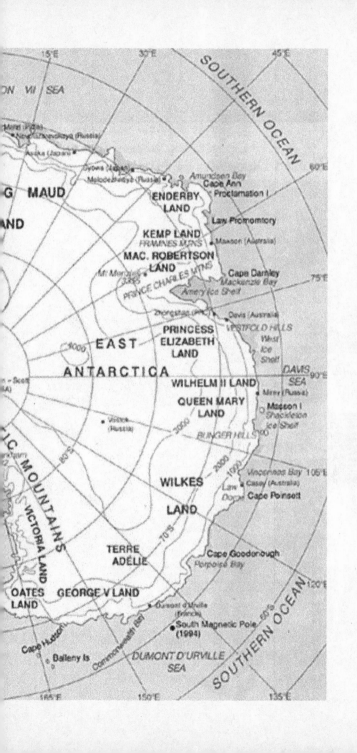

PART ONE

DISCOVERY

1

DISCOVERY MINUS SIX MINUTES
EAST ANTARCTICA

LIEUTENANT COMMANDER TERRANCE DRAKE of the U.S. Naval Support Force, Antarctica, paced behind a snow dune as he waited for the icy gale to pass. He badly needed to take a leak. But that would mean breaking international law.

Drake shivered as a blast of polar air swept swirling sheets of snow across the stark, forsaken wasteland that seemed to stretch forever. Fantastic snow dunes called *sastrugi* rose into the darkness, casting shadows that looked like craters on an alien moonscape. Earth's "last wilderness" was a cold and forbidding netherworld, he thought, a world man was never meant to inhabit.

Drake moved briskly to keep himself warm. He felt the pressure building in his bladder. The Antarctic Treaty had stringent environmental protection protocols, summed up in the rule: "Nothing is put into the environment." That included pissing on the ice. He had been warned by the nature geeks at the National Science Foundation that the nitrogen shock to the environment could last for thousands of years. Instead he was expected to tear open his food rations and use a bag as a urinal. Unfortunately, he didn't pack rations for reconn patrols.

Drake glanced over his shoulder at several white-domed fiberglass huts in the distance. Officially, the mission of the American "research team" was to investigate unusual seismic activity deep beneath the ice pack. Three weeks earlier the vibes from one of those subglacial temblors had sliced an iceberg the size of Rhode Island off the coast of East Antarctica. Floating off on ocean currents at about three miles a day, it would take ten years to drift into warmer waters and melt.

Ten years, thought Drake. That's how far away he was from nowhere. Which meant anything could happen out here and nobody would hear him scream. He pushed the thought out of his mind.

When Drake first signed up for duty in Antarctica back at Port Hueneme, California, an old one-armed civilian cook who slopped on the mystery meat in the officers' mess hall had suggested he read biographies of men like Ernest Shackleton, James Cook, John Franklin and Robert Falcon Scott—Victorian and Edwardian explorers who had trekked to the South Pole for British glory. The cook told him to view this job as a test of endurance, a rite of passage into true manhood. He said a tour in Antarctica would be a love affair—exotic and intoxicating—and that Drake would be changed in some fundamental, almost spiritual way. And just when this hostile paradise had seduced him, he was going to have to leave and hate doing so.

Like hell he would.

From day one he couldn't wait to get off this ice cube.

Especially after learning upon his arrival from his subordinates that it was in Antarctica that the old man back in Port Hueneme had lost his arm to frostbite. Everyone in his unit had been duped by the stupid cook.

Now it was too late for Drake to turn back. He couldn't even return to Port Hueneme if he wanted to. The navy had closed its Antarctica training center there shortly after he arrived in this frozen hell. As for the one-armed cook, he was probably spending his government-funded retirement on the beach, whistling at girls in bikinis. Drake, on the other hand, often woke up with blinding headaches and a dry mouth. Night after night the desertlike air sucked the moisture from his body. Each morning he awoke with all the baggage of a heavy night of binge drinking without the benefits of actually having been drunk.

Drake shoved a bulky glove into his pocket and felt the frozen rabbit's foot his fiancée, Loretta, had given him. Soon it would dangle from the rearview mirror of the red Ford Mustang convertible he was going to buy them for their honeymoon, courtesy of his furloughed pay. He was piling it up down here. There simply was no place to blow it. McMurdo Station, the main U.S. outpost in Antarctica, was 1,500 miles away and offered its two hundred winter denizens an ATM, a coffeehouse, two bars, and a male-female ratio of ten-to-one. Real civilization was 2,500 miles away at "Cheech"—Christchurch, New Zealand. It might as well be Mars.

So who on earth was going to see him paint the snow?

Drake paused. The gale had blown over. At the moment, the katabatic winds were dead calm, the silence awesome. But without warning the winds could come up again and gust to a deafening 200 mph. Such was the unpredictable nature of Antarctica's interior snow deserts.

Now was his chance.

Drake unzipped his freezer suit and relieved himself. The nip of the cold stung like an electric socket. Temperatures threatened to plunge to 130° below tonight, at which point exposed flesh would freeze in less than thirty seconds.

Drake counted down from thirty under his foggy breath. At T minus seven seconds he zipped up his pants, said a brief prayer of thanks, and looked up at the heavens. The three belt stars of the Orion constellation twinkled brightly over the barren, icy surface. The "kings of the East," as he called them, were the only witnesses to his dirty deed. Wise men indeed, he thought with a smile, when suddenly he felt the ice rumble faintly beneath his boots before fading away. Another shaker, he realized. Better get the readings.

Drake turned back toward the white domes of the base, his boots crunching in the snow. The domes should have been a regulation yellow or red or green to attract attention. But attention was not what Uncle Sam wanted. Not when the Antarctic Treaty barred military personnel or equipment on the Peace Continent, except for "research purposes."

Drake's unofficial orders were to take a team of NASA scientists deep into the interior of East Antarctica, charted by air but never on foot. They were to follow a course tracking, of all things, the meridian of Orion's Belt. Upon reaching the epicenter of recent quakes and building the base, the NASA team immediately began taking seismic and echo surveys. Then came the drilling. So the "research" had something to do with the subglacial topography of the ancient landmass two miles beneath the ice.

What NASA hoped to find buried down here Drake couldn't imagine, and General Yeats hadn't told him. Nor could he imagine why the team required weapons and regular reconn patrols. The only conceivable threat to the mission was the United Nations Antarctica Commission (UNACOM) team at Vostok Station, a previously abandoned Russian base that had been reactivated a few weeks earlier. But Vostok Station was almost four hundred miles away, ten hours by ground transport. Why NASA should be so concerned about UNACOM was as much a mystery to Drake as what was under the ice.

Whatever was down there had to be at least twelve thousand years old, Drake figured, because he'd read someplace that's how long ice had covered this frozen hell. And it had to be vital to the national security of the United States of America, or Washington wouldn't risk the cloak-and-dagger routine and the resulting international brouhaha if this illegal expedition were exposed.

The command center was a prefab fiberglass dome with various satellite dishes and antennae pointed to the stars. As he approached the dome, Drake set off loud cracking pops when he passed between several of dozens of metal poles placed around the base. The bone-dry Antarctic air turned a human being into a highly charged ball of static electricity.

The warmth generated by thermal heaters placed beneath the banks of high-tech equipment welcomed Drake as he stepped inside the command center. He had barely closed the thermal hatch when his radio officer waved him over.

Drake stomped over to the console, shaking off snow. He discharged his fingers on a grounded metal strip along the console edges. The sparks stung for a second, but it was less painful than inadvertently zapping the computers and frying their data. "What have you got?"

"Our radio-echo surveys may have triggered something." The radio officer tapped his headset. "It's too regular to be a natural phenomenon."

Drake frowned. "On speaker."

The radio officer flicked a switch. A regular, rhythmic rumble filled the room. Drake lowered his parka hood to reveal a tuft of dark hair standing on end. He tapped the console with a thick finger and cocked his ear. The sound was definitely mechanical in nature.

"It's the UNACOMers," Drake concluded. "They're on to us. That's probably their Hagglunds snow tractors we're picking up." Already Drake could picture the impending international flap. Yeats was going to go ballistic. "How far away, Lieutenant?"

"A mile below, sir," the bewildered radio officer replied.

"Below?" Drake glanced at his lieutenant. The humming grew louder.

One of the overhead lights began to swing. Then rumbling shook the ground beneath their feet, like a distant freight train closing in.

"That's not coming from the speaker," Drake yelled. "Lieutenant, raise Washington on the SAT-COM now!"

"I'm trying, sir." The lieutenant flicked a few switches. "They're not responding."

"Try the alternate frequency," Drake insisted.

"Nothing."

Drake heard a crack and looked up. A small chunk of ice from the ceiling was falling. He stepped out of the way. "And the VHF band?"

The lieutenant shook his head. "Radio blackout."

"Damn!" Drake hurried to the weapons rack, removed an insulated M-16 and moved to the door. "Get those satellite uplinks online!"

Drake opened the hatch and burst outside. The rumbling was deafening. Breathing hard, heaving with each long stride, he ran across the ice to the perimeter of the camp and stopped.

Drake raised his M-16 and scanned the horizon through the nightscope. Nothing, just an eerie green aura highlighted by the swirling polar mist. He kept looking, expecting to soon make out the profile of a dozen UNACOM Hagglunds transports. It felt like a hundred of them. Hell, maybe the Russians were moving in with their monster eighty-ton Kharkovchanka tractors.

The ground shook beneath his feet. He glanced down and saw a jagged shadow slither between his boots. He jumped back with a start. It was a crack in the ice, and it was getting bigger.

He swung his M-16 around and tried to outrun the crack back to the command center. There were shouts all around as the tremors brought panicked soldiers tumbling out of their fiberglass igloos. Then, suddenly, the shouts were silenced by a shriek of wind.

Freezing air rushed overhead like a wind tunnel. The katabatic blast knocked Drake off his feet. He slipped and fell flat onto the ice pack, the back of his head slamming the ground so hard and fast that he instantly lost consciousness.

When Drake came to, the winds had stopped. He lay there for several minutes, then lifted his aching, throbbing head and looked out from beneath his snow-dusted parka hood.

The command center was gone, devoured by a black abyss, a huge crescent chasm about a hundred yards wide. The cold was playing tricks on him, he hoped, because he could swear this abyss stretched out across the ice for almost a mile.

Slowly Drake dragged himself toward the scythelike gorge. He had to find out what happened, who had survived and needed medical attention. In the eerie silence he could hear his freezer suit scrape along the ice, his heart pounding as he reached the edge of the abyss.

Drake peered over and aimed a flashlight into the darkness. The beam bathed the glassy blue-white walls of ice with light and worked its way down.

My God, he thought, this hole has to be at least a mile deep.

Then he saw the bodies and what was left of the base. They were on an ice shelf a few hundred yards down. The navy support personnel in their white freezer suits were hard to distinguish from the broken fiberglass and twisted metal. But he could easily pick out the corpses of the civilian scientists clad in multicolored parkas. One of them was lying on a small ice ledge apart from the others. His head was bent at an obscene angle, framed in a halo of blood.

Drake's mind swirled as he took in the remnants of his first command. He had to check the other bodies to see if anyone was still breathing. He had to find some equipment and get help. He had to do something.

"Can anybody hear me?" Drake called out, his voice cracking in the dry air.

He listened and thought he heard chimes. But the sound turned out to be the frozen limbs of his radio officer, clinking like glass as they dangled over smashed equipment.

He shouted into the wind. "Can anybody hear me?"

There was no response, only a low howl whistling across the abyss.

Drake looked closer and saw some sort of structure protruding from the ice. It wasn't fiberglass or metal or anything from the base camp. It was something solid that almost seemed to glow.

What the hell is that? he thought.

An appalling silence fell across the wasteland. Drake knew then with chilling clarity that he was alone.

Desperately he searched for a satellite phone in the debris. If he could just get a message out, let Washington know what had happened. The hope that help was on the way from McMurdo Station or Amundsen-Scott might give him the strength to set up some sort of shelter, to make it through the night.

A sudden gust shrieked. Drake felt the ground give way beneath him, and he gasped as he plunged headlong into the darkness. He landed with a dull thud on his back and heard a sickening snap. He couldn't move his legs. He tried to call for help but could only hear a hard wheezing from his lungs.

Overhead in the heavens, the three belt stars of Orion hovered in indifferent silence. He noticed a peculiar odor, or rather a change in the quality of the air. Drake could feel his heart pumping in some unfamiliar but regular pattern, like he was losing control of his body. Still, he could move his hands.

His fingers crawled along the ice and grasped his flashlight, which was still on. He scanned the darkness, moving the beam across the translucent wall. It took a moment for his eyes to adjust. He couldn't quite make out what he was looking at. They looked like pieces of coal in the ice. Then he realized they were eyes, the eyes of a little girl staring straight at him out of the icy wall.

He stared back at the face for a moment, a low moan forming at the back of his throat when he finally turned his head away. All around him were hundreds of perfectly preserved human beings, frozen in time, their hands reaching out in desperation across the ages.

Drake opened his mouth to scream, but the rumbling started again and a glistening avalanche of ice shards crashed down upon him.

2
DISCOVERY
PLUS TWENTY-ONE DAYS
NAZCA, PERU

CONRAD YEATS SCALED THE SIDE of the plateau under the blazing Peruvian sun and looked across the plains of Nazca. The empty, endless desert spread out hundreds of feet below him. He could pick out the gigantic figures of the Condor, Monkey, and Spider etched on the baked expanse that resembled the surface of Mars. The famous Nazca Lines, miles long and thousands of years old, were so enormous that they could be seen only from the air. So could the tiny dust cloud swirling in the distance along the Pan-American Highway. It settled near the van he had parked off to the side. Conrad pulled out his binoculars and focused below. Two military jeeps pulled up to the van and eight armed Peruvian soldiers jumped out to inspect it.

Damn, he thought, how did they know where to find me?

The woman on the opposite line adjusted her backpack and said in a flat French accent, "Trouble, Conrad?"

Conrad glanced at her cynical blue eyes framed by a twenty-four-year-old baby-smooth face. Mercedes, the daughter of a French TV mogul, was his producer on *Ancient Riddles of the Universe* and helped him scout locations.

"Not yet." He put the binoculars away. "And it's Doctor Yeats to you."

She pouted. Her ponytail swung out the back of her Diamondbacks baseball cap like an irritated thoroughbred's tail flicking flies. "Doctor Conrad Yeats, world's greatest expert on megalithic architecture," she intoned like the B-actor announcer for their show. "Discarded by academia for his brilliant but unorthodox theories about the origins of human civilization." She paused. "Adored by women the world over."

"Just the lunatics," he told her.

Conrad eyed the last ledge beneath the plateau summit. He was stripped to the waist. Strong and muscular, his body had been toughened and tanned from tackling the hills of the world's geographical and political hot spots. His dark hair was too long, and he had it tied back with a strip of leather. His lean thirty-nine-year-old frame and chiseled features made him look tired and hungry, and he was. Tired of life's journey, hungry for answers.

It was his quest for the origins of human civilization—the "Mother Culture" which had birthed the world's most ancient societies—that drove him to the earth's remote corners. His obsession, a nun once told him, was really his quest for the biological parents who had vanished after his birth. Perhaps, he thought, but at least the ancient Nazcans left him more clues.

Conrad grabbed the ledge overhead and gracefully

pulled himself onto the summit of the flat plateau. He reached down, took hold of Mercedes's dusty hand and pulled her up to the ledge. She fell on top of him, deliberately, and he sprawled on his back. Her playful eyes lingered on his for a moment before she looked over his shoulder and gasped.

The summit was sheered off and leveled with laser-like precision. It was like a giant runway in the sky over the Nazcan desert, and it afforded breathless views of some of the more famous carvings.

Conrad stood up and brushed off the dust while Mercedes relished the view. He hoped she was taking it all in, because her next vista would be from behind bars unless he figured out some way to elude the Peruvians below.

"You have to admit it, Conrad," she said. "This summit could have been a runway."

Conrad smiled. She was trying to get a rise out of him. Since the carvings could only be seen from the air, some of his wacky archaeologist rivals had suggested that the ancient Nazcans had machines that could fly, and that the particular mount on which he and Mercedes stood was once a landing strip for alien spaceships. He wouldn't mind one showing up about now to take him away from Mercedes and the Peruvians. But he needed her. The show was all he had left to fund his research, and she was his only line of credit.

Conrad said, "I suppose it's not enough for me to suggest that aliens who could travel across the stars probably didn't need airstrips?"

"No."

Conrad sighed. It was hard enough for him to contend with the sands of time, foreign governments, and goofball theories in his quest for the origins of human civilization without ancient astronauts eroding what little respect he had left in the academic community.

At one time Conrad was a groundbreaking, postmodern archaeologist. His deconstructionist philosophy was that ancient ruins weren't nearly so important as the information they conveyed about their builders. Such a stand ran against the self-righteous trend toward "preservation" in archaeology, which in Conrad's mind was code for "tourism" and the dollars it brought. He became a maverick in the press, a source of bitter jealousy among his peers, and a thorn in the side of Near East and South American countries who laid claims to the world's greatest archaeological treasures.

Then one day he unearthed dozens of Israelite dwellings from the thirteenth century B.C. near Luxor in Egypt that offered the first physical proof for the biblical account of the Exodus. But the official position of the Egyptian government was that their ancient forefathers never used Hebrew slaves to build the pyramids. Moreover, only the Egyptian government had the right to announce discoveries to the media. Conrad didn't discuss his find with them before talking to the press, thus violating a contract that every archaeologist working in Egypt had to sign before starting a dig. The head of Egypt's Supreme Council of Antiquities called him "a stupid, lazy jerk" and banned him forever from Egypt.

Suddenly, the tables had turned, and Conrad the iconoclast had become Conrad the preservationist, demanding international protection for his "slave city." By the time Egypt allowed camera crews to the site, however, the crumbling foundations of the Israelite dwellings had been bulldozed into oblivion to make way for a military installation. There was nothing left to preserve, only a story nobody believed and a reputation in tatters.

Now he was worse off than ever. Stripped of his stature. Strapped for cash. In the arms of Mercedes and her crazy reality TV show that peddled entertainment, not archaeology, to the masses. He couldn't go back to Egypt, and soon the same would be said of Peru and Bolivia and a growing number of other countries. Only the hard discovery of humanity's Mother Culture could rescue him from ancient astronauts and this purgatory of cheap documentaries and even cheaper flings.

Concern clouded Mercedes's face. "We could blow a whole day just getting a crew up here for your stand-up," she said, brooding for a moment before her face suddenly brightened. "Much better to stick with an aerial from the Cessna and a voice-over."

Conrad said, "That kind of defeats the purpose, Mercedes."

She shot him a quizzical glance. "What are you talking about?"

"I see it's time we perform a sacred ritual," he told her, taking her hand. "One that will unleash a revelation."

Conrad dropped to his knees, pulling her down next to him. Mercedes's eyes sparkled in expectation. "Do as I do, and behold a great mystery."

Mercedes leaned next to him.

"Dig your fingers into the dirt."

They slowly dug their fingers through the hot, black volcanic pebbles into the cool and moist yellow clay beneath.

"This in your script?" she asked. "It's good."

"Just rub the clay between your fingers."

She did, and then lifted a small clump to her nostrils and smelled it, as if to experience some cosmic epiphany.

"There you go," he told her.

A look of confusion crossed her face. "That's it?"

"Don't you see?" he asked. "This ground is too soft for the landing of wheeled aircraft." He smiled at her in triumph. "So much for your fantasies of ancient astronauts."

He should have known his simple, scientific test wouldn't go over well with her. Her eyes turned into steely blue slits of rage. He had seen the transformation before. That's how she got to where she was in TV, that and her father's money.

"The show needs you, Conrad," she said. "You think differently than others. And you've got credentials. Or had them anyway. You're a twenty-first-century astro-archaeologist, or whatever the hell you are. Don't piss it away. I want to keep you on. But I'm under pressure to deliver ratings. So if you don't play ball, I'll get some toothy celebrity who plays an archaeologist on TV to take your place."

"Meaning?"

"Give the freaks who are watching what they want."

"Ancient astronauts?"

A serene smile broke across her baby face as she adopted a fawning, adoring gaze. He groaned inwardly.

"Professor Yeats," she gushed, wrapping her arms around him and kissing him on the mouth.

Unable to extract himself, or come up for air, he kissed her back contemptuously, feeling her body respond to his own self-hatred. Obviously what the French dramatist Molière said about playwrights applied to archaeologists as well. He was the prostitute here. He started out doing it for himself, then for a few friends and universities. Hell, he might as well get paid for it.

Suddenly the wind picked up and Mercedes's ponytail slapped him across the face. A gleaming metallic object hovered in the sky. He shaded his eyes and recognized the shape of a Black Hawk military chopper fitted with side-mounted machine guns.

Mercedes followed his gaze and frowned. "What is it?"

"Trouble."

Conrad reached behind her and pulled out a Glock 9 mm automatic pistol from her backpack. Mercedes's eyes grew wide. "You sent me through customs with that?"

"Nah, I bought it in Lima the other day." He pulled out a loaded clip from his belt pack and rammed it into the butt of the pistol. He tucked the gun behind his belt. "I'll do the talking."

Mercedes, speechless, nodded.

The chopper descended, the wind from its blades kicking up red dust as it touched down. The door slid open, and six U.S. Special Forces soldiers in field uniforms stepped down onto the summit and secured the area before a lanky young officer in a blue USAF flight suit clanked down the metal steps to the ground and walked up to Conrad.

"Doctor Yeats?" the officer said.

Conrad looked him over. He appeared to be about his own age, a slim, easygoing man Conrad had seen somewhere before. He wore a single black leather glove on his left hand. "Who wants to know?"

"NASA, sir. I'm Commander Lundstrom. I work for your father, General Yeats."

Conrad stiffened. "What does he want?"

"The general needs your opinion on a matter of vital interest to the national security."

"I'm sure he does, Commander, but the national interest and my own are two different things."

"Not this time, Doctor Yeats. I understand you're persona non grata at the University of Arizona. And in case you hadn't noticed, an armed goon squad is climbing up that cliff. You can come with me, or you could spend a few weeks in a Peruvian jail cell."

"So you're saying I can either see my father or go to jail? I'll have to think about it."

"Think about this," Lundstrom said. "Your little friend there might not want to bail you out of jail when she discovers you've been using her to smuggle a stolen Egyptian artifact into the country so you can pawn it off to a wanted South American drug lord."

"Another lie coming out of Luxor. Where did I allegedly find this artifact?"

"The Egyptians say you looted it from the National Museum of Baghdad when the city fell to invading American forces during the Iraq war. They got the Iraqis to confirm it. At least that's what they're telling the Peruvians, Bolivians, and anybody else who will listen."

Conrad tried to muffle his rage at the Egyptians even as he calculated the chances of Mercedes letting him rot in prison. He concluded she'd probably let the guards have a few whacks at him before bailing him out.

"Very nice," Conrad told Lundstrom. "But all the same, I'm going to have to pass up this wonderful opportunity." Conrad offered his hand to wish Lundstrom a hearty good-bye.

But the commander didn't budge. "There's more, Doctor Yeats," he said. "We've found what you've spent your whole life looking for."

Conrad looked him in the eye. "My biological parents?"

"Next best thing. You'll be briefed when we get there."

"'There' almost got me killed last time, Commander. Look, why don't you find somebody else?"

"We tried." Lundstrom paused, letting the reality sink in that Conrad wasn't at the top of anybody's list these days. "But if her disappearance is any indication, it appears that Dr. Serghetti has already been retained by another organization to investigate this matter."

"Serena?"

Lundstrom nodded.

Conrad's mind raced through a number of scenarios, all of them entirely unpleasant and utterly thrilling at the same time. Just hearing her name made him come alive. And the thought that he and Serena and his father and the distinct worlds each of them inhabited would for the first time collide made him wonder if the space-time continuum could handle it or if the universe itself would explode.

"This isn't going to end well, Commander, is it?"

"Probably not. But General Yeats is waiting."

"Give me a minute."

Conrad turned and walked back to Mercedes, who had been watching the exchange with a furrowed brow, and kissed her. "I'm sorry, baby. But I'm going to have to go."

"Go?" she said. "Go where?"

"To visit a real ancient astronaut."

Conrad reached into her pack again and took out a gold Nineteenth Dynasty Egyptian statuette of Ramses II, who was pharaoh during the alleged Exodus. He had found it in the slave city, and it was the one thing left in his life that proved he wasn't insane. He gave it to Mercedes.

"Now you never knew where this came from, just in case the nice gentlemen coming over the ledge ask you when they escort you back to Lima."

Mercedes's mouth dropped as Conrad and Lundstrom climbed into the Black Hawk. The door shut and the military chopper lifted up and away.

Conrad looked down at the shrinking plateau. By the time he remembered to wave good-bye to Mercedes, the militia men had reached the summit and the chopper was over the side of a mountain.

Conrad turned to Lundstrom. "So what on earth does my father want with me?"

"It's where on earth," said Lundstrom, throwing him a white polar "freezer" suit. "Catch."

3
DISCOVERY
PLUS TWENTY-TWO DAYS
ACEH, INDONESIA
ROME

DR. SERENA SERGHETTI SKIMMED across the emerald rice fields at two hundred feet, careful to keep the chopper steady. The sun had burst through the dark clouds, but thunder rumbled across the lush mountainside, and rain threatened.

She was nearing the town of Lhokseumawe in the war-torn corner of Indonesia that used to be known as the Dutch West Indies. There were twenty thousand orphans in the province, casualties of a decades-long struggle between Acehnese separatists and the Indonesian military. Now Al Qaeda terrorists had injected themselves into the mix on the Muslim side, making the situation even more combustible. She had to do something to help these children whom the rest of the world had forgotten.

As she passed over the wetlands, she glanced down and saw the sun glint off the oil slick. A discharge from an oil well in Exxon Mobile's Cluster II had contaminated the local paddy fields, orchards, and shrimp farms.

It had happened before, but this leak looked far more threatening. The widows and orphans in the nearby villages of Pu'uk, Nibong Baroh, and Tanjung Krueng Pase would be devastated. They would have to move to another area for at least six months, maybe a year, their sustenance wiped out.

She was about to flick on the onboard remote camera when a voice spoke in her headphone in heavily accented English. "Welcome to Post Thirteen, Sister Serghetti."

She glanced starboard and saw an Indonesian military chopper with side-mounted machine guns keeping pace with her chopper. The voice spoke again. "You are going to land on the helipad in the center of the complex."

She banked to the right and started to climb when four bullets raked the side. "Land immediately," the voice said, "or we'll blow you out of the sky."

She gripped the joystick tightly and dropped lower toward the helipad. She lightly touched down on the platform as soldiers in field greens surrounded her chopper, fingers gripping their M-16s.

They were Kopassus units—Indonesian special forces—based at nearby Camp Rancong, she realized as she stepped out of the chopper with her hands up. Camp Rancong, the site of many reported tortures, was owned by PT Arun, the Indonesian oil giant, which was itself partially owned by Exxon Mobile, which facilitated Post Thirteen.

The wall of Kopassus forces parted as a jeep drove up. It braked to a halt and an officer, a colonel judging by his shoulder boards, stepped out and sauntered over.

He was a slim young man in his twenties. Behind him straggled an older, bloated Caucasian civilian, whom by his lethargic and nervous demeanor Serena guessed to be the site's token American oil executive.

"What is the meaning of this?" she demanded.

"The infamous Sister Serghetti," the colonel said in English. "You speak Acehnese like a native but certainly do not look like one. Your pictures in the media don't do your beauty justice. Nor hint of your skills as a pilot."

"I learned on the job, Colonel," she said dryly in her native Australian accent.

"And which job would that be? You seem to have so many of them."

"Dropping food and medical supplies to the poorest of the poor in Africa and Asia because their governments are so corrupt that U.N. shipments rarely make it to their intended villages," she said. "They either disappear or rot on the docks because the roads are impossible to drive."

"Then you're in the wrong place, ma'am," said the American in a southern drawl. "I'm Lou Hackett, the chief executive for this here operation. You should be in East Timor helping the Catholics stand up to Muslims. What the hell are you doing here in a pure Muslim province like Aceh?"

"Documenting human rights abuses, Mr. Hackett," she said. "God loves Muslims and Acehnese separatists too. Maybe even as much as American businessmen."

"Rights abuses? Not here," Mr. Hackett said. He was keenly watching her chopper, now being stripped by a crew of Kopassus technicians.

Serena looked him in the eye. "You mean that's not

your oil slick out there soaking the local shrimp farms, Mr. Hackett?"

"I would hardly call an innocent accident a human rights violation."

Mr. Hackett wiped the sweat from his brow with an old, worn handkerchief. She noted a logo on it. It was the seal of the president of the United States. A trinket, no doubt, from some campaign fund-raiser.

"So your company didn't build the military barracks here at Post Thirteen where victims of human rights abuses claim to have been interrogated?" she went on, glancing at the Indonesian colonel. "Or provide heavy equipment so the military could dig mass graves for its victims at Sentang Hill and Tengkorak Hill?"

Mr. Hackett looked at her as if she were the problem and not his oil discharge. "What do you want, Sister Serghetti?"

The Indonesian colonel answered for her. "She wants to do to Exxon Mobile and PT Arun what she did to Denok Coffee in East Timor."

"You mean break the grip of a cartel controlled by the Indonesian military and let the people sell their goods at market prices?" she asked. "Hmm, now that's a thought."

Hackett had clearly had enough. "Hell, if the East Timorese want to be slaves for Starbucks, that's their business, Sister. But when you threw the military out of the coffee business, they took a special interest in mine."

"Here's another thought, Sister Serghetti," the colonel said, handing her a sheet of paper. It was a fax. "Leave."

She looked the fax over twice. It was from Bishop Carlos in Jakarta, winner of the 1996 Nobel Peace Prize.

It said she was urgently needed in Rome. "The pope wants to see me?"

"The pope, the pontiff, the Holy See, whatever the hell you call him," said Mr. Hackett. "I'm a Baptist myself. Just call yourself lucky to walk out of here."

She turned toward her chopper in time to see several soldiers carry away the dismantled cameras from its belly.

"And the people of Aceh?" she pressed Mr. Hackett as the colonel nudged her toward his jeep. He was apparently keeping her chopper. "You can't pretend this isn't happening."

"I don't have to pretend anything, Sister," Mr. Hackett said, waving her a smug good-bye. "If it ain't in the news, it ain't happening."

Twenty-four hours later, Serena leaned back in the rear of the unmarked black sedan as old Benito nudged it through the angry protesters and camera crews in Saint Peter's Square. That she could arouse such strong sentiments seemed impossible. And yet the demonstrations outside were meant for her.

She was only twenty-seven, but she had already made a lifetime's worth of enemies in the petroleum, timber, and biomedical industries or anyone who put profit ahead of people, animals, or the environment. But her efforts inadvertently left a few of the people she had hoped to save jobless. Well, maybe more than a few, judging by the mob outside.

Dressed in her trademark urban uniform of an Armani suit and high-top sneakers, she hardly looked the part of a former Carmelite nun. But that was the point. As "Mother Earth" she made headlines, and with recognition came influence. How else would the style-over-substance media, the secular world, and, ultimately, Rome take her seriously?

God was another matter. She wasn't sure what he thought of her, and she wasn't sure she wanted to know.

Serena stared through the rain-streaked window. Vatican police were pushing back the crowds and paparazzi. Then, out of nowhere, *whap!*—there was a loud crack, and she jumped. A protester had managed to slap his placard against the glass: FIND ANOTHER PLANET, MOTHER EARTH.

"I think they miss you, *signorina*," said the driver in his best English.

"They mean well, Benito," she replied, looking at the throngs with compassion. She could have addressed him in Italian, French, German, or a dozen other languages. But she recalled Benito wanted to work on his English. "They're scared. They have families to feed. They need someone to blame for their unemployment. It might as well be me."

"Only you, *signorina*, would bless your enemies."

"There are no enemies, Benito, just misunderstandings."

"Spoken like a true saint," he said as they left the mob at the gate and curved along a winding drive.

"So, Benito, do you know why His Holiness has summoned me to the Eternal City for a private audience?" she asked, casually smoothing her pants, trying to hide the anxiety building inside.

"With you it is always hard to say." Benito smiled in the mirror, revealing a gold tooth. "So much trouble to choose from."

Too true, she thought. When she was a nun, Serena was usually at odds with her superiors, an outcast within her own church. Even the pope, an ally, once told *Newsweek* magazine, "Sister Serghetti is doing what God would do if only he knew the facts." That made good copy, but she knew that no court of public opinion could protect her within these gates.

Born of an illicit affair between a Catholic priest and a housemaid outside Sydney, Serena Serghetti was filled with shame as a little girl. She grew up among sordid whispers and hated her father, who denied his patrimony to the end and died a drunken fraud. She silenced the whispers by pledging sexual purity at age twelve, excelling in her study of linguistics and, most shocking of all, joining a convent at sixteen. Within a few years she had become a living example of redemption to the Church and a walking, talking reminder to humanity of its ecological sins.

It was a good run while it lasted, which was almost seven years. Then, a few months after a personal crisis in South America, she returned to Rome for moral guidance and instead discovered that the Vatican was refusing to pay its water bills, hiding behind its status as a sovereign state and the obscure Lateran Treaty of 1929, which established that Italy must provide water for the 107-acre enclave for free but made no provision for sewage fees. "We neither render unto Caesar the taxes we owe Caesar, nor render unto God the honor we owe God as his stewards of Creation," she said when she publicly renounced her vows and embraced the environment.

It was then that the media dubbed her "Mother Earth." Ever since, she couldn't stop people from addressing her as such, or as "Sister Serghetti." She was probably the world's most famous former nun. Like the late Princess Diana before she died, Serena was no longer part of the church's royal family and yet somehow had become its "Queen of Hearts."

Swiss Guards in crimson uniforms snapped to attention as her sedan pulled up to the entrance of the Governorate. Before Benito could open the door for her and offer her an umbrella, she was already climbing the steps in the rain at a leisurely pace, her sneakers splashing in the puddles as she looked up to the sky and enjoyed feeling a few drops on her face. If her history with the Vatican was any guide, this was probably the last breath of fresh air she'd be enjoying for a while. A guard smiled as she passed through the open door.

It was warm and dry inside, and the young Jesuit waiting for her recognized her instantly. "Sister Serghetti," he said cordially. "This way."

There was the buzz of activity from various offices as she followed the Jesuit down a maze of bureaucratic corridors to an old service elevator. To think it all started with a poor Jewish carpenter, she thought as they stepped inside and the door closed.

She wondered if Jesus would find himself as much a stranger in his church as she did.

She frowned at her reflection in the metal doors of the elevator and smoothed out her lapels. So ironic she should care, she realized, knowing the silk and wool were spun by the sweat of some poor child in a Far East factory to feed the global consumer market. The clothes and the image they projected represented everything she hated, but she used them to raise money and consciousness in a media age more obsessed with a former nun's look than her charity. So be it.

But would Jesus wear Armani?

It was an insane world, and she often wondered why God had either made it that way or had simply allowed it to mutate into such an abomination. She certainly would have managed things differently.

The office she was looking for was on the fifth floor and belonged to the Vatican's intelligence chief, a cardinal named Tucci. It was Tucci who would brief her and escort her to the papal residence for her private audience with the pope. But the cardinal was nowhere to be found. Still, the young Jesuit ushered her inside.

The study seemed older and more elegant than befit Tucci's reputation. Medieval paintings and ancient maps graced the walls rather than the more modern, contemporary art that Tucci was reputed to favor.

Older and more elegant still was the man seated in a high-back leather chair with a pair of seventeenth-century Bleau globes on either side. The white regalia with the gold lace at the throat perfectly offset the silver hair. He looked every bit an urbane, handsome man of the faith, and the eyes, when he glanced up from the file he was reading, were clear and intelligent.

"Sister Serghetti," said her Jesuit escort, "His Holiness."

The pope, whom Serena instantly recognized, needed

no introduction. "Your Holiness," she said as the Jesuit closed the door behind her.

The great man seemed neither stern nor beatific to her. Rather, he radiated the businesslike aura of a CEO. Except that this corporation was not traded daily on the exchanges of New York, London, and Tokyo. Nor did it forecast its future growth in terms of quarters, years, or even decades. This enterprise was in its third millennium and measured its progress in terms of eternity.

"Sister Serghetti." The pope's voice conveyed genuine affection as he gestured to a chair. "It's been too long."

Surprised and suspicious, she sank into a leather chair while he looked over her Vatican file.

"Ozone protests outside the United Nations headquarters in New York," he read aloud in a quiet yet resonant voice. "Global boycotts against biomedical companies. Even your Internet home page registers more hits than mine."

He looked up from the file in his lap with quick, bright eyes. "I sometimes wonder if your obsession to save Earth from the human race is motivated by some deeper, inner desire to redeem yourself."

She shifted in her leather seat. It felt hard and uncomfortable. "Redeem me from what, Your Holiness?"

"I was acquainted with your father, you know."

She knew.

"Indeed," the pope went on, "I was the bishop to whom he came for advice upon learning that your mother was pregnant."

This Serena did not know.

"He wanted your mother to have an abortion."

"That doesn't surprise me," she said, scarcely able to contain the bitterness in her voice. "So I take it you advised him not to?"

"I told him that God can make something beautiful even out of the ugliest of circumstances."

"I see."

Serena didn't know if the pope expected her to thank him for saving her life or was simply relating historical events. He was studying her, she could tell. Not with judgment, nor pity. He simply looked curious.

"There's something I've always wanted to ask you, Serena," the pope said, and Serena leaned forward. "Considering the circumstances of your birth, how can you love Jesus?"

"Because of the circumstances surrounding his birth," she replied. "If Jesus was not the one, true Son of God, then he was a bastard and his mother, Mary, a whore. He could have given in to hatred. Instead he chose love, and today the Church calls him Savior."

The pope nodded. "At least you agree the job is taken."

"Indeed, Your Holiness," she replied. "He gave you a pretty good job too."

He smiled. "A job which I'm told you once said you'd like to have someday."

Serena shrugged. "It's overrated."

"True," the pope replied and eyed her keenly, "and rather unattainable for former nuns who have repeated the sins of their fathers."

Suddenly her camera-ready facade crumbled and she felt naked. With this pope, a private audience was more like a therapy session than an inquisition, and she had run out of righteous indignation to prop herself up.

"I'm not sure I understand what His Holiness is getting at," she stammered, wondering just how much the pope knew. Then, remembering the fate of those who so often underestimated him, she decided it was best to come clean before she further embarrassed herself. "There was one close call, Your Holiness," she said. "But you forget I'm no longer a nun nor bound by my vows. You'll be happy to know, however, that I plan to remain celibate until I marry, which I suspect will be never."

The pope said, "But why then did—"

"Just because we did not physically consummate our relationship did not mean we did not emotionally," Serena explained. "And my feelings left me no room for doubt that I could not be a bride of Christ in this life and burn with passion for a man. Not without being a hypocrite like my father. So if you're thinking of using this issue to undermine my credibility—"

"Nonsense," said the pontiff. "Doctor Yeats's name came up in an intelligence report, that's all."

"Conrad?" she asked, awed by the Vatican's operatives.

"Yes," said the pope. "I understand you met him in Bolivia during your former life as our most promising linguist."

She leaned back in her chair. Perhaps a manuscript had turned up that required translation. Perhaps His Holiness had a job for her. She began to breathe easier. She was relieved to escape the subject of her celibacy, but the pope's reference to Conrad had aroused her curiosity.

"That's right. I was working with the Aymara tribe of the Andes."

"An understatement," the pope said. "You used the Aymara language to develop translation software for the Earth Summit at the United Nations. This you accomplished with a personal laptop computer after experts at a dozen European universities using supercomputers failed."

"I wasn't the first," she explained. "A Bolivian mathematician, Ivan Guzman de Rojas, did it in the 1980s. Aymara can be used as an intermediate language for simultaneously translating English into several other languages."

"Six languages only," the pope said. "But you've apparently unlocked a more universal application."

"The only secret to my system is the rigid, logical structure of Aymara itself," she said, her confidence returning in force. "It's ideal for transformation into computer algorithm. Its syntactical rules can be spelled out in the kind of algebraic shorthand that computers understand."

"I find this all quite fascinating," he told her. "As close to hearing the whisperings of God as man may likely get in this life. Whyever did you give it up?"

"I still make a contribution now and then, Your Holiness."

"Indeed, you are quite the freelancer. Not only are you Mother Earth and an official goodwill ambassador for the United Nations, but I see you worked on the *Latinatis Nova et Vetera*," he said, referring to the Vatican's "new look" Latin dictionary designed by traditionalists to catapult the ancient tongue of Virgil into the new millennium.

"That's right, Your Holiness."

"So we have you to thank for coining the Latin terms for *disco* and *cover girl*—*caberna discothecaria* and *terioris paginae puello.*"

"Don't forget *pilamalleus super glaciem.*"

The pope had to pause to make the mental translation. "Ice hockey?"

"Very good, Your Holiness."

The pope smiled in spite of himself before growing very serious. "And what do you call a man like Doctor Yeats?"

"A *sordidissimi hominess*," she said, not skipping a beat. "One of the dregs of society."

The pope nodded sadly. "Is this man the reason why you chose to suppress your gifts, leave the Church, and run off to become Mother Earth?"

"Conrad had nothing to do with my decision to devote my energies to protecting the environment," she said, sounding more defensive than she intended.

The pope nodded. "But you met him while working with the Aymara tribe in Bolivia, shortly before you left the Church. What do you know about him?"

She paused. There was so much she could say. But she would stick with the essentials. "He's a thief and a liar and the greatest, most dangerous archaeologist I've ever met."

"Dangerous?"

"He has no respect for antiquity," she said. "He believes the information gleaned from a discovery is more important than the discovery itself. Consequently, in his haste to uncover a virgin find he will often destroy the integrity of the site, future generations be damned."

The pope nodded. "That would explain why the Egyptian Supreme Council of Antiquities has forbidden him from ever setting foot in Luxor again."

"Actually, the council's director general lost some money to Conrad in a card game when they were consulting on the Luxor Casino in Las Vegas," Serena said. "The way I heard it was that he paid Conrad off with a Nineteenth Dynasty statuette and that Conrad's been trying to unload it on the black market ever since. He needs the money, badly I understand, in order to keep going. It would make a wonderful addition to our collection here if you're interested."

The pope frowned to show he did not appreciate her dry sense of humor. "And I take it the story is the same in Bolivia, where Doctor Yeats was barred a year after your encounter with him?"

Serena shrugged. "Let's just say that he found a certain *generalissimo's* daughter to be more interesting than the ruins."

"Do I detect a note of jealousy?"

Serena laughed. "There will always be another woman for a schemer like Conrad. The treasures of antiquity, on the other hand, belong to all of us."

"I'm getting a clear picture. Whatever did you see in him, Sister Serghetti, if I may ask?"

"He's the most honest soul I've ever met."

"You said he was a liar."

"That's part of his honesty. What does he have to do with all this?"

"Nothing, really, beyond his effect on you," the pope said, but Serena felt there was more to it than that.

"But what am I to you, Your Holiness, if you'll forgive my asking? I'm no longer a Catholic nun or Vatican linguist or any other official appendage of the Church."

"Be it as a nun or lay specialist we contract with, Serena, you'll always be part of the Church and the Church will always be part of you. Whether you or I like it or not. Right now, our chief interest is in how the Aymara came up with their language. It's so pure that some of your colleagues suspect it didn't just evolve like other languages but was actually constructed from scratch."

She nodded. "An intellectual achievement you'd hardly expect from simple farmers."

"Exactly," said the pope. "Tell me, Sister Serghetti, where did the Aymara come from?"

"The earliest Aymara myth tells of strange events at Lake Titicaca after the Great Flood," she explained. "Strangers attempted to build a city on the lake."

"Tiahuanaco," said the pope, "with its great Temple of the Sun."

"Your Holiness is well informed," Serena said. "The abandoned city is said to have originally been populated by people from 'Aztlan,' the lost island paradise of the Aztecs."

"A lost island paradise. Interesting."

"A common pre-Flood myth, Your Holiness. Many myths speak of the lost island paradise and have a deluge motif. There's the ancient Greek philosopher Plato's account of Atlantis, of course. And the Haida and Sumerian, too, share a similar story of their origins."

The pope nodded. "And yet it's hard to imagine two more different cultures than the Haida and Sumerian, one in the rainy Pacific Northwest of America and the other in the arid desert of Iraq."

"That a common myth of some event is shared by disparate cultures isn't evidence that such an event took place," she said dryly, the academic in her taking over. "Fossil records and geology, for example, tell us there was a flood, an ice age, and the like. But whether there was a Noah who built an ark, and whether he was Asian, African, or Caucasian, is pure speculation. And there's certainly no proof of any island paradise."

"Then what do you make of these similar stories?"

"I've always considered them to be indicators of the universality of the human intellect."

"So to you Genesis is nothing more than a metaphor?"

She had forgotten the pope's habit of turning their every conversation back to her faith. She slowly nodded. "Yes, I suppose so."

"You don't seem so sure."

"Yes, definitely." There, she said it. He had forced her to say it.

"And the Church itself? Just a good idea gone bad?"

"Like all human institutions, the Church on earth is corrupt," she said. "But it's given us hospitals, orphanages, and hope for the human race. Without it civilization would sink into a moral abyss."

"I'm glad to hear you say that." There was tenderness in the pope's eyes and a tone of disbelief in his voice as he asked her, of all people: "Sister Serghetti, I want you to pause and consider whether the Spirit is prompting you in your heart to take on a holy mission that may truly make you worthy of your calling as Mother Earth."

The only thing the Spirit was telling her was that something wasn't right here. She had rebuked the Vatican and left the Church. Now the pope was asking her to be his official emissary. "What sort of mission?"

"I understand you are an official observer and adviser to the implementation of the international Antarctic Treaty."

"I'm an adviser for the Treaty's Committee for Environmental Protection," she explained. "But I represent Australia, Your Holiness, not the Church."

The pope nodded and tapped his fingers on his armrest. "You know those recent news reports about seismic activity in Antarctica?"

"Of course, Your Holiness. A glacier the size of Delaware was sliced off last month after the most recent temblor. And another one the size of Rhode Island broke away before that. In short order it may all add up to the equivalent of the entire eastern seaboard of the United States."

"What if I told you that our intelligence sources have located a secret and illegal American military expedition in Antarctica, in land claimed by your own homeland, Australia?"

"I'd say the Americans are violating the Madrid Protocol of 1991, which established Antarctica as a zone of peace reserved exclusively for scientific research purposes. All military activities are banned from the continent." Serena leaned forward. "How do you know this?"

"Three U.S. spy satellites recently disappeared from orbit," he explained.

She blinked. How long had the Vatican been in the business of tracking foreign spy satellites? "Perhaps they stopped working or were deliberately destroyed," she suggested.

"Dead U.S. satellites are usually left in orbit," the pope explained as easily as if he were discussing New Testament hermeneutics. "And if one satellite, let alone three, had died, congressional overseers would have made more noise than Vatican II. That did not happen."

"I'm afraid we've stepped beyond my area of expertise, Your Holiness," Serena said. "What are you suggesting happened?"

"The satellites were placed into orbits that would move more slowly across the skies than other high-altitude spy cameras, giving them more time to photograph targets."

"Targets?"

"Military strikes are usually mounted immediately before a spy satellite passes overhead, so they can record the damage before the enemy has time to cover it up. But after the latest seismic activity in Antarctica, no known spy satellites would have passed over the affected area. That suggests that one or more of the missing satellites may be watching."

"Are you suggesting the U.S. military is actually causing those seismic shock waves?" she asked.

"That's what I want you to find out."

She sat back in her chair. The pope had no reason to lie to her. But there must be more to this than what he was telling her. Why else would the Holy See take such profound interest in an empty continent populated by more penguins than Catholics?

"Is there something more you want to tell me?" she asked. "Does it involve Doctor Yeats?"

The pope nodded. "He apparently has joined the American expedition in Antarctica."

So it did involve Conrad, she realized, but in an altogether unexpected scenario. "Why would the American military need an archaeologist?"

The pope said nothing, and Serena knew in an instant that the Vatican was enlisting her help as a linguist and not as an environmentalist. All of which meant the Americans had found something in Antarctica. Something that would require the expertise of archaeologists and linguists. Something that had clearly rattled the Vatican. The only reason the pope was reaching out to her was because he had no other choice. The Americans obviously weren't consulting with him. But perhaps they should have, she suddenly realized.

"You have something to show me, don't you, Your Holiness?"

"I do." With gnarled fingers, the pope unfurled a copy of a medieval map across his desk. It was dated 1513. "This was discovered in the old Imperial Palace in Constantinople in 1929. It belonged to a Turkish admiral."

"Admiral Piri Reis," she said. "It's the Piri Reis World Map."

"You recognize it, then." The pope nodded. "So you've undoubtedly seen this too."

He passed across an old U.S. Air Force report. It was dated July 6, 1960, code-named Project Blue Book.

"No, I haven't," she said with interest, picking up the slim report. "Since when does the Vatican have access to classified American military intelligence?"

"This old report?" the pope said. "I'd hardly call it classified. But the addendum is."

She thumbed through the pages, written by the chief of the cartographic section of Westover Air Force Base in Massachusetts. The conclusion of Air Force officials was that the Antarctic portions of the Piri Reis World Map did accurately depict the Princess Martha Coast of Antarctica and the Palmer Peninsula.

Her eyes lingered on the last page, where Lieutenant Colonel Harold Z. Ohlmeyer of the Eighth Reconnaissance Technical Squadron wrote:

The geographical detail shown in the lower part of the map agrees very remarkably with the results of the seismic profile made across the top of the ice cap by the Swedish-British-Norwegian Antarctic Expedition of 1949. This indicates *the coastline had been mapped before it was covered by the ice cap.* The ice cap in this region is now about a mile thick. We have no idea how the data on this map can be reconciled with the supposed state of geographic knowledge in 1513.

Then came the Pentagon addendum, dated 1970 and handwritten in bold strokes by USAF Colonel Griffin Yeats. She knew that this was Conrad's father, and it made the hair on her neck stand on end. The note said:

All future reports regarding Piri Reis World Map and Project Sonchis shall be passed through this office and classified accordingly.

"Sonchis," she repeated, closing the report.

"Any significance?"

"There was an Egyptian priest named Sonchis who allegedly provided Plato with his detailed account of Atlantis."

"Admiral Reis's map states it is based on even earlier source maps going back to the time of Alexander the Great."

"You're saying what exactly, Your Holiness?"

"Only an advanced, worldwide maritime culture that existed more than ten thousand years ago could have created these source maps."

Serena blinked. "You believe that Antarctica is Atlantis?"

"And its secrets are buried under two miles of ice," he said. "What we are dealing with is not just a lost ancient civilization, but the lost mother culture your friend Doctor Yeats has been searching for, one possessing scientific knowledge that we have yet to comprehend."

"If this turns out to be real it will throw many things into question," Serena replied, "including the Church's interpretation of the Genesis account in the Bible."

"Or uphold it," the pope said, although he didn't

sound hopeful. "But should that be the case, we are all the worse for it."

"You've lost me, Your Holiness."

"God has shown me a prophecy about the end of time," he said. "But I have not revealed it to the Church because it is too terrible to contemplate."

Serena sat on the edge of her seat. Her usual concerns aside, this pope certainly seemed to have control of his senses and be of sound mind. "What did you see, Your Holiness?"

"I saw a beautiful rose frozen in ice," the pope said. "And then the ice cracked, and out of the crack came fire and a war waged by the sons of God against the Church and all mankind. In the end the ice melted and tears rolled off the petals of the rose."

Serena recalled the sixth chapter of Genesis, which said that the "sons of God" ruled the Earth in an ancient epoch of time. Their offspring, born of women, did so much evil that God destroyed them and the entire human race in the Great Flood, save for Noah and his family. But Serena also recalled that apocalyptic visions, whether from the Bible or from the mouths of young Portuguese shepherds, do not detail the future in high-definition clarity. Instead they synthesize it and set it against a unified, timeless backdrop of symbols that require interpretation.

"So Your Holiness feels that this vision, the myth of Atlantis, and the current American military activities in Antarctica are altogether one and the same?"

"Yes."

She tried to mask her doubt, but each element alone strained credulity. "I see."

"No, you don't," he said. "Look closer." The pope held a rolled-up parchment in his hand. "This is one of the source maps we believe Admiral Reis used. The map, really."

Serena slowly reached forward and took the map from the pope's hand. As soon as she clutched it in her own, she felt a jolt of anticipation surge through her veins.

"It has Sonchis's name on it," the pope said. "But the rest of the writing is pre-Minoan."

She said, "Give me a few weeks and—"

"I was hoping you could decode it on the way to Antarctica," the pope said. "I have a private jet fueling up on the runway for your journey."

"My journey?" Serena said. "You said it yourself, Your Holiness. This city, if it truly exists, is buried under two miles of ice. It might as well be on Mars."

"The Americans have found it," the pope insisted. "Now you must find them. Before it is too late."

The pope placed one hand on the terrestrial globe to his right and the other on the celestial globe to his left.

"These globes were painted by Dutch master cartographer Willem Bleau in 1648," he said. "At the time they, too, displayed the 'modern world.' Unfortunately, they depict an entirely wrong version of the planet and the heavens. Look, California is an island."

She looked at the terrestrial globe and saw monsters in the sea. "I'm familiar with Bleau's work, Your Holiness."

"What everybody once thought was true is false," he replied. "A warning that the way we see the world today will probably look equally wrong a few centuries hence. Or a few days."

"A few days?" Serena repeated. "Your prophecy is to

be fulfilled within a few days and you have not revealed it to the Church?"

"There are bitter spiritual, political, and military implications, Sister Serghetti," the pope said, continuing to address her as a nun, a member of the family, and not an outsider. "Just consider what would happen should moral anarchy reign on Earth because humanity has cast aside the Judeo-Christian tradition."

"I have, Your Holiness, and that day came a long time ago to the rest of the world outside Rome."

The pope said nothing for an uncomfortable minute. Finally, he cleared his throat and said, "Have you ever wondered why you chose to join such a secure and predictable surrogate family as the Church?"

Serena remained silent. It was a question she took pains to avoid asking herself. The truth was that despite her public differences with it, she believed the Church was the hope of humanity, the only institution that kept an amoral world from spinning out of control.

"Perhaps because as a nun you felt it would be easy for you to be right with God," the pope said. "Perhaps because you desperately needed to know beyond a shadow of a doubt that you were acceptable to him."

The pope was probing so close to the truth that it was almost too unbearable for Serena to remain in the room. She wanted to run away and hide.

"It's not by my good deeds but by God's mercy through Christ's atoning death on the cross that my immortal soul is saved, Your Holiness."

"My point exactly," the pope said. "What more do you hope to add?"

Serena could feel the emptiness inside her like a dull ache. She had no answer for the pope but wanted to say something, anything. "Banishing me to Antarctica to expose the Americans isn't going to—"

"Finally make you worthy of your calling as Mother Earth?" The pope looked at her like a father would his daughter. "Sister Serghetti, I want you to go to nature's 'last wilderness' and find God—away from all this." He gestured to the books and maps and works of art. "Just you and the Creator of the universe. And Doctor Yeats."

4

DISCOVERY
PLUS TWENTY-THREE DAYS,
SIX HOURS
ICE BASE ORION

THE COMMAND CENTER OF ICE BASE ORION was a low-ceilinged module crammed with consoles and crew members watching their flickering monitors in the shadows. But to Major General Griffin Yeats it was a triumph of Air Force logistics, erected in less than three weeks in the most alien terrain on planet Earth.

"Thirty seconds, General Yeats," said Colonel O'Dell, Yeats's neckless executive officer, from the shadows of his glowing console.

An image of Antarctica hovered on the main screen. The ice-covered continent was an eerie blue from the vantage point of space, a great island surrounded by a world ocean and an outer ring of landmass, the navel of the Earth.

Yeats stared at the screen incredulously. He had seen that very picture of the Southern Hemisphere once before, from the window of an Apollo spacecraft. That was almost a lifetime ago. Still, some things never changed, and a sense of awe washed over him.

"Satellite in range in fifteen seconds, sir," O'Dell said.

The video image blurred for a moment. Then a gigantic storm cloud jumped into view. Yeats saw what looked like the legs of a spider swirling clockwise around Antarctica. There were twelve of these legs or "strings of pearls"—low-pressure fronts endemic to the region.

"That's one hell of a storm," Yeats said. "Give me the specs."

"Looks like we've got four separate storms merging into a double-low, sir," O'Dell reported. "Almost four thousand miles wide. Big enough to cover the entire United States."

Yeats nodded. "I want the runway cleared again."

The room got quiet, only the low hum and soft beeps of the computers and monitors. Yeats was aware of the stares of his officers.

O'Dell cleared his throat. "Sir, we should warn six-nine-six."

"Negative. I want radio blackout."

"But, sir, your—Doctor Yeats is on board."

"We've got forty men on that transport, Colonel. And a fine pilot in Commander Lundstrom. No transmissions. Buzz me on their approach."

"Yes, sir," said O'Dell with a salute as Yeats marched out of the command center.

The floor-to-ceiling window in General Yeats's quarters framed the yawning ice gorge outside, offering him a skybox seat of the excavation. Pillars of bluish, crystal plumes billowed out of the abyss. And at the bottom was everything he and Conrad had been searching for.

Yeats poured himself a Jack Daniel's and sat down behind his desk. He hurt like hell and wanted to howl like the katabatic winds outside. But he couldn't afford to let O'Dell or the others see him at less than his best.

He propped his right boot on the desk and pulled his pant leg back to reveal a scarred and disfigured limb, his parting gift from his first mission to this frozen hell more than thirty-five years ago. The pain throbbed a few inches below the knee. Goddamn tricks the cold played on him down here.

But damn if it didn't feel good to be in charge again, he thought, catching a dim reflection of himself in the reinforced plexiglass window. Even now, in his sixties, he still cut a commanding figure. Most of the baby faces on the base had no idea who he used to be way back when. Or, rather, who he was supposed to have been.

Griffin Yeats should have been the first man on Mars.

The *Gemini* and *Apollo* space veteran had been tapped for the job in 1968. The Mars shuttle, as originally formulated by rocket pioneer Wernher von Braun in 1953 and later revised by NASA planners, was scheduled to depart the American space station Freedom on November 12, 1981, reach the red planet on August 9, 1982, and return to Earth one year later.

If only politics were as predictable as the orbit of the planets.

By 1969 the war in Vietnam had sapped the federal budget, and the moon landing had temporarily satiated Americans' appetite for space exploration. With congressional opposition to the mission mounting, President Nixon rejected the Mars mission and space station program. Only the space shuttle would get the green light. It was a catastrophic decision that set the Mars program back for decades, left the space shuttle all dressed up with no place to go, and cast a rudderless NASA adrift in the political backwaters of Washington without a clear vision.

It also killed Yeats's dreams of greatness.

The desk console buzzed and broke Yeats's trance. It was O'Dell in the command center. "Sir, we think we've picked them up on radar. Twenty minutes to landing."

"Where are we with the runway?"

"Clearing it now, sir, but the storm—"

"No excuses, Colonel. I'll be there in a minute. You better have an update."

Yeats took another shot of whiskey and stared outside. At the time Nixon decided to scrap the Mars mission, Yeats was here in Antarctica, in the middle of a forty-day stay in a habitat specifically designed to simulate the first Martian landing. They were a crew of four supported by two Mars landing modules, a nuclear power plant, and a rover for exploring the surrounding territory.

Antarctica was as cold as Mars, and nearly as windy. Its snowstorms packed the same kind of punch as Martian dust storms. Most of all, the continent was almost as remote as the red planet, and in utter isolation a crew member's true character would reveal itself.

For Yeats it was an experience that would forever change his life, in ways he never imagined. Four men walked into that mission. Only one limped out alive. But

54   THOMAS GREANIAS

to what? To roam the subbasement corridors of the Pentagon as a creaky relic of the old space program? To raise an orphaned boy? To lose his wife and daughters as a result? Everything had been taken away from him.

Today he was taking it back.

5
DISCOVERY
PLUS TWENTY-THREE DAYS

IT WAS FREEZING IN THE FUSELAGE of the C-141 Starlifter transport when Conrad woke with a start. Groggy and sore, he rubbed his eyes. He was strapped in with two dozen Special Forces commandos sporting polar freezer suits and insulated M-16s.

He felt another jolt. For most of the flight they had soared through clear skies and over endless white. But now they were floating in some murky soup, and the turbulence grew worse by the second. The giant cargo containers in the rear shifted, straining their creaky tie-downs with each shock.

Conrad glanced at his multisensor GPS watch, which used a network of twenty-seven satellites to pinpoint his location anywhere on the globe and was accurate to within a hundred feet. But the past sixteen hours aboard various military craft must have chewed up the lithium batteries, because the longitudinal and latitudinal display was blanked out. The built-in compass, however, spun wildly—NE, SE, SW, NW. They must be nearing a polar region, he realized, most likely the South Pole.

He turned to the stone-faced commando sitting next to him and shouted above the whine of the turboprop engines, "I thought military personnel were banned from Antarctica."

The commando checked his M-16, stared ahead, and replied, "What military personnel, sir?"

Conrad groaned. This was precisely the sort of bullshit he had to put up with his entire life as the son of Griffin Yeats, a washed-out NASA astronaut who had somehow managed to march through the shadowy corridors of power at the Pentagon to become an Air Force general. Yeats firmly believed that truth should be divulged strictly on a "need to know" basis, starting with the circumstances surrounding Conrad's birth.

According to Yeats's official version of events, Conrad was allegedly the product of a one-night tryst between a Captain Rick Conrad and a nameless Daytona Beach stripper. When Captain Conrad died in Antarctica during a training mission, the woman dropped off their bastard child at the doorstep of the Cape Canaveral infirmary. A short time later she herself died of a drug overdose. NASA, eager to maintain the squeaky clean image of its astronauts, was only too eager to cut the red tape and let Captain Conrad's commanding officer and best friend, Major Griffin Yeats, adopt him.

Growing up, however, Conrad began to doubt the veracity of Yeats's story. His stepmother, Denise, certainly did. From the beginning she suspected that Yeats was Conrad's biological father and that he used Captain Conrad's death as a convenient cover to explain the birth of his own illegitimate son. No wonder she divorced

Yeats when Conrad was eight and moved away with her daughters, ages eleven and nine, the only friends Conrad had.

Finally, after years of base hopping and misery, Conrad had become enough of a rebel to have been tossed out of several schools and to confront Yeats. Not only did Yeats deny everything, but he refused to use his government contacts to help Conrad decisively identify his biological parents. That alone gave Conrad all the reason he needed to hate the man.

But by then it was obvious that General Yeats didn't really seem to care what Conrad or anybody else thought of him. Despite his failed career as an astronaut, Yeats went from one promotion to another until he finally got his star, and with it command of the Pentagon's mysterious Defense Advanced Research Projects Agency, or DARPA. Thanks to the financial backing of the Reagan administration throughout the 1980s, Yeats and his team of extremist military planners invented the Internet, the global positioning system, stealth technology, and the computer mouse, among "other things."

This mission, Conrad concluded, no doubt fell into the latter category of "other things." But what, specifically? Conrad had long suspected that a fabulous discovery lay under the ice in Antarctica. After all, East Antarctica was an ancient continent and at one time tropical. Yeats had obviously found something and needed him. Or maybe this was merely a sorry attempt at some sort of father-son reconciliation.

Two big turbo jolts brought Conrad back to the freezing fuselage of the C-141. Without asking permission, he unbuckled his strap and stumbled toward the cockpit, grabbing an occasional strut in the fuselage for support.

The glass flight deck was deceptively bright and airy. Conrad could see nothing but white beyond the windshield. Lundstrom sat in the pilot's seat, barking at his copilot and navigator. But the engines were whining so loudly that Conrad couldn't catch what he said.

Conrad shouted, "Could I at least see this phenomenal discovery before you kill me?"

Lundstrom definitely looked annoyed when he glanced back at him over his shoulder. "Get back to your seat, Doctor Yeats. Everything's under control."

But the pilot's eyes betrayed his anxiety, and suddenly Conrad knew where he had seen him before. Until four years ago, Conrad recalled, Lundstrom had been a space shuttle commander. His leather glove, now tightly gripped around the steering column, disguised a hand that had been badly burned and disfigured along with a third of his body in an explosion on the launch pad before his aborted third mission.

Conrad said, "Come on, Lundstrom, riding the space shuttle couldn't have been this bumpy."

Lundstrom said nothing and returned his attention to the steering column.

Conrad scanned the weather radar and saw four swirling storms converging into a double-low.

"We're flying into that?"

"We're going to slip between the back side of one low and the front side of the other before they merge," Lundstrom said. "McMurdo advises us that back side winds of the first low won't exceed a hundred knots. Then we ride the front side of the other low, tailwinds of about a hundred and twenty knots pushing us downhill all the way to the ice."

"In one piece?" McMurdo, Conrad knew, was the largest American station on the continent. "I thought McMurdo had a big airstrip. Why can't we land there and try again here tomorrow? What's the rush?"

"Our window is closing fast." Lundstrom tapped the radar screen. "Tomorrow those two lows will have merged into one big nasty mother. Now get back to your seat."

Conrad took a seat behind the navigator. "I am."

Lundstrom glanced at his copilot. Conrad could see their reflections in the windshield. Apparently they had decided he might as well stay.

Lundstrom said, "Your file warned us that you were trouble. Like father, like son, I suppose."

"He's not my real father, I'm not his real son." At least at this moment Conrad hoped not. Like most Americans he had suspected the existence of a database with information about him somewhere in Washington. Now Lundstrom had confirmed it. "Or wasn't that information in my file?"

"That along with some psychiatric evaluations," Lundstrom said, obviously enjoying this exercise at Conrad's expense. "Nightmares about the end of the world. No memories before the age of five. You were one screwed-up kid."

"Guess you missed the joys of being breastfed milk tainted with LSD and other hallucinogens," Conrad said. "Or having full-blown flashbacks when you were six. Or kicking the asses of little Air Force brats who said you were a screwed-up kid."

Lundstrom grew quiet for a moment, busying himself with the controls.

But Conrad's interest was piqued. "What else does my file say?"

"Some shit you pulled the first time we went to war with Iraq in the 1990s."

Conrad was still in grad school back then. "Ancient history."

"That's what I heard," said Lundstrom. "Something about Soviet MiGs and the Ziggurat at Ur."

Conrad nodded. Four thousand years ago Ur was the capital of Sumer in the land of Abraham. Today it was buried in the sands of modern-day Iraq. "Something like that."

"Like what?" Lundstrom seemed genuinely curious. Apparently Conrad's file didn't include everything.

"The Iraqis had a nasty habit of building military installations next to archaeological treasures as shields for protection," Conrad said. "So when U.S. satellites detected two Soviet MiG-21 attack jets next to the ruins of the ancient Ziggurat at Ur, the Pentagon concluded the Iraqis were parking the MiGs there to avoid bombing."

Lundstrom nodded. "I remember hearing that."

"Well, they also suspected Hussein himself was holed up inside the ziggurat," Conrad went on. "So I gave them the targeting information they needed to launch a Maverick missile at the site."

"A Maverick? That was first-generation bunker buster. You're shitting me."

"Only a Maverick could burrow its way beneath the pyramid and destroy it from the inside out and make the explosion look like an Iraqi mishap."

"So you'd wipe an eternal treasure from the face of the earth just to kill some *despot du jour?*" Lundstrom actually seemed shocked. "What the hell kind of archaeologist are you?"

"The kind you nice people apparently need," Conrad said. "So now why don't you tell me—"

Suddenly a throbbing whine alerted the crew. Lundstrom gripped the controls. The copilot checked his instruments.

The navigator shouted, "Side winds at two-fifty G have shifted around to eighty G!"

"Wind sheer," said Lundstrom, adjusting the yoke. "Damn, she's stiff. Looks like we found the jet stream."

Conrad braced himself against his seat as the plane hit heavy turbulence and the gyros began to wander and go wild.

"Gyro's tumbling," called the navigator.

Lundstrom shouted, "Give me a celestial fix."

The navigator swung to the overhead bubble sextant that protruded out the topside skin of the plane and tried to read their location from the stars. But he shook his head. "Soup's too thick to extrapolate a reading."

"Ever heard of GPS?" Conrad shouted over the din.

"Useless with the EMP."

Electromagnetic pulse? thought Conrad. Those kind of microwaves, generated by small explosions of the nuclear variety, had a tendency to knock out all sophisticated technological gear. That explained why they were flying in such an old crate. What the hell was Yeats doing down there on the ice?

Conrad said, "What about a goddamn Doppler navigation system?"

"Negative."

"Listen to me, Lundstrom. We have to radio the tower at McMurdo for help. How far away are we?"

"You don't get it, Conrad," said Lundstrom. "We're not landing at McMurdo. Our designated landing site is elsewhere."

"Wherever 'elsewhere' is, we're not going to make it, Lundstrom," he said. "You've got to change course for McMurdo."

"Too late," said Lundstrom. "We passed our point of safe return. We're committed."

"Or should be," said Conrad, "along with Yeats and your whole sorry bunch in Washington."

The navigator shouted, "Headwinds skyrocketing—a hundred knots! Ground speed dropping fast—a hundred fifty knots!"

The plane's four engines strained to push against the headwinds. Conrad could feel the resistance in the vibrations in the floor beneath his boots. The turbulence rose through his legs like coils of unbridled energy until his insides seemed to melt. For a dead man he felt very much alive and wanted to stay that way.

"Keep this up and we'll be flying backward," he grumbled.

"Headwinds a hundred seventy-five knots," the navigator shouted. "Two hundred! Two twenty-five!"

Lundstrom paused a moment and apparently considered a new strategy. "Cut and feather numbers one and four."

"Copy," said the engineer, shutting down two engines.

"Ground speed still dropping," said the navigator, sounding desperate. "Fuel's almost spent."

Conrad said, "What about an emergency landing on the ice pack?"

"Possible," said Lundstrom. "But this is a wheeled bird. Not a ski bird."

"Belly land her!" Conrad shouted.

"Negative," said Lundstrom. "In that stew downstairs we'd probably cream into the side of a berg."

Another side wind blast hit them so hard that Conrad thought the plane would tip over on its back and spiral down to the ice. Somehow Lundstrom managed to keep her level.

"You've got to do something," Conrad shouted. "Jettison the cargo!"

"General Yeats would sooner jettison us."

"Then we have to radio for help."

"Negative. We have radio blackout. Radio's useless."

Conrad didn't believe him. "Bullshit. This is a black ops mission. There's no goddamn radio blackout. Yeats just wants to keep this quiet." Conrad slipped behind the radio and tried to put on a headset. But the shaking made it difficult.

"What do you think you're doing?" Lundstrom demanded.

Conrad slipped the headset on. "Calling for help."

Conrad heard a click near his ear. But it wasn't the headset. It was the sliding of a sidearm receiver. He turned to see Lundstrom pointing a shiny Glock 9 mm automatic pistol at his head. Conrad recognized it as his own, which he was relieved of upon boarding the chopper back in Peru. "Get your ass back in your seat, Doctor Conrad."

"I'm in my seat." Conrad flicked on the radio switch. A low hum crackled. "You can't kill me. You need me, Lundstrom. God knows why, but you do. And you better put my gun away. It's been known to go off accidentally. If this ride gets any bumpier you might miss my head and put a hole through the windshield."

Lundstrom looked outside at the raging skies. "Damn you, Conrad."

Conrad leaned over the radio microphone, aware of the barrel of the pistol wavering behind his head as he adjusted the frequency. "What's our call sign and frequency?"

Lundstrom hesitated. Then a huge jolt almost ejected him out of his seat. Lundstrom lowered the pistol as the turbulence rocked the cockpit. "We're six-nine-six, Conrad," Lundstrom shouted, reaching over to adjust the frequency.

Conrad clicked on the radio microphone. "This is six-nine-sixer. Requesting emergency assistance."

There was no response.

"This is six-nine-sixer," Conrad repeated. "Requesting emergency assistance."

Again, no response.

"Look!" shouted the navigator. "Ice Base Orion."

"Ice Base Orion?" Conrad repeated.

The mist parted for a moment, opening a window

onto the wasteland below. A panorama of mountains poked up out of the ice, filling the entire horizon as far as Conrad could see. The flanks of jagged peaks dribbled whipped-cream snow into the bottom of a great valley marked by a black crescent-shaped crack in the ice. Perched on the concave side of the crack was a human settlement of domes, sheds, and towers. Conrad saw it flash by before they were swallowed up by the mist again.

"This is it?" Conrad asked.

Lundstrom nodded. "If only we can find the strip."

"The strip?" asked Conrad when a thunderous bolt of turbulence almost knocked him out of his chair. If he hadn't strapped himself in, he realized, his head would now be part of the instrument panel.

"The runway," Lundstrom explained. "Bulldozed out of the ice."

"We're making a white-on-white approach?" Conrad stared at the swirling snow outside the flight deck windshield. Strobe lights and boundary flares were useless against the glare of a whiteout. With the sky overcast, there were no shadows and no horizons. And flying over a uniformly white surface makes it impossible to judge height or distance. Even birds crash into the snow. "You guys are borderline lunatic."

The radio crackled.

"Six-nine-sixer, this is Tower." A gruff, monotone voice came in. "Repeat. This is Tower calling six-nine-sixer."

"This is six-nine-sixer," said Lundstrom, grabbing the microphone. "Go ahead, Tower."

The controller on the other end said, "Winds fifteen cross and gusting to forty knots, visibility zero-zero."

Conrad could tell Lundstrom was doing the math, wondering whether to go for it or go into holding and pray for a miracle.

"Winds shifting to dead cross, gusting to sixty knots, sir," shouted the navigator.

Conrad grabbed the microphone back. "Trying to land this tin crate on a giant ice cube is suicide and you know it."

"Search-and-rescue teams standing by," the controller said. "Over."

Conrad looked hard into the mist as Lundstrom brought them in. Visibility was nil in the fog and blowing snow. Suddenly the curtain parted again and a row of black steel drums appeared on approach dead ahead. The strip itself was marked in Day-Glo signboards.

"We're coming in too low," he said.

"Commence letdown," Lundstrom ordered.

The copilot gently throttled back, working to keep the props in sync.

The radio popped. "Begin your final descent at the word 'now,'" the controller instructed.

"Copy."

"You are right on the glide slope."

"Copy," said Lundstrom when a nerve-wracking dip shook the plane from front to back. Conrad tightened the straps of his seat harness and held his breath.

"You are now below the glide slope," the controller warned. "Decrease your rate of descent and steer two degrees left."

"Copy." Lundstrom gently tugged the steering column and Conrad could feel the C-141 level off.

"You are now back on the glide slope," the controller said. "Coming right down the pike at two miles to touchdown . . ."

Conrad could still see nothing out the windshield but a white wall.

". . . right on at one mile to touchdown . . ."

". . . right on at one-half mile . . ."

". . . one-quarter mile . . ."

". . . touchdown."

Conrad and Lundstrom stared at each other. They were still floating.

"Tower?" repeated Lundstrom.

An eternity of silence followed, then a slamming crunch. The commandos toppled like dominos over one another and then dangled weightlessly from their web-like seats. The tiedowns in the rear snapped apart and the cargo shifted forward.

Conrad heard the crack and looked back to see several metal containers fly through the main cabin toward the cockpit. He ducked as something whizzed past his ear and struck Lundstrom in the head, driving the pilot's skull into the controls.

Conrad reached for the steering column just as the ice pack smashed through the windshield and everything collapsed into darkness.

6

DISCOVERY
PLUS TWENTY-THREE DAYS,
SEVEN HOURS

IT WAS THE BLEEPING SOUND of the C-141's homing beacon that finally brought Conrad back to consciousness. He blinked his eyes open to a flurry of snow. Slowly the picture came into focus. Through the broken fuselage he could see pieces of the transport scattered across the ice sheet.

He glanced at Lundstrom. The pilot's eyes were frozen open in terror, his mouth gaping in a fixed scream. Then Conrad saw a metal shard protruding from Lundstrom's skull. He must have died on impact.

Conrad swallowed hard and gasped for breath. The Antarctic air seemed to rush inside and freeze his lungs. He felt punchy, light-headed. This is no good, he told himself, no good at all. His internal, core temperature was dropping. Hypothermia was setting in. Soon he'd lose consciousness and his heart would stop unless he took action.

He fumbled for his seat buckle, but his fingers

wouldn't move. He glanced down. His right hand was frozen to the seat. His fingertips were white with frost-bite. He knew that meant the blood vessels had contracted and the tissue was slowly dying.

Conrad surveyed the cockpit, trying not to panic. Using his numb but gloved left hand, he grasped a thermos from behind Lundstrom's corpse. He worked it until the top popped open. Then he poured the hot coffee over his right hand, watching a cloud of steam rise over his sizzling hand as he peeled it away from the chair. He looked at his seared palm. It was bloody red and blistered, but he was too numb with cold to feel any pain.

He dragged himself over to the copilot and put an ear to his lips. He was breathing, just barely. So was the navigator. Conrad could hear a few low groans from the commandos in back.

Conrad reached for the transmitter. "This is six-nine-sixer," Conrad said breathlessly, leaning over the microphone. "Requesting emergency assistance."

There was no answer. He adjusted the frequency.

"This is six-nine-sixer, you bastards," he repeated.

But no matter which frequency he dialed, he was unable to break through. After several minutes of empty hissing, the transmitter finally went dead.

Nobody could hear him, he realized.

Conrad worked his way through the cockpit debris, searching for a backup radio. But he couldn't find one. Surely they had to have a beacon, an EPIRB signal at the least. But perhaps Lundstrom and his team didn't want to be found in a case like this.

The only thing he discovered was a single flare, and that from his own pack. A lot of good it would do him.

What a sorry way to die, he thought, staring at the flare in his gloved fist. You survive an airplane crash only to turn into a Popsicle. God, how he hated the cold. It was all he ever knew as a child, and to die in the snow was the last way he wanted to go. It would signify he had not traveled as far from home as he once dreamed. And he would never reconcile with his father.

How's that for irony? he thought as he scanned the temperature reading on his multisensor watch. The digital thermometer displayed -25° F. Then he took a closer look and realized he had missed a digit. -125° F.

Conrad slumped to the floor with the rest of the crew, his eyelids starting to get heavy. He fought to stay awake, but it was a losing battle, and he had begun to drift off into unconsciousness when suddenly the plane started to shake and he thought he heard a dog barking.

He opened his eyes, dragged himself over to his backpack on the floor, and managed to sling it over his shoulder. He then fumbled for his flare, his fingers working slowly, slid down through a hole in the fuselage, and fell onto the ice.

The thud sharpened his senses.

Conrad staggered to his feet and looked across the barren ice. But there was nothing to see. If anything, the snow was coming down even harder. Then, out of the mist, a huge tractorlike vehicle appeared.

It looked like one of those big Swedish Hagglunds. Its two fiberglass cabs were linked together and ran on rubber treads that left wide waffle tracks in the snow.

Conrad quickly broke his flare and started waving his hands. His arms felt heavy and he couldn't feel the flare in his fist.

The Hagglunds plowed to a stop in front of him. The forward cabin door opened. A white Alaskan husky jumped out and ran past Conrad to the wreckage. Conrad heard clanking and saw the white boots of a large figure emerge from the Hagglunds and descend the rungs of the small ladder to the ice pack.

Conrad could tell from the towering frame and crisp, spare movements that it was his father. Stiff in a white freezer suit with charcoal under his goggles to block the snow glare, Yeats marched toward him, his powerful strides crunching deeply into the snow.

"You broke my radio blackout orders, son." Yeats stood there like a statue, snow flying all around him. "You blew our twenty."

"It's good to see you, too, Dad."

Yeats took the flare from Conrad's hand, dropped it into the snow, and ground it under his boot. "You've attracted enough attention."

A geyser of anger suddenly erupted inside Conrad. Anger at Yeats and at himself for letting his father reach out across time and pull him back into this personal frozen hell.

"Lundstrom's dead along with half your men," Conrad gestured with his frostbitten hand toward the plane.

Yeats spoke into his radio. "S and R teams," Yeats barked. "See what you can salvage from the cargo hold before the storm buries us alive."

Conrad glanced back at the wreckage and men, which

would soon be forgotten under the merciless snow. Then the husky trotted out with a wristwatch in his mouth. Its face was smeared with frozen blood. Conrad felt the husky brush past his leg and looked on as it ran for the Hagglunds.

"Nimrod!" Yeats called out after the dog. But the husky was already scratching at the door of the forward cab.

"Nimrod's the only one here with half a brain." Conrad marched toward the Hagglunds. But when he reached the forward cab and grasped the door handle, Yeats blocked it with a stiff arm.

"Where do you think you're going?" Yeats demanded.

Conrad cracked open the icy cab door, letting Nimrod jump into the warm cab first. "Don't piss in your pants, Dad. In this cold, something might fall off."

Conrad glanced at his bandaged hand as he followed Yeats down an insulated corridor inside the mysterious Ice Base Orion. A medic in the infirmary had dressed the hand as best he could. But now that it was thawing, it hurt like the living daylights.

Classical music was piped in through hidden speakers. Only the thin polystyrene walls separated them from the furious storm raging outside. Eight inches and what sounded like the faint strains of Symphony No. 25 in G Minor.

"Mozart," Yeats said. "Some bullshit experiments proved that classical music has a positive effect on the cardiovascular system. A decade from now it will be blues or rap or whatever turns on the geeks."

They passed through another air lock into a new module and Conrad felt a weird sensation of vertigo. The upper half of the module looked exactly like the bottom half. And the ceiling area was packed with instrument panels, circuit breakers, temperature dials, and dosimeter gauges. The panel clocks, like Yeats's wristwatch, were set on central time—Houston.

Then Conrad noted the NASA markings all around and suddenly realized that Ice Base Orion was never intended for use on Earth. It must have been designed to be an orbiting space station or a colony on one of the polar caps of Mars, where the ice would be tapped for water and life support.

"What the hell is this place you've built down here?" Conrad asked.

"Welcome to the most inaccessible human settlement on the planet, son."

They turned a corner, and Conrad followed Yeats down another long corridor. Conrad could hear a low hum beneath the music as they walked. And every now and then, a shudder seemed to pass through the entire base like a train had just rumbled by.

"We've got a command center, biodome, mobile servicing center, an astrophysics lab, an observatory, and modules for materials processing, remote sensing, and medical research," Yeats said.

"You forgot the drill rig," Conrad said. "That would explain the shaking."

Yeats pretended he hadn't heard him and pointed in the opposite direction. "The brig is that way."

This whole base is a brig, thought Conrad as he

looked down a tunnel toward a sealed-off air lock. "Where is anybody going to go that you need to lock him up?"

"The harsh conditions here are known to send men over the edge," Yeats said.

Conrad looked at his father. "Is that what happened to you?"

Yeats stopped and turned around abruptly in front of a door marked PERSONNEL ONLY. As if anybody else was around to violate security procedures.

"Follow me through this door, son," said Yeats, his hand resting on the release bar, "and you just might go over the edge yourself."

Standing on a platform inside the cavernous laboratory was a pyramid about ten feet tall. A solid piece of rock with an almost reddish glow, it was marked by four grooves or rings around its sides. The rings began halfway up the slopes and grew closer together toward the top.

Conrad let out a low whistle.

"Pentagon satellites picked up a dark anomaly beneath the ice shortly after the last big quake some weeks ago," Yeats said. "We put a survey team on the ground, but they couldn't pick up anything solid. The anomaly appeared to be invisible to radio-echo surveys. That's when we started drilling. We hit the stone a mile beneath the ice cap. Clearly it's not a natural rock formation."

No it wasn't, Conrad thought with growing excitement

as he studied the stone. The U.S. State Department's official position was that no human had set foot on Antarctica before the nineteenth century. Yet this rock was at least as old as the ice that covered it—twelve thousand years. That strongly suggested the remains of a civilization twice as old as Sumer, the oldest known on Earth.

Conrad ran his hand across the smooth face of the stone and inserted a finger into one of the strange grooves. This find could be it, he thought, nearly trembling now, the first evidence of the Mother Culture he had been seeking his entire life.

"So where's the rest of it?" he asked.

Yeats seemed to be holding back. "Rest of what?"

"The pyramid," Conrad said. "This is a benben stone."

"Benben?"

Now Yeats was just playing dumb, clearly eager to see if his investment in him was worth the cost. Conrad didn't mind singing for his supper, but he wasn't going to settle for crumbs.

"An ancient Egyptian symbol of the bennu bird—the phoenix," Conrad said. "It represents rebirth and immortality. It's the capstone or pyramidion placed on top of a pyramid."

"So you've seen it before?"

"No," Conrad said. "They're missing from all the great pyramids of the world. We know them mostly through ancient texts. They were replicas of the long-lost original benben stone, which was said to have fallen from heaven."

"Like a meteorite," finished Yeats, staring at the rock.

Conrad nodded. "But a benben this size means the pyramid beneath it would have to be enormous."

"A mile high and almost two miles wide."

Conrad stared at Yeats. "That's more than ten times the size of the Great Pyramid in Giza."

"Eleven point one times exactly," said Yeats. So his father had indeed done his homework. "Bigger than the Pentagon. And more advanced. Its exterior is smoother than a stealth bomber, which may explain why it's been invisible to radio-echo surveys. These grooves on this capstone are P4's only distinguishing exterior character-istic. Beyond its sheer size, of course."

Conrad touched the benben stone again, still incredu-lous that civilization existed on Earth at an earlier date and at a more advanced level than even he previously imagined.

"P4," Conrad repeated. So that's what they were call-ing it. Shorthand for the Pyramid of the Four Rings. It made sense. "And it's at least twelve thousand years old."

Yeats said, "If it's as old as this benben stone, then P4 is at least six billion years old, son."

"Six billion?" Conrad repeated. "That's impossible. Earth is only four and a half billion years old. You're telling me that P4 could be older than the planet?"

"That's correct," Yeats said. "And it's right under our feet."

7

DISCOVERY
PLUS TWENTY-FOUR DAYS,
FIFTEEN HOURS

YEATS COULD HEAR THE FAINT STRAINS of Mozart beneath the drone of two ventilation fans pumping air inside his compartment as he watched Conrad analyze the data from P4 on his laptop.

Cupping a mug of hot coffee in his bandaged hand, Conrad shook his head. "Nothing ever changes with you, Dad, does it?"

Yeats stiffened. "Meaning?"

"You never taught me how to fly a kite or how to throw a split-fingered fastball when I was growing up," Conrad said. "No, I had to learn that kind of stuff on my own. With you it was always, 'What do you think of this weapons system design, son?' or 'How'd you like to watch the launch of my new spy satellite?' And whenever I see you on this stinking planet, the scenery is always the same. It's always some military base. Always dark. Always cold. Always snowing."

Yeats glanced out the picture window at the storm raging outside. The whiteout was so bad he couldn't even see the ice gorge anymore. What was left of the C-141 was long buried by now. He was relieved Conrad had survived the crash, and he was happy to see him. But it was clear Conrad didn't feel the same way, and that hurt.

"Maybe I bring it with me." Yeats poured himself a third shot of whiskey and nodded to the laptop data. "Anyway, the carbon dating appears conclusive."

"For the benben stone only," Conrad began as another wave of those trainlike shudders passed through the room.

"That was ours," Yeats said, referring to the drilling being done to clear the ice around the top of P4 at the bottom of the abyss. "You'll know the real jolt when you feel it."

"And you think P4 is causing the earthquakes?"

"You're the genius, son. You tell me."

Conrad sipped his coffee and grimaced. "What the hell is this? Diesel sludge?"

"It's the water. The station's supply comes from melted snow. The soy-based food is even worse."

Conrad pushed the coffee away. "Just because P4's benben stone is allegedly six billion years old doesn't mean the rest of the pyramid is that old or that aliens built it."

"Who said anything about aliens?" Yeats tried to maintain a blank expression, but Conrad was way ahead of him.

"Meteorites have been bombarding the earth since the planet was first formed—like that four-and-a-half-billion-year-old Martian rock they found here in

Antarctica a few years back," Conrad said. "Humans could have found a meteorite billions of years later and carved it into a benben stone."

Yeats downed his Jack Daniel's. "If that makes you feel better."

"Well, *somebody* built P4," Conrad said. "And they built it long before ice covered Antarctica or any human civilization was thought to exist. Whatever else the builders of P4 were, they were advanced, possibly more advanced than present-day human civilization."

Yeats nodded. "Which means whoever gains access to their technology theoretically could alter the world's balance of power."

"Still paranoid about asymmetrical force?" Conrad said. "No wonder you're willing to risk lives and break international law by fielding a military presence in Antarctica."

Yeats paused. "You mean Atlantis."

"Atlantis? You think there's a city down there?"

Yeats nodded. "For all we know P4 is only the tip of the iceberg, so to speak."

"Atlantis is just a name, a myth," Conrad said. "Maybe that myth is based on what you think you've found. Maybe not. Maybe it's our long-lost Mother Culture. Maybe not. A proper excavation of P4 alone would require decades of research."

That was just like Conrad, Yeats thought. It wasn't enough to find the greatest discovery since the New World. No, Conrad had to be "right" about it, lest he be another Columbus who had discovered what had always been there.

"We don't have decades, son," Yeats explained. "We have days. Now I saw one of your TV specials and you said flat out that Antarctica was Atlantis."

Yeats clicked on his computer and an *Ancient Riddles* promo popped up. Yeats glanced at Conrad, who grimaced in embarrassment.

"Atlantis," boomed the baritone announcer. "The ancient city of fantastic wealth and military power described by the ancient Greek philosopher Plato in his *Dialogues* in the fourth century B.C. An entire civilization swallowed up by the sea in a single day. Its survivors sought refuge all over the world and built the pyramids of Egypt, the ziggurats of South America, and other ruins of unexplained origins. Come explore the unexplained with astro-archaeologist Doctor Conrad Yeats."

Yeats turned it off. "Well?"

"What I said is that Antarctica is the only place on Earth that *literally* fits Plato's description of Atlantis," Conrad explained. "I never said I actually believed Plato's account was true. Remember, it's a publish-or-perish world in academia, Dad, and only the wildest ideas garner attention."

Yeats frowned. "You're saying Plato is a liar?"

Conrad shrugged. "Plato was simply an idealist who dreamed up a perfect paradise, Atlantis, to express his yearnings."

Yeats was disappointed in Conrad's flippant response and narrowed his eyes. "Whereas you have no ideals."

"Every archaeologist has his favorite address for Atlantis," Conrad said. "Most think it's the island of Thíra in the Mediterranean, which sank into the sea after its volcano exploded. That was nine hundred years before Plato penned his account of Atlantis. Others favor the North Atlantic or Troy in Turkey, a city which itself was considered a myth until its ruins were recently discovered. Still others suggest that Atlantis was really the Americas and that the lost city could well lie beneath Lake Titicaca, or Los Angeles for that matter."

Yeats said, "But none of these were anything like the high-tech civilization Plato insisted was destroyed almost twelve thousand years ago."

"True."

"So this could be Atlantis."

"It could be." Conrad shrugged. "Look, all I'm saying is that if you throw a dart at a world map you'll find somebody's idea of Atlantis," Conrad said. "Or, if you're like my show's producer, you could throw darts at solar systems on celestial charts. The possibilities are infinite. I can't draw any conclusions until I get inside P4."

"I can't promise you'll get inside, son," Yeats said. "Not yet. This is a military operation. So if you've got a theory about P4, put up or shut up."

"Fine. Then I'll take my frequent flier miles and go home."

"Goddamn it, Conrad." Yeats smashed his fist into the tabletop. "You're not going anywhere. And if you want to get inside P4, you better tell me something I don't already know."

Conrad stood up and walked over to the window. For a wild moment Yeats worried that Conrad would pick up a metal chair and try to shatter the reinforced glass. But he simply stared outside as the wind howled. The man had learned to master the rage that had consumed him as a boy.

"OK then," Conrad finally said without turning around. "My best guess is that P4 may well be the original on which the Great Pyramid in Giza was modeled, except on a much grander scale. In other words, P4 is the real deal and the Great Pyramid that Khufu built is an inferior clay replica."

"Your best guess?" Yeats repeated. "I can't work off hunches, son."

"It's more than that," Conrad said. "Your own data says the base is aligned at the cardinal points—north, south, east, and west. It's also sloped at an angle of fifty-one degrees, fifty-two minutes—just like the Great Pyramid. And knowing what I do about the Great Pyramid, up close and personal, I can make some educated guesses about P4."

Yeats exhaled. "Like what?"

"Like the probability that P4 is a representation of the Southern Hemisphere of Earth."

"Whereas the Great Pyramid in Egypt is a representation of the Northern Hemisphere of Earth," Yeats said. "I get it. So what?"

Conrad crossed the floor to the desk and tapped a few keys on his laptop. "The hemisphere is projected on flat surfaces as is done in mapmaking." He turned his laptop around so Yeats could see the graphic on his screen. It looked like a German cross. "This is the pyramid if we flattened it out. The apex represents the South Pole, and the perimeter represents the equator."

"Go on."

"This is the reason why the perimeter is in relation two pi to the height," Conrad explained. "P4 thus represents the Southern Hemisphere on a scale of one to forty-three thousand two hundred."

"Represents the Southern Hemisphere in relationship to what?" Yeats asked.

"The heavens," said Conrad. "The ancients associated certain meanings with various constellations. Once I determine this pyramid's celestial counterpart in the skies we'll have a better idea of its function."

"Function?" Yeats repeated. "It's a tomb, right?"

"Pyramids themselves were never designed to serve as burial places, although they were used that way in some cases," Conrad said. "Their higher purpose was connected to the ancient king's quest for eternal life. To attain it he would have to participate in the discovery of a revelation that would unveil the mystery of 'First Time.'"

"First Time?" Yeats stared hard at him. "What's that?"

"It's the secret of Creation," Conrad said. "How the universe was formed, how we got here, where we're going."

"Where we're going? Now how the hell would the builders of P4 know that?"

"The ancients believed that the cosmic calendar resets itself every twenty-six thousand years or so," Conrad said. "Each epoch of time ends in some cataclysm leading to a new creation or age. Survivors of such global extinction events would naturally want to warn future generations."

"So this secret goes all the way back to Genesis?"

"Earlier than that," Conrad said. "According to Aztec and Mayan myths, there have been at least five Suns or Creations. This is allegedly the Fifth Sun we're living in."

"What happened to the Fourth Sun?" Yeats demanded.

"Well, according to the ancients, it was destroyed by the Great Flood," Conrad said. "Based on the four rings we found on the benben stone, my guess is that P4 was built at the very dawn of the Fourth Sun, just after the destruction of the Third Sun, right around the time the biblical story of Genesis says God created the heavens and the earth."

"You just told me P4 goes further back than that."

"That's because inside the pyramid I expect to find a repository of knowledge from the previous three Suns," Conrad said. "It might even contain the secret of First Time itself, something older than the known universe."

Yeats started pacing back and forth, unable to contain his excitement. His bum leg was killing him, but he didn't care. "You sure about all this?"

"Won't be until I get inside." Conrad's face darkened. "But it's fair to assume that, whatever else is down there, P4 holds a legacy of knowledge at least as great as our own."

"Which is why we have to get inside first," Yeats concluded. "Because it won't be long before we have company."

Conrad asked, "You find the entrance yet?"

"I've got a drill crew working out of a rig we've set up on P4's summit," Yeats said. "The top of the pyramid, about fifty feet of it, sticks out of the bottom of the abyss like the tip of an iceberg. The crew has been drilling a hole down the east face toward the base. That's where the computer models say we'll find the entrance. We're about halfway there."

Conrad said, "You're drilling in the wrong place."

Yeats took a deep breath. "OK, then. Where should I be drilling?"

"The north or south face, although with P4 I'd favor the north face," Conrad said. "Less than a half mile down the drill crew will most likely find the entrance to a large shaft that will take us into the heart of P4."

"Most likely?" Yeats huffed. "You want me to pull my team off mission just to follow your instinct?"

"Look, if P4 is indeed the original on which the Great Pyramid was modeled, then I suspect we'll find two shafts radiating from the center of the pyramid out the south and north faces of the exterior. If the similarities I'm seeing continue to play out, then we can use these shafts to get inside P4 in half the time it's going to take you right now."

"And what exactly is the function of these shafts? If they exist."

"I have an idea," Conrad said. "But I'd have to get inside P4 to be certain."

"Naturally," Yeats grumbled.

"I thought the price of admission to P4 was to tell you something you didn't already know," said Conrad when the intercom buzzed. "I just did."

"What you told me means nothing if we can't find this shaft you allege exists," Yeats said.

"You will," Conrad insisted when the com beeped again.

Irritated, Yeats flicked on his screen. It was O'Dell in the command center. "What is it?"

"One of our long-range patrols just reported in," O'Dell said. "Looks like Doctor Yeats's little distress call attracted some attention. We've got company."

8
DISCOVERY
PLUS TWENTY-FOUR DAYS,
SIXTEEN HOURS

THE AIR LOCK DOOR SLID OPEN and a blast of polar air blew in with a flurry of snow. An ethereal figure emerged from the cloud in a green Gore-Tex parka. And even before the fur-lined hood dropped and the ultraviolet glasses came off, Conrad instinctively knew who it was.

"Serena," he said.

Every man has his own Atlantis, Conrad knew, a part of his past or himself that seems submerged and gone forever. Serena Serghetti was his Atlantis, and now she had suddenly resurfaced.

Serena said nothing for a minute, simply smiled at him and looked around. Then Nimrod trotted up to her and licked her wool mitten. She scratched the appreciative husky's ear.

Conrad glanced at Yeats, who was standing silently next to him, and at the two armed MPs in freezer suits behind Serena. All seemed to be waiting for some sort of utterance.

Finally, Serena spoke her first words to Conrad in five years. "You have a permit for her?" she asked, petting Nimrod.

Conrad blinked, incredulous. Perhaps he was so lost in the moment he hadn't heard her correctly. "For the dog?"

Serena nodded. "Huskies have been banned from the continent since 1993, as have any species not indigenous to Antarctica. I think that includes you, Conrad, along with your friends here."

Yeats stared, jaw open. "You two know each other?"

"Don't you recognize her?" Conrad said. "This is Serena Serghetti, aka Mother Earth, formerly the Vatican's top linguist and now an environmentalist and official pain in the ass."

"Only if you're an ass," Serena said brightly and extended a mitten toward Yeats. "General Yeats, you look warm-blooded in person. Not at all like Conrad described you."

Conrad looked at Yeats, who let the dig slide. "The Vatican?"

"Actually, I'm here as a representative of the Australian Antarctic Preservation Society and an adviser to the environmental committee of the United Nations Antarctica Commission. This land belongs to Australia, you see, according to Article Four of the Antarctic Treaty, of which the United States is a member. All members are required to give notice of expeditions, stations, and military personnel and equipment active in Antarctica. You haven't stated your business on our territory, General Yeats."

Conrad's mind was reeling, trying to take in her mysterious appearance in this frozen hell, let alone this bizarre exchange with his father about arcane minutia in international law.

Yeats cleared his throat. "Article Four, while recognizing that some nations lay claim to territory, expressly states that those claims do not have to be honored by other nations," Yeats said evenly. "In other words, seventy nations instead of seven could have territorial claims here, Sister Serghetti, but the United States does not recognize their validity."

"Maybe so," Serena replied. "But there's no ambiguity to Article One, which clearly and forcefully bans any measure of a military nature, which is tough luck for you."

"Unless such measures are for scientific purposes."

"And what purpose is that, Conrad?"

Conrad realized she was addressing him. And he said the first thing that popped into his head. "We're mounting a salvage operation."

He studied her reaction as she looked around and took in the command center doors down the corridor and soldiers with polar-protected M-16s.

"You mean for that C-141 that crashed?" she asked. "I saw the wreckage when I landed on your runway."

Conrad glanced at Yeats, who seemed impressed. Not only was she Mother Earth. She was also the Flying Nun. No wonder Yeats's jaw was on the floor. "You landed a plane?" Yeats asked.

"Your base is hard to miss with a fissure as wide as the Colorado River snaking around it. Did you cause that crack?"

"It was already there," Yeats said defensively.

"Then you won't mind if I have a look," she said. "The Antarctic Treaty provides for the right of access and inspection to all bases. Consider us official inspectors."

She stepped aside and Conrad saw behind her four well-built young men with dark, deep-set eyes. Video and sound equipment rested heavily on their broad shoulders.

Conrad said, "Who are they?"

"My camera crew. As long as we're making an inspection, I assume we can take pictures?"

"Sure," said Yeats, who motioned to the MPs to relieve the men of their equipment. "You can inspect everything from the brig."

Conrad watched Serena and her crew in their respective cells on two monitors in the command center. The men were sitting quietly on the floor like caged foxes. Serena, meanwhile, was stretched across her bunk like Sleeping Beauty.

"You can't just lock up Mother Earth," he told Yeats. "The world's going to find out."

But Yeats was focused on the other monitors that showed various grainy images of the P4 Habitat and a drill rig atop the flat summit of P4, where a work crew was tunneling down the north face of the pyramid as Conrad had instructed.

"You better pray your hunch about a shaft pays off, son. Or I just might lock you up too. And, frankly, in your case, the world won't give a shit."

Conrad opened his mouth to say something when Colonel O'Dell walked up with a file. Conrad caught his disapproving glance and realized he was the only civilian running loose on the base. O'Dell looked itchy to toss him into the brig with the rest of them.

"Here's that NSA report on Sister Serghetti, sir."

"Thank you, Colonel."

Conrad watched as Yeats scanned the file. "The NSA keeps files on nuns?"

"Nuns who develop a universal translator based on the Aymara language," Yeats said. "The NSA has been trying to get its hands on Sister Serghetti's system ever since. The Aymara language is so pure that the NSA suspects it didn't just evolve like other languages but was constructed from scratch."

"Explain that to us, Doctor Yeats," O'Dell blurted out.

Yeats shot O'Dell a nasty glare, but Conrad didn't flinch.

"The earliest Aymara myth says that after the Great Flood, strangers attempted to build a city on Lake Titicaca," Conrad said. "We know what's left of it as Tiahuanaco, with its great Temple of the Sun. But the builders abandoned it and disappeared."

"And just where on earth did these builders come from?" Yeats asked him in earnest.

"According to legend, they came from the lost island paradise of Aztlan. The Aztec version of Atlantis," Conrad said, staring at his father. "So what are you saying?"

Yeats closed the file. "The Good Sister might know the language of the people who built P4."

• • •

Serena had always pictured Antarctica as a symbol of peace and harmony, a model for how humans could live with one another and all species with which they shared the planet. She had also held similar such illusions about her relationship with Conrad. But now as she looked around her cell inside Ice Base Orion, her dream had melted away to reveal four cold walls, a tiny sink, and a urinal.

There was a hidden camera somewhere, she was sure, and General Yeats and that tosser Conrad no doubt were watching her every move. But they couldn't read her mind. So she sat on her bunk and pretended to be alone with her thoughts.

As an Australian she felt more kinship with Antarctica than the Americans. So often as a little girl she would look across the sea and know that the great white continent was on the other side. Australia was the closest of the world's nations to Antarctica and claimed 42 percent of it, including most of East Antarctica and the very ground—or ice over the ground—on which the Americans had constructed this secret facility.

But for all her work in Antarctica—mostly saving leopard seals or minke whales—her experience had been confined to the spectacular landscapes on the fringes of the continent. There the wildlife was wonderful and the auroras glorious. But this mission into the interior snow deserts had proven Antarctica to be an empty continent indeed. Even now within the warmth of this American base, she could sense the barrenness.

Serena also thought she could hear crackling noises from the shell's expansion joints. Stations built on ice tend to sink under their own weight as the heat they generate melts the surrounding ice. This station, probably days old, was just settling in.

She remembered her capture at the secret airstrip carved out of the ice and her subsequent escort to Ice Base Orion. The Hagglunds tractor in which the Americans transported her had passed a power plant along the way. It was buried a hundred yards away from the living quarters behind a protective snow dune. Too far way to service diesel engines in this cold, she thought. That's when she realized it was probably a compact nuclear plant. Probably a 100-kilowatt system.

At first she was outraged. How dare the Americans bring nuclear materials onto the continent! she thought. Ninety percent of all the ice in the world was here. Any meltdown could cause global catastrophe. This alone was more than enough to bust the Americans with the U.N.

But now her fury at the Americans for breaking every international law on the books had turned to fascination. However cool she played it with Conrad and General Yeats back at the air lock, she was in fact burning with excitement. There was Conrad, of course. But clearly her mission here involved much more than protecting the unspoiled Antarctic environment from the Americans.

Something momentous had been found down here, she realized, just like the pope said. Something that could turn history—and the Judeo-Christian tradition—on its head. In spite of all this, however, she felt exhilarated. Of all the candidates His Holiness could have chosen to be his eyes for this historic event, he had chosen her.

She heard the door unlock with a buzz and turned.

When the MP opened the door of the brig and ushered Conrad in, Serena was sitting on the edge of her bunk, sipping diesel tea from a Styrofoam cup. Conrad noted the silver bride of Christ band on her left ring finger that signified her spiritual union to the one and only Son of God. That would be Jesus to her, unfortunately, and not some disreputable scoundrel like Conrad Yeats. He wondered why she was still wearing it. Probably to keep his likes at bay.

"Conrad." Serena managed a smile. "I figured they'd send you. You always did have odd ideas for a secret rendezvous."

Conrad saw she was down to her wool sweater now, her black hair falling softly over her shoulders. Underneath she was probably wearing polypropylene inner liners to move sweat away from her skin, or acrylic thermal underwear. As for what was wrapped under that, Conrad didn't have to imagine, and he realized he was the one sweating.

"What's so odd?" He reached over and touched her face. "You're still cold."

"I'm fine. What happened to you?"

He looked at his bandaged hand. "Occupational hazard."

"Like Yeats? I would have put you and me together before I ever thought I'd see you with your father."

"Like you and your *GQ* boys in the next—"

"Cell?" She smiled. "Worried about some competition, Conrad?" she asked. "Don't be. If I were the last woman on earth and you were the last man, I'd become a nun again."

Conrad stared into her soft brown eyes. It was the first time they had been alone, face-to-face, in five years, and Conrad secretly felt she looked more beautiful than ever. He, on the other hand, felt old and worn down. "What are you doing here, Serena?"

"I thought I might ask you the same question, Conrad."

He was itching to tell her about the ruins beneath the ice, that his theories were true. But he couldn't. After all, they had never dealt with the ruins of their own lives on the surface.

"You're not just here to save the environment," Conrad stated. "When you came through that air lock, you weren't surprised to see me."

"You're right, Conrad," she said softly and put a warm hand to his face. "I missed you and had to see you."

Conrad pulled back. "You are so full of it, and you know it."

"Oh, and you're not?" The floor began to rumble. Serena sat back in her bunk and glanced at her watch. She's timing the shakers, he thought to himself. Suddenly she said, "When were you going to inform the rest of the world about your discovery?"

Conrad swallowed hard. "What discovery?"

"The pyramid under the ice."

Conrad blinked in disbelief but said nothing. Still,

there was no use fighting the fact that somehow she knew as much or more than he did about this expedition.

"So what else did God tell you?"

"I'd say the team has been drilling exploratory tunnels in the ice around the pyramid," she said. "And I'd bet that by now your cowboy father has probably found a door."

There was a minute of silence. They were no longer locked in their typical give-and-take banter but were fellow truth-seekers. Conrad was glad she was there and angry at the same time. He was worried about her safety and yet felt threatened by her presence, as if somehow she was standing in his way.

"Serena," he said softly. "This isn't some oil platform that you can chain yourself to in order to protest the production of fossil fuels. A few dozen soldiers have already died on this expedition, and it's practically a miracle you and I are even talking."

A cloud of sober reflection passed over Serena's face. She was processing her own thoughts. "I can take care of myself, Conrad," she said. "It's you I'm worried about."

"Me?"

"Your father hasn't told you everything."

"What else is new?" Conrad shrugged. "Passing along a piece of information for him is like passing a kidney stone. So he's hiding something. So are you, Serena. A lot more. Look, neither the United States nor the Vatican is going to be able to keep a lid on something this big."

Her eyes narrowed. "Conrad, I know you're not this naive, so it must be denial," she said. "Tell me, how did Yeats lure you down here? Did he promise you credit for the find of the ages? Maybe more help in finding your true parents?"

"Maybe."

"Trust me, Conrad," she said, the pain of personal experience in her eyes, "there are some answers you don't want to know."

"Speak for yourself, Serena."

"Conrad, this isn't about you and this isn't about me. It's about the world at large and the greater good. You have to consider other people."

"I am considering them. This is an unprecedented development in human history. And I want to share it with the world."

"No, you want to magnify the great name of Doctor Conrad Yeats," she said. "To hell with the rest of the world. But why should you care? It's the information about Earth that's more important than the planet or its people. Isn't that how it goes with you? You haven't changed a bit."

"If you're referring to our relationship, you knew exactly what you were doing then, Miss High and Mighty. You just didn't want to take responsibility for your actions."

"I was pure as the driven snow, Conrad. But you pissed on me. Just like you're going to piss on this planet."

"Hey, it's not like we actually did anything."

"My point exactly," she said. "But you didn't do much to contradict the rumors, did you?"

"I am not the bad guy here."

"Aren't you?" she asked. "You're nothing but a pawn

of the United States, willing to betray everything you believe in about international cooperation and the brotherhood and sisterhood of humanity to satisfy your selfish curiosity."

"I don't want to change the world," he told her. "I just want to understand it. And this is our best shot yet to make sense of who we are and where we came from. You make it sound like the fruit of forbidden knowledge. One bite and we'll all be cursed."

"Maybe we already are, Conrad. Isn't that what attracted you to me in the first place? I was your forbidden fruit. Just like these ruins you've found under the ice."

"Try the other way around, Serena," he said. "And my mind is made up."

Serena nodded. "Then you might as well take me down with you."

Conrad stared at her incredulously. The only reason he was here was because he was the world's leading authority on megalithic architecture and the son of the general leading the expedition. Serena didn't have a prayer. "You've got to be kidding."

"What happens when you come across some inscription down there?" she asked simply. "Who's going to figure it out? You?"

Not only had he failed to extract any meaningful information from her, Conrad thought with a sinking feeling, but she also had directed their conversation to precisely this point. The point that Yeats had just predicted this would all come to. And somehow, Serena knew as much.

"Granted, I'm no linguist, but here and there I've picked up a thing or two."

"Like a venereal disease?" she shot back. "For all you know, Conrad, the only reason you're here is because they thought they couldn't get me."

The thing that bothered Conrad the most was that she said it with absolute humility. It wasn't a boast, but a plausible probability. Then Conrad realized she was playing to the security camera near the ceiling. She had been talking to Yeats all along.

"You're unbelievable, you know that?" he told her. "Absolutely unbelievable."

She flashed him a warm smile that could melt the ice caps. "Would you have me any other way?"

9

DISCOVERY
PLUS TWENTY-FOUR DAYS,
SIXTEEN HOURS
U.S.S. *CONSTELLATION*,
SOUTHERN OCEAN

"**DAMN YEATS,**" cursed Admiral Hank Warren.

The short, powerfully built Warren scanned the blacked-out silhouettes of his carrier group's battle formation with his binoculars from the bridge of the aircraft carrier U.S.S. *Constellation*. They were twenty miles off the coast of East Antarctica, and Warren's mission was to keep his battle group undetected until further orders.

To that end, all radars and satellite sets were turned off. Only line-of-sight radios capable of millisecond-burst transmissions were allowed. Extra lookouts with binoculars were posted on deck to sweep the dawn's horizon for enemy surface ship silhouettes and submarine periscope feathers.

The idea was to get the battle force in close to the coast without betraying their position and then strike at the enemy without warning. A nuclear-powered carrier was good at that. But who the hell was the enemy down here? He and his battle force were freezing their asses trying to avoid detection, and the only enemy they were intimidating was the penguins.

Meanwhile, an unidentified aircraft using a U.S. Navy military frequency had placed a distress call before disappearing from radar. And if the crew of the *Constellation* heard it, then others had heard it too.

All he knew was that this had something to do with that crazy bastard Griffin Yeats, and that made him even more uneasy.

Way back when, Warren had done some time with the U.S. Naval Support Task Force, Antarctica. It was his rescue team that found Yeats wandering in a stupor back in '69 after forty-three days in the snow deserts, the sole survivor of a training mission for a Mars launch that never happened. The nut insisted on dragging three NASA supply containers with him even though the navy had its own. Not a care about the three bodies he left behind. Only later did Warren's team learn that the containers Yeats dragged out with him were radioactive. But that's the kind of man Yeats was, unconcerned with the havoc he wreaked in other people's lives if they got in the way of his own agenda. When Warren filed a complaint, all he got was the "classified" and "need to know" bullshit.

Now, more than thirty-five years later and bearing the rank of admiral, Warren was still in the dark when it came to Yeats. And it frustrated him to no end. His crew had just picked up a short-burst distress call from what appeared to be some black ops flight calling itself 696, which apparently crashed on approach to some phantom landing strip. Yeats's fingerprints were all over this debacle, and Warren was personally going to see to it that the man got the early retirement he deserved.

"Conn, Sonar," shouted the sonar chief from his console.

"Conn, aye." Warren had the conn for the morning watch. It was important for the crew to see him in command and even more important for him to feel in command.

"Lookouts report unknown surface vessel inbound at two-zero-six," the sonar chief reported. "Range is under a thousand yards."

"What!" the admiral blurted. "How the hell did we miss it?"

Warren lifted his binoculars and turned to the southwest. There. A ship. The letters across the bow said MV *Arctic Sunrise*. It was a Greenpeace ship, and on board was a guy pointing a video camera with a zoom lens at the *Constellation*.

"Helmsman, get us out of here!"

"Too late, sir," said a signalman. "They've marked us."

The signalman pointed to a TV monitor.

"This is CNN, live from the *Arctic Sunrise*." The reporter was broadcasting from the bow of the Greenpeace ship. "As you can see behind me, the U.S.S. *Constellation,* one of the mightiest warships ever made, is cruising off the coast of Antarctica, its mission shrouded in secrecy. But first, CNN has captured on video large cracks in this Antarctic ice shelf, which suggest that the collapse of the shelf is imminent."

A scruffy college type, the kind who wouldn't last a

week at Annapolis, came on-screen to say, "Scientists consider the rapid disintegration of this and other ice shelves around Antarctica a sign that dangerous warming is continuing."

Footage appeared of an iceberg that had split off the coast a few weeks ago. The reporter's voice-over noted that the towering ice cube covered two thousand square miles, with sheer walls rising almost two hundred feet above the waterline and had an estimated depth of one thousand feet.

"And now a bizarre new twist to the global warming phenomenon has surfaced regarding accusations of unauthorized nuclear tests by the United States in the interior snow deserts of Antarctica."

The CNN report concluded with a long shot of the *Constellation*'s ominous profile on the ocean horizon at dawn.

"Aw, hell," said Warren. MSNBC and the other network news shows would soon give out the same information. It couldn't get any worse. "Damn you, Griffin Yeats."

10
DISCOVERY
PLUS TWENTY-FOUR DAYS,
SIXTEEN HOURS

SERENA SAT ON HER BUNK, listening to the whirring of the two fans pumping air and God knew what else into the cold brig. She shivered. Images she had trained herself to suppress had resurfaced after seeing Conrad. Now, as she hugged her body to keep warm, the memory of their last time together came flooding back.

It had been March, six months after they first met at the symposium of Meso-American archaeologists in La Paz, Bolivia's capital. She was still a nun then, and they were seeing each other almost daily, working side by side on a research project in the lost city of Tiahuanaco high in the Andes.

Conrad Yeats was intelligent, attractive, witty, and sensitive. He was almost more spiritual than her colleagues from Rome, and what attracted her to him most was the purity of his calling. Some found his unorthodox theory of a Mother Culture threatening, but to her it made a wild kind of sense, based on her own studies of world mythologies. She and Conrad were approaching the same conclusion from different ends, he from archaeology and she from linguistics.

On the last night of their field studies program he invited her to join him for a "revelation" on Lake Titicaca, about twelve miles away from Tiahuanaco.

It was a curious place for good-byes, she thought as she strolled the shore. Locals and tourists alike were bustling about and drinking beers at the lakeside taverns as the sun began to set.

Then a tanned and handsome Conrad showed up in an elegant reed boat, like some Tiahuanacan visage come to life. The boat came from the lake's island of Suriqi. It was a fifteen-footer made from bundled totora rushes, wide amidships and narrow at either end with a high curving prow and stern. Tight cords held the bundles of reeds in place.

"Look familiar?" he asked as he beckoned her aboard. "Just like the boats made from papyrus reeds that the pharaohs used to sail the Nile during the Age of the Pyramids."

"And I suppose, Doctor Yeats, that you can explain how these strikingly similar designs could arise in two such widely separated places?" she asked, playing along.

It was just one of the many mysteries of Lake Titicaca, he said in his best tour guide twang and offered to take her to the middle of the lake to show her his "revelation."

She had a pretty good idea what that revelation was and smiled. "There's nothing you can show me in the middle of the lake that you can't show me here."

"I wouldn't go that far," he told her.

She shouldn't have gone with him. The sisters had a policy of traveling in pairs and never being alone with a man in a room with the door closed. It wasn't out of fear or paranoia but for appearances' sake. There must not be a hint of impropriety that would harm the cause of Christ.

But Conrad, as usual, was too persuasive to resist.

He paddled with long, powerful strokes and they glided across the silvery surface. At 12,500 feet above sea level, Lake Titicaca was the highest lake in the world, and it felt like it. Serena thought she could almost touch the heavens.

"Now the odd thing about this lake is that it's located hundreds of miles from the Pacific, yet it contains ocean-variety fish, seahorses, crustacea, and marine fauna," Conrad lectured with a wink.

"And you think it's seawater from the Genesis flood?" Serena asked.

Conrad shrugged. "When the waters receded, some got dammed up here in the Andes."

"I guess that explains the docks in Tiahuanaco."

Conrad smiled. "Right. Why else would the ruins of a city twelve miles away have docks?"

"Unless it was once a port and the south end of this lake extended twelve miles and more than a hundred feet higher," Serena concluded. "Which means civilization flourished here before the flood and Tiahuanaco is at least fifteen thousand years old."

"Imagine that."

She could. She wanted to. A world before the dawn of

recorded history. What was it like? Were people really that much different from us today? she wondered. There must have been women like me back then, she thought, and men like Conrad. He had dropped his skeptical pose and opened up so beautifully out here. So different from his posture before the academics.

The night air was chilly, and Serena was huddled in the bow. Conrad paddled slowly. The twilight sky above was a magnificent turquoise blue, and the lake stretched on like glass for eternity.

For the longest time they were silent, gliding along the reeds with only the dip of Conrad's paddle making soft lapping sounds like an ancient metronome. Then, when they were in the middle of the glistening waters, he pulled up his paddle and let them drift beneath the stars.

"What's wrong?" she asked.

"Nothing." He produced a basket of food and wine. "Absolutely nothing at all."

"Conrad," she began, "I really should be getting back. The sisters will worry."

"As well they should."

He sat beside her and kissed her, then pushed her gently backward until she was lying down. He stroked her face and kissed her on the lips, and she shivered.

"Conrad, please."

Their eyes locked, and she thought of his childhood pain, their connection, thought that if there was ever any man to do this with, any time of her life and any place on the planet, this was it.

"Tomorrow I go back to Arizona and you go back to

Rome," he whispered in her ear. "And we can remember our last night in Bolivia as the night that never happened."

"You got that right," she said, and pushed him overboard to a satisfying splash.

Inside his compartment, as he packed his gear for the impending descent to P4, Conrad, too, was thinking about that night with Serena on the reed boat.

He had always been in awe of her determination and courage. And her beauty was unmatched. Yet she wore it so effortlessly, as if she didn't care whether she was seventeen or seventy. She was charming and self-effacing, even funny. But that night it had been her glimmering eyes, almost glowing under the dark hair that draped down onto his chest, that had mesmerized him.

She told him she had always admired his purity and single-mindedness. He was what he was, she said, and not like herself—someone able to pretend to be what she was not. He wondered what dark secret she was about to confess but soon realized she had none. Her only sin was being an unwanted child.

It was then, for a fleeting moment, that he came closest to knowing her. For the first time he grasped her holy death wish and understood her drive to be a martyr, a saint, a woman who counted. If anything, he realized, her works of compassion were her way of avoiding intimacy. She feared being "found out" and thus not measuring up to her standards, much less God's. She would do anything to avoid those feelings of not being needed, of feeling worthless, a "mistake" like her birth. But she didn't fear that rejection from him. She knew he loved her.

And that's how he knew she truly loved him.

He felt he had come to the end of his lifelong quest, had found the Temple of God. That he was a thief in the sacred shrine, taking what did not belong to him, only made the experience more exciting, dangerous, and satisfying than any relic or ancient artifact he had ever taken, before or since.

But he knew it was over when she pushed him off the reed boat and into the freezing waters of Lake Titicaca. When he climbed back on board, she wasn't laughing. It hadn't been a prank. Instead the fear had returned to her eyes.

Suddenly Conrad realized she was the one who had stolen something from him. "Where do you think you're going?" he asked.

"Back to Tiahuanaco," she said, "before anybody realizes I'm missing at breakfast."

"Be a risk taker. Let's enjoy what time we have."

"I'm disappointed in you, Doctor Yeats," she said, handing him the paddle. "I didn't think you were the kind of man who took advantage of nuns."

Conrad, a man with no small ego, was disappointed that she had spurned his advances. Worse, she was denying her own complicity. "And I didn't think you were the kind of nun who cares what other people think."

"I'm not," she shot back.

She was right, of course. That much was obvious to anybody. But Conrad also sensed that what she was truly afraid of was her feelings for him, of losing control. And if Serena Serghetti could be defined as any kind of nun, she was most definitely the kind who made damn well sure she was always in control.

Their parting was not happy. She acted as if she had made a huge mistake and had potentially blown her whole future with their night together. In truth, however, she didn't regret it for a minute. At least that's what Conrad eventually concluded. What Serena feared was further intimacy. Like she had something to hide. Then he understood. It was herself. She had disappointed herself and as a result felt unworthy of him.

She was wrong, he knew, and he vowed to prove to her that she was worth something without the title of Sister and that he was worth the price of her sacrifice. But she would have none of it.

The last memory he had of her was standing at the shore, trying to kiss her good-bye, and watching her run to hail a cab. He waved to her, but she never looked back. He tried to reach her in Rome by phone a week later, and after months of unreturned calls, he even showed up at one of her conferences unannounced. Now she had become famous, throwing herself so fully into her work that he wondered if it was the unwanted child in her she wanted to forget, or him.

In any case, a private audience with Mother Earth, he soon discovered, was about as probable as he discovering his beloved lost Mother Culture.

Until now.

• • •

The nun's got titanium balls, Yeats thought as he reviewed Serghetti's exchange with Conrad on a video monitor in the command center. I have to give her that. The pope knew exactly what he was doing when he sent her.

"How does she know so much, sir?" asked O'Dell, who was standing next to him.

"Moot point now," said Yeats. "I doubt the Vatican wants her to talk. But for all we know, she's right. Her presence may even be necessary for what's ahead."

"And your son, sir?"

Yeats looked at O'Dell. "What about him?"

"I've seen the DOD report." O'Dell looked concerned. "Your boy's been in therapy since kindergarten. Nightmares of cataclysmic doom. Visions of the end of the world. With all due respect, sir, he's a lunatic."

"So he had a traumatic childhood," Yeats said, wishing O'Dell would put a lid on it. "Didn't we all? Besides, the DOD doesn't have his complete file. Trust me, I wrote it."

Yeats was about to turn his attention back to the monitor when Lieutenant Lopez, one of his communications officers, walked up. Besides Sister Serghetti, young Lopez was the only other woman at Ice Base Orion.

"General Yeats," she reported. "I think you better see this."

Yeats followed her to the big screen and saw the U.S.S. *Constellation* on TV with a CNN logo in the lower right corner.

"Warren," Yeats cursed under his breath. He stared at the intrepid Greenpeace vessel juxtaposed on-screen with the mighty *Constellation*. Goddamn that sausage in a sailor suit!

O'Dell said, "How did they know, sir?"

"Take a wild guess, Colonel." Yeats pointed to Sister Serghetti in her cell on the little monitor. "She's been stalling the whole time, waiting for the cavalry to arrive. It's only a matter of time before an army of U.N. weapons inspectors comes knocking at our door."

Which meant the insertion team had to be in and out of P4 before then, Yeats concluded, and he mentally began to make the calculations. P4 would have to be wiped clean of significant technology or data before any internationals reached the site.

"It gets worse, sir," Lopez said. "McMurdo reports that Vostok Station intercepted our communications with Flight six-nine-six. They've already dispatched a UNACOM team."

Yeats groaned. "I knew it. Who's leading the team?"

"An Egyptian air force officer," she said, handing him a report. "Colonel Ali Zawas."

"Zawas?" Yeats looked at the photo of a handsome man in uniform with dark, thoughtful eyes and black wavy hair. "Holy shit."

O'Dell said, "He wouldn't be related to—"

"He's the secretary-general's nephew," Yeats said. "And he's a graduate of the United States Air Force Academy. Flew with the Allies during the first Gulf War and downed two Iraqi jets for us. Damned fine officer and gentleman." Yeats handed the report back to Lopez. "What kind of backup does Zawas have, Lieutenant?"

"Well, there are the Russians at Vostok under the command of a Colonel Ivan Kovich. And the Aussies are offering support from Mawson Station." She paused. "So are some of our own American scientists from Amundsen-Scott who have been kept out of the loop."

"Damn it!" Yeats growled. "The whole world's going to be here in a few hours."

"Not with this storm kicking up again, sir," O'Dell said. "ETA six hours. WX Ops says this thing is going to slam us hard. Might pin everybody down for three weeks."

Yeats looked out the window. The skies had darkened. Snow pelted the glass like bullets. "The storm might stop the Aussies, but it will only slow down Zawas and his UNACOM team." Yeats turned to O'Dell. "You hold off the barbarians here on the surface while I take the insertion team down to P4."

O'Dell said, "And how am I going to explain holding Mother Earth against her will?"

"You won't have to," Yeats said. "I'm taking her with us. Now."

PART TWO
DESCENT

11

DESCENT HOUR ONE
THE ABYSS

THE SKY OVER THE CHASM turned an ominous deep black, and Serena felt the wind pick up with a sudden chill. If this was supposed to be a lull in the polar storm, she didn't want to stick around for the real deal. Mist boiled up from the abyss below, where the nearest shelter, the so-called P4 Habitat, was a one-mile drop.

"You sure you're up for this, Sister?"

It was Yeats, sliding down the icy wall above her in his white freezer suit, grinning like the devil under the blinding light of his headtorch. Back on the surface, he had detailed the risks to her about coming down with the insertion team. But what other choice did she have? To wait back at the base with the rest of the world until the team resurfaced would be to remain in the dark.

"Technically, it's Doctor Serghetti, General," she said, digging the crampon attached to her plastic boot into a toehold. "And I climbed Everest with my first Mother Superior."

"She give you the garter?"

Yeats was pointing to Serena's harness. It actually did look like a red garter belt with two loops around her thighs. In case of a fall it would spread the shock evenly throughout her lower body.

"No, just this." Serena pulled out her ice ax and hammered an ice screw into the frozen wall before attaching a new line with a carabiner. She wanted to show Yeats she was more than up to the challenge. But in fact she was feeling strange. Her heart was pounding and she was breathing rapidly. "Do you smell something?"

"Yeah," said Yeats. "Your story."

She had never met the infamous Griffin Yeats until Ice Base Orion, only heard about him from Conrad. But she didn't trust him. Like Emerson said: "Who you are speaks so loudly I can't hear what you're saying." The guy was a rogue at heart, just like this expedition. He simply did a better job of hiding it than Conrad, who was refreshingly honest and even charming about his shortcomings. She also concluded that Yeats hadn't agreed to let her join the team out of the kindness of his heart or even because he valued her for her expertise as a linguist.

"Tell me again why you changed your mind and let me tag along?"

"If anything, I learned from NASA that women are always a pleasant addition to astronaut crews."

She had expected something sexist like that coming from him. "Gee, I thought it was because women are actually better with precision tasks, more meticulous, and more flexible at multitasking than men."

"Whenever they're not too emotional or easily upset," Yeats replied and dropped out of sight just as Conrad rappeled alongside her.

"Anything wrong?" Conrad asked.

Serena sighed and shook her head. "Your father never stops, does he?"

"It's not in his nature," Conrad answered without feeling. "Once he's programmed, he keeps going and going until he finishes the job."

"And leaves a trail of bodies behind him."

"Then we better not let him get too far ahead of us," Conrad said, rappeling down.

She went after him. He was an expert climber in tropical climates. But overconfidence could be fatal in icy conditions like this. And she was worried for him. For his soul. For her own too. Because in trying to save him once before she felt she had condemned them both.

Conrad was within reach now, and she dropped down a few feet and found a hold. The color of the ice was a beautiful blue and almost seemed to glow. "Pretty," she said.

"Don't stop, Serena. Keep going." Conrad spoke rapidly.

Serena continued to ease up on her line. But Conrad's physiology concerned her. Was he hyperventilating? Serena didn't know and could feel her own breathing quicken to an unnaturally fast pace. Her heart too. The pounding was regular but fast.

She eased up a bit more when Conrad motioned with a gloved hand. "Down there," he said. "See it?"

Serena peered into the mist below. A hole parted and she could see a grid of lights, like a landing pad. "I see."

"No, do you see it?"

Suddenly Serena could see that the landing pad was in fact the flattened summit of a gleaming white pyramid rising sharply through the floor of the abyss. She had to shade her eyes from the glare of the lights off the pyramid's surface.

"P4," she heard herself saying under her breath.

"Don't ask me how it got here," Conrad said, now sporting his sunglasses. "I can't explain it yet. But I will."

The conviction in his voice inspired confidence. His excitement was pure, unadulterated, and moving. Not a trace of fear, she thought with envy, just genuine curiosity and enthusiasm. She had almost forgotten what that felt like.

She slipped on her sunglasses. The flat summit, brighter than the whitest snow, was blinding. So this was why the pope had sent her down, she realized. She had suspected something spectacular, but she was completely unprepared for the sight or dimension of this monument. It was gigantic.

She was staring at it in wonder when she heard her line creak.

"Just some slack," Conrad assured her. "No worries."

She heard a sharp crack and the ping of metal. The piton holding her line in the ice popped out, and she thought she was falling.

"Conrad!" she shouted as she buried her ice ax into the wall and hung on.

But Conrad said nothing. She looked to her side. He was gone. It was his piton that had popped out.

She looked down in time to see Conrad fall into the mist.

"Conrad!" she screamed.

Yeats rappeled down beside her.

"You couldn't wait until afterward to bury him?" he asked, scanning the billowing mist below. Yeats flicked Conrad's line with the back of a gloved finger. "He's still floating."

She heard a crack and looked up to see the ice screw on her own line start to slip. She instinctively pulled out her ice ax and swung it at Yeats, who put up a defensive arm. "Hold this," she said and suddenly felt herself plunging into space.

She fell through the cloud a few seconds later, hurtling toward the lights below when her line snapped tight and she stopped with a jolt. For a moment she feared she had shattered her pelvis. But her harness had done its job.

She caught her breath and could hear her windproof parka squeaking against the nylon rope as she swung back and forth.

"Conrad?" she called.

"Over here," he replied. "I found something."

She swung her head in the direction of his voice, and her headtorch found him swinging ten feet from the wall, unable to get a hold.

"Hang on," she said as she swung over.

It took three tries before her arc was wide enough to reach him. As she swung toward him, she held out her hand, and he gripped it tight, holding her next to him. They swung together in space for a few seconds, clinging to each other.

"Finished bungee jumping, Conrad?" she asked, trying to mask her anxiety with sarcasm.

"Look!" he said.

She turned in the darkness and her headtorch bathed the wall with light. There was something in the ice. Then her eyes focused and Serena found herself face-to-face with a little girl, frozen in time.

"Dear Jesus," she whispered.

"Remember when you told me the only way we'd get together again was when hell freezes over?" he told her. "Well, here we are."

The mist lifted and the light from below flooded the entire wall. In an instant Serena could see hundreds of human beings, their faces frozen in fear. All of them seemed to shout out at once. Serena covered her ears, only to realize that she was the one screaming.

12
DESCENT HOUR THREE
HABITAT MODULE

AN HOUR LATER, inside the warm P4 habitat module, Conrad was concerned as he looked at Serena on the fold-out surgical table. Her eyes blinked rapidly beneath the high-intensity lights, an oxygen mask over her mouth and several EKG electrodes attached to her chest. Her hair was brushed back from her face and the belt around her cargo pants loosened.

Conrad pointed out the fogged-up porthole at the American flag Yeats had planted atop the pyramid summit.

"Focus on the flag and breathe deeply," he told her as he administered the oxygen from a heavy yellow canister.

Her parka and outerwear were gone, and he tried not to gaze at her full breasts rising and falling beneath her wool undershirt. She had been hyperventilating since they reached the bottom of the ice gorge, spooked, it seemed, by the frozen graveyard that entombed them. Conrad glanced at the EKG monitor. Only now was her heart rate returning to the upper register of the normal range.

"Better?" he asked her after a minute.

She looked at him like he was a lunatic for asking.

Conrad looked around the cramped habitat perched atop P4's flat summit at the bottom of the gorge. It was a single module, fifty-five feet long and fourteen feet in diameter. Yeats was huddled with the three technicians by the monitors. One was Lopez, a female officer Conrad recognized from Ice Base Orion. The other two were fair-haired steroid freaks who answered to the names of Kreigel and Marcus. They were clearly Yeats's muscle down here.

Conrad turned to Yeats. "Was there any particular reason why you forgot to mention the frozen bodies?"

"Yeah," said Yeats. "I wanted to see your reaction."

Conrad gestured at Serena and glared at Yeats. "Satisfied?"

"Quit whining." Yeats stood up, a hypodermic in hand. He flicked the syringe with his finger, and a clear liquid squirted into the air. Serena squirmed.

Conrad watched in alarm as Yeats grabbed hold of Serena's arm. "What are you doing to her?" he demanded.

"Giving her a shot of the stimulant eleutherococcus," said Yeats, injecting it into Serena's arm before Conrad could stop him. "It's a plant extract of the ginseng family. Deep-sea divers, mountain rescuers, and cosmonauts take it to resist stress while working under inhospitable conditions. About the only damn usable thing the Russians ever contributed to our space program."

The drug seemed to be working. Conrad looked at Serena, who was breathing more evenly now, although there was anger in her eyes. Clearly this wasn't a woman who was used to being taken care of.

"She'll be fine," said Yeats. "Now, if you don't mind,

I've got to check my drill team's search for that mythical shaft of yours."

"As mythical as P4," Conrad called out as Yeats opened the hatch and stepped outside. Subzero polar air whooshed inside.

"You seem to be holding up just fine, Conrad," Serena said, catching him off guard. She had removed her oxygen mask. "I take it this isn't the first time you've seen frozen bodies at least twelve thousand years old?"

He looked down at her, barely able to contain his excitement. It wasn't every day he found evidence for his theories, or proof that he wasn't crazy. "Those bodies explain how the pyramid got here."

"Got here?" She managed to sit up, the color returning to her high cheekbones. "What are you talking about? Did it move?"

Conrad dug into his pack and produced a frozen orange. "I chipped this out of the wall," he said. "This proves Antarctica was once a temperate climate."

Serena looked at the orange. "Until it suddenly froze over one day, I suppose?"

Conrad nodded. "Hapgood's theory of earth-crust displacement."

"Charles Hapgood?" Serena asked.

"That's right. Dead for years. So you've heard of him?"

"The university professor, yes, but not this displacement theory."

Conrad always relished an opportunity to tell Mother Earth something she didn't know. Holding up the orange, he said, "Pretend this is Planet Earth."

"OK." She seemed willing to humor him.

He snapped open a pocket knife and carved an outline of the seven continents on the thawing peel. "Hapgood's theory says the ice age was not a meteorological phenomenon. Rather, it was the result of a geological catastrophe about twelve thousand years ago." Conrad rotated the orange upward so that the United States was in the Arctic Circle and Antarctica was closer to the equator. "This was the world back then."

Serena lifted an eyebrow. "And what happened?"

"The entire outer shell of Earth's surface shifted, like the skin of this orange." Conrad rotated the orange downward until it resembled Earth as they knew it. "Antarctica is engulfed by the polar zone while North America is released from the Arctic Circle and becomes temperate. Ice melts in North America while it forms in Antarctica."

Serena frowned. "What caused this cataclysmic shift?"

"Nobody really knows," said Conrad. "But Hapgood thought it was an imbalance of ice in the polar caps. As ice built up, they became so heavy they shifted, dragging the outer crust of the continents in one piece to new positions."

Serena eyed him. "And you'd be willing to stake what's left of your reputation on this earth-crust displacement theory?"

Conrad shrugged. "Albert Einstein liked the idea. He believed significant shifts in Earth's crust have probably taken place repeatedly and within a short time. That could explain weird things, like mammoths frozen in the Arctic Circle with tropical vegetation in their stomachs.

Or people and pyramids buried a mile beneath the ice in Antarctica."

Serena put a soft hand on Conrad's shoulder. "If that helps you make sense of the world, then good for you."

Conrad stiffened. He thought she'd be as excited as he was by the evidence. That they were two of a kind. Instead she was attacking the conclusion he had drawn. More than that, she was attacking him personally. He resented this cavalier dismissal—by a woman of religious faith, no less—of a plausible scientific hypothesis from one of the greatest minds in human history. "Does the Vatican have a better theory?"

Serena nodded. "The Flood."

"Same difference," Conrad said. "Both fall under the God-Is-a-Genocidal-Maniac Theory." But as soon as the words were out, he was sorry he had said them to her.

"Hey, mister, you watch your mouth," said a female voice from behind.

Conrad turned to see Lopez looking cross at him. Another Catholic, he realized. Lopez looked at Serena and asked, "You want me to kick his ass for you?"

Serena smiled. "Thanks, but he gets it kicked enough already."

"Well, the offer stands," Lopez said before returning to her work. The Aryan twins, Kreigel and Marcus, looked disappointed. Conrad figured they must be Lutheran, agnostics, or simply of good German stock who in another time and place might have distinguished themselves as poster boys for Hitler's SS.

Serena reached for her parka and slipped her arms

through the sleeves. "What are you suggesting, Conrad?" She was trying to zip her parka, but the EKG wires were in the way. "That God is to blame for humanity's every famine, war or lustful leer?"

He realized she was looking straight at him now, her warm, brown eyes both accusing him and forgiving him at the same time. It irritated the hell out of him. So maybe he had been watching her breasts a little longer than he should have, he thought. He was only human. So was she, if she'd only admit it.

"I saw the way you looked at the little girl in the ice," Conrad said softly. "It was like you were looking at yourself. Hardly the wicked sort the Genesis flood was intended to punish."

"The rain falls on the just and the unjust," she said absently. "Or in this case the ice."

Conrad could tell her thoughts were someplace else. She couldn't see her EKG numbers jumping again.

Conrad pointed to the monitors. "Look, maybe we should take you back up and bring down an able-bodied replacement." He reached over to help her with the EKG wires. "I don't want you to get hurt."

She angrily knocked him away with her shoulder and ripped off the EKG leads. "Speak for yourself, Doctor Yeats."

Conrad rubbed his head and stared at her in disbelief. "Could you send signals that are possibly more mixed?"

She zipped up her parka and jumped to her feet. "Who's mixed up here, Doctor Yeats?"

Conrad stood still, aware of Lopez staring at him with interest. So were Kreigel and Marcus. The soldiers looked like they were just itching for the good nun to give the evil archaeologist a hard knee to the groin.

Then the hatch door opened and another blast of cold shot into the module with Yeats.

"You're right, Yeats," Conrad said coolly. "She's fine."

"Good. Now gear up. We're going into P4," Yeats said. "The drill team just found your shaft."

13

DESCENT HOUR FOUR
UPPER CHAMBER

THE SHAFT WAS ABOUT SEVEN FEET WIDE and seven feet high, Serena guessed, and sloped into total darkness. A coin toss had won her the bragging rights of being the first inside, this after the drill team had sent a twenty-two-pound, six-wheeled modified Mars Sojourner down the shaft with a blowtorch and camera. The remote robot confirmed what Conrad had suspected: the shaft led directly to a chamber in the heart of P4.

As Serena stood on the landing the Americans had erected along the north face of P4 and looked into the mouth of the shaft, she could feel her heart racing. She was still disturbed by the little girl frozen in the ice, she realized, not to mention the sudden, cataclysmic end to an entire society. If only the child hadn't looked so terrified.

She had always taken comfort in the theory that Genesis was a myth and the flood a theological metaphor. Yes, fossil evidence suggested a natural cataclysm. And no, she harbored little doubt that there was some sort of global deluge. But as divine retribution for humanity's wickedness? That was simply Moses's opinion.

Unfortunately, she found the alternative worldview, that impersonal cycles of nature wiped out entire species in random fashion, even more distressing, if only because it sapped any meaning from her righteous indignation.

Perhaps it had something to do with her own childhood, she could hear the Holy Father telling her. She had seen herself as a child, an innocent victim, encased in ice, frozen in time like parts of her own personality. Or maybe it was simply the failure of her faith to provide any genuine comfort regarding the inexplicable evil and suffering in this world. It was as if Satan had his own guardian angel—God. But then that would make God the Devil, a thought too terrible for Serena to dwell on.

Her trance was broken by Conrad's voice behind her.

"If you'd like, Serena, I could always take the lead."

She glanced over her shoulder at Conrad and frowned. He was cocky now that he had found a back door into the pyramid. The implication in his eyes was that once again he was right, as always. Not just about P4 but about everything else, including her. As if in time he could figure her out like any other archaeological riddle.

Infuriated, she said, "So you can translate ancient alien inscriptions too?"

"The written word is but one form of communication, Sister Serghetti, as you well know," Conrad replied.

She hated this sort of academic posturing, probably because she was so often guilty of it herself. Or maybe because, like their exchange in the habitat module, it denied the intimacy she felt they had established during the descent down the ice chasm.

"Besides," Conrad added, "I don't think we'll find any inscriptions inside."

"How would you know that?"

"Just a hunch." Conrad ran his hand across the shiny white surface of the pyramid. "Now notice the interlocking casing stones that sheath the whole structure."

If there were any fine grooves, she couldn't see them because of the brilliant reflection. "So how come our pyramids don't shine white like this?"

"The sheathings were stripped for mosques during the Middle Ages," Conrad explained. "The pyramids became cheap quarries. Feel it."

Serena ran her glove across the surface. There was a glassy feel to the stone. "A different ore?"

Conrad smiled. "You noticed. No wonder radio-echo surveys never detected the pyramid. You were right, Yeats. This stuff is slicker than a stealth bomber."

"And harder than diamonds," Yeats added impatiently from somewhere behind Conrad. "Broke all our drills trying to bore holes before we found the shaft. We don't have a name for it yet. Now if we could move ahead and—"

"*Oreichalkos*," Conrad answered.

Conrad's voice seemed to bounce up and down the shaft walls. Serena asked, "What did you say?"

"*Oreichalkos* is the name of the enigmatic ore or 'shining metal' Plato said the people of Atlantis used," Conrad said. "It was a pure alloy they mined, an almost supernatural 'mountain-copper.' It sparkled like fire and was used to cover walls—and for inscriptions. I'm betting the outer six feet of the pyramid is made of this stuff."

He seemed way too sure of himself. She said, "You think you have all the answers, don't you?"

"We won't know until we get inside, will we?"

"And what if the builders laid a trap?" she said.

"The Atlanteans are the ones who got trapped, remember?" Conrad said. "Besides, the builders never intended entrants to penetrate from the sky, through this shaft. The only booby traps, if any, are scattered around P4's base and any tunnels leading up to key chambers."

She looked over Conrad's shoulder at Yeats, whose brow was furrowed with either concern or, more likely, impatience. Lopez, Kreigel, and Marcus, standing next to him, were as stone-faced as ever.

"Let's find out," she said and stepped into the shaft.

Conrad was right about the *oreichalkos*, she soon discovered. About seven or eight feet into the shaft, the surface of the walls changed to a rougher, darker kind of stone or metal. It scraped lightly on her Gore-Tex parka, but she found that she could creep down the shaft with both feet by leaning back and holding her line taut. The light from her headtorch could only pierce about fifty feet of the darkness ahead.

"How are we doing down there?" called Yeats. His voice sounded flat and tinny in the shaft.

"Fine," she replied.

But she didn't feel fine. The air was heavy and suffocating. The wet, dense walls seemed to close in on her the farther they descended down the thirty-eight-degree grade. As she crept along the shaft, a tingling sensation started in the small of her back and slowly rose up her spine.

Twenty minutes later they emerged from the shaft into a massive, somber reddish room that seemed to radiate tremendous heat and power. It was completely empty.

"There's nothing here, Conrad," she said, her voice echoing. "No inscriptions. Nothing."

"Don't be so certain."

She turned and watched Conrad rappel off the wall from which the shaft emptied, followed by Yeats and his three officers.

Conrad swept the room with his floodlight, revealing walls made of massive granitelike blocks. The floor and ceiling were likewise spanned by gigantic blocks. The chamber was longer than a football field and Serena guessed more than two hundred feet high. Yet it felt like the walls were pressing down on her.

"Talk about megalithic architecture," Conrad said as he ran his light beam across the ceiling. "The engineering logistics alone for this are amazing."

Conrad was right about the architecture, she thought. It revealed much about its builders. That's what made linguistics so intriguing to her. Language often tried to hide or manipulate meaning. In so doing it revealed the true nature of the civilization behind the artifacts.

But there were no inscriptions here. There was nothing. Even in the sparest of digs she could usually find an object that connected her in some way to the people of those times. A shard of pottery, a figurine. They were more than artifacts. They belonged to thinking, feeling human beings. It was like looking through her father the priest's personal items after he died and finding the most trivial yet telling clues about her past.

She felt no connection here. Nothing. Just absolute emptiness, and it was chilling. Not even a sarcophagus—a burial coffin, which if her memory of Egyptian pyramids served her, should have been at the western end of this chamber, but wasn't. At least a tomb was built for someone. But this place was cold, utilitarian, aloof.

"I don't see any other shafts," she said. "You said we'd find another one. And there are no doors. We're stuck."

"There it is." Conrad's beam caught the shaft in the southern wall. It looked just like the one they had emerged from.

Serena said, "All we're going to find at the end of it is the ice pack."

Conrad took a closer look and nodded. "In the Great Pyramid in Giza, the southern shaft led the deceased pharaoh to his reed boats to sail his earthly kingdom. The northern shaft was for him to join the stars in the celestial kingdom."

"That's nice," she said. "But I don't see the burial coffin of a deceased pharaoh in here."

Serena watched as Conrad walked to the center of the room. His footsteps seemed to reverberate more loudly the closer to the center he went.

"What are you doing?" she asked.

"If there's nothing inside the room, then we have to look at the room itself." Conrad walked over to the western wall and turned to face east. He took out what looked like a pen and bounced a thin laser beam off the walls. Then he checked his readings. "This chamber forms a perfect one-by-two rectangle," he announced. "And the height of this room is exactly half the length of its floor diagonal."

"So?"

"Since the chamber forms a perfect one-by-two rectangle, the builders have expressed a golden section, phi."

"Phi?" asked Yeats.

"Phi is an irrational number like pi that can't be worked out arithmetically," Conrad explained. "Its value is the square root of five plus one divided by two, equal to 1.61803. Or, the limiting value of the ratio between successive numbers in the Fibonacci series—the series of numbers beginning 0, 1, 1, 2, 3, 5, 8, 13—"

"In which each term is the sum of the two previous terms," said Serena, completing his lecture. "What's your point?"

"The builders left nothing to chance here. Every stone, every angle, every chamber has been systematically and mathematically designed for some grand purpose. This isn't only the oldest and largest structure on the planet. It's the most perfect too."

She swallowed hard. "Meaning?"

"Meaning it's humanly impossible."

Serena studied him carefully and concluded that he believed what he was saying. She didn't yet, but she was impressed with his brilliance. It was rare she met a man smarter than she was. Only Conrad was perhaps too brilliant for his own good, like the geniuses used by the Americans to build the atomic bomb during World

War II. And too sure of himself. He obviously somehow fancied he was going to take something out of P4 and stake his claim in history.

But Yeats would never allow it, she knew, glancing at the American general. His cold, stone-faced expression told her that once Conrad had served his usefulness he would be disposable. Not as his son, but certainly as an archaeologist. Conrad, however, was too smart to be disposable. Which is why she wasn't worried so much by what Conrad was saying as by what he wasn't saying.

"So now you're concluding that P4 is alien?" She shook her head. "The bodies we found in the ice are human. Yeats said the lab autopsies proved as much."

"That doesn't mean those people built P4," Conrad said. "This thing might have been here long before they arrived."

The way he referred to "this thing" bothered her. P4 wasn't a thing. It was a pyramid. Or was it? Without any inscriptions, she was powerless to find any meaning for this monument or argue with Conrad, except to say, "You don't know that for sure."

"Have some faith." Conrad crossed the room and walked over to the opposite shaft. He then pulled out a handheld device from his belt.

"What are you doing?" she said.

"Launching my astronomical simulator." Conrad pushed a button to call up a graphic on the display. "The northern shaft we came through is angled at thirty-eight degrees twenty-two minutes. This southern shaft is angled at fifteen degrees thirty minutes."

Serena walked over. "You lost me."

"You're forgetting this pyramid may be a meridian instrument to track the stars," Conrad said as he glanced at the palm display. "The shafts in the king's chamber of the Great Pyramid, for example, target Orion and Sirius. My hunch is that they were modeled after this. All we have to do is match the shafts with various celestial coordinates throughout history and we can date P4 to the precise—" Conrad stopped short. He was staring at his display.

"Go on," Serena said.

"Wait." Conrad frowned. "This can't be right."

"What is it?"

"Something wrong, Conrad?" asked Yeats, who was still looking up the southern shaft with his flashlight.

"The angle of the shafts targets certain stars in a certain epoch," Conrad said. "This shaft targets Alpha Canis Major in the constellation of the Great Dog. It was known as Sirius to the ancients, who associated it with the goddess Isis, the cosmic mother of the kings of Egypt."

"As opposed to the cosmic king Osiris," Serena said.

Conrad's eyes lit up. "Whose constellation Orion is rising in the east right now."

"You told me all this back at Ice Base Orion." Yeats was now impatiently looking over Conrad's shoulder.

"You don't understand," Conrad explained, and Serena herself was trying to catch up. "This shaft targets Alpha Canis Major right now, on the cusp of the Age of Aquarius, as seen from the South Pole at sunrise on the spring equinox."

Yeats said, "It's September, Conrad."

"For you northerners," Serena reminded Yeats. "It's

spring here and in the rest of the Southern Hemisphere." She turned to Conrad. "So what's the meaning?"

"Well, from a fixed point on the ground, the skies are like the odometer on a car. The heavens change over one complete cycle every twenty-six thousand years," he explained. "Meaning either this pyramid was built twenty-six thousand years ago, during the last Age of Aquarius. Or—"

"Or what?" she demanded.

"Or it was built to align with the stars at a date in the future." He looked her in the eye, and she felt her spine tingle. "For this present moment, right now."

14

DESCENT HOUR FIVE
ICE BASE ORION

INSIDE ICE BASE ORION ON THE SURFACE, O'Dell was lying on his bunk, listening to Chopin, waiting for some word from Yeats and the team below, when suddenly the walls began to shake and the Klaxon sounded.

Every so often the daily monotony of the base was broken by a "sim," or simulation. A Klaxon would sound, and the crew would rush to their posts in the command center, where warning light panels and the diagnostic computers were located. A flashing SIM light on the panel was the crew's notification that the emergency was not real.

But since O'Dell was the man who ordered sims, and he didn't order this event, he knew no SIM light would be flashing. He could feel his pulse quicken and his adrenaline spike as he darted out of his wardroom and headed for the command center module, where the crew was already gathered around the main monitor screen.

"We've got a breach at the outer perimeter, sir," said the lieutenant on duty. "Sector Four."

O'Dell looked at the grainy picture of swirling snow.

And then a large gray object emerged through the mist. "It's the Russians," he cursed as he recognized the Kharkovchanka tractor.

"Breach in Sector Three," shouted another officer, followed by several others.

"Sector Two breach, sir!" another said.

"Sector One!"

"Sector Three!"

O'Dell looked around the room at the monitors: Kharkovchanka tractors everywhere. The Russians had surrounded the base. He stood very still, the gravity of the situation slowly sinking in. Then he felt a tap on his shoulder. "Sir?"

O'Dell turned to see his communications officer. He blinked. The officer's lips were moving, but O'Dell couldn't hear anything. "What?"

"I said the Russians are hailing us, sir. Do you want to respond?"

O'Dell took a breath. "Can we reach General Yeats?"

"We lost contact with his party as soon as they penetrated P4."

Before O'Dell could reply, a call came over the intercom from the east air lock. "Ivans at the gate!" O'Dell heard the Russians banging against the door with what sounded like the butts of their AK-47s. He exhaled and turned to his communications officer. "Inform the Russians that a reception committee will greet them at the east air lock."

"Yes, sir."

"Meanwhile, let's hide everything we can."

O'Dell marched out of the command center and into

a maze of polystyrene corridors lined with bright, reinforced glass windows. A glance outside at the village of cylindrical modules and geodesic domes told him it would be impossible for him to hide what his team was doing here.

He passed through an air lock into a module where the strains of a Mozart symphony grew louder. He passed a cleanup crew outside the lab containing the benben stone. The double doors with the PERSONNEL ONLY sign had disappeared behind a fake glass window that was conveniently fogged up. He just hoped the Russians wouldn't look too closely. But it was probably too much to ask for, much like his prayer that they would miraculously be blinded to the dosimeters located in various panels to measure radiation from the base's nuclear reactor. That alone qualified as a smoking gun that would effectively end his career, O'Dell realized. Yeats would then end his life.

Two unarmed MPs were waiting for him by the air lock. O'Dell nodded, and slowly the heavy inside door opened. The icy air took his breath away as two figures—one large and squat, the other tall and slim—came in and stomped their boots. The squat man lifted his hood and O'Dell saw the ugliest red swollen face of his life.

"I am Colonel Ivan Kovich," he said triumphantly in English but with a thick Russian accent. "And you are in very big trouble. Very big."

Before O'Dell could reply that Ice Base Orion was simply a humble research station, Kovich began to cough uncontrollably. His tall, lanky aide pounded his commanding officer on the back until Kovich waved him off.

"Read it to him, Vlad," Kovich said, and by way of introduction added, "This is Vladimir Lenin, great-great-grandson of Lenin himself."

O'Dell watched with interest as the young officer produced a crumpled piece of paper from his parka and smoothed it out. Apparently this Lenin hadn't risen quite so high in the ranks as his ancestor. In halting English he said, "You are in violation of Article One of international Antarctic Treaty. No military allowed. Treaty gives us right to inspect base."

The young Lenin glanced at Kovich, who nodded, and then put the piece of paper away.

"Any questions?" Kovich asked O'Dell.

O'Dell said, "How many of you will be joining us?"

"As many Russians as there are Americans here on this base and at the bottom of that gorge outside," Kovich said.

"What about Colonel Zawas and his team?"

"We hope you tell us," Kovich said. "We have not heard from his patrol. They have vanished into thin air."

15
DESCENT HOUR FIVE

THERE WAS SILENCE INSIDE the chamber. Yeats looked at Conrad and could tell from his expression that something had gone horribly wrong with his calculations. The nun could tell too, he thought.

Yeats said, "Any chance you—"

"No mistake," Conrad said. "The southern shaft, which we know was built at least twelve thousand years ago, is designed to align with the star Sirius as it appears in our skies present day. The northern shaft likewise targets Al Nitak, the middle star in Orion's belt."

There was more, Yeats could tell, but Conrad wasn't talking, and Yeats knew why. Serena was also studying Conrad closely.

"Even if you're right about the astronomical alignments, why now?" she asked Conrad. "Do you think P4 has anything to do with the recent earthquakes?"

To Yeats's relief, Conrad said nothing.

"I think we ought to call Ice Base Orion before we proceed any farther." Yeats pulled out his radio and adjusted the frequency. "Ice Base Orion, this is Team Phoenix."

There was no response, just hissing and popping.

"Ice Base Orion," Yeats tried again. "Do you copy?"

Again, no answer.

"Damn," Yeats said. "These walls must be interfering."

"They didn't interfere with the video that the probe sent," Serena said. "Maybe your base isn't there anymore. Maybe it's been buried by the snowstorm."

"Look, Sister Serghetti—" Yeats snapped.

"Doctor Serghetti," she corrected.

"Look, Doctor Serghetti, we've got a case of radio blackout probably caused by this polar storm. That's all. Considering the weather on the surface, I say we wait it out down here. And as long as we're here, we do what we're supposed to do. Lopez, Marcus, Kreigel!"

The three officers snapped to attention. "Sir!"

"Set up a new command and logistics post inside this chamber. The habitat is probably unstable. Bring whatever you need down here." Yeats put a hand on Conrad's shoulder. "You said something back on the surface about four shafts in the pyramid."

"Yes," said Conrad. "I suspect the other two shafts, if they exist, are in a lower chamber. We'll need to find it to be sure."

"To be sure of what?" Serena pressed.

Conrad said, "I'll know when we get there."

"And just how are you going to get there?" she asked.

"Through that door."

"What door?" Yeats asked.

"That door."

Yeats watched Conrad turn toward the shaft they had emerged from and scan the wall to the right with his flashlight. There in the corner, to Yeats's amazement, was an open passageway. It had been behind them.

"That wasn't there before," Serena said hoarsely.

"Yes, it was," Conrad said. "It's always been there."

Once again Conrad's sense of space and dimension awed Yeats. He wouldn't be surprised if Conrad already had mapped out the entire interior of P4 in his head.

"I'm telling you it wasn't," Serena insisted.

"And I'm telling you that you missed it," Conrad said. "Chill out, OK?"

"Fine." She took a step toward the open door. "Then what are we waiting for?"

Yeats blocked her with his arm. "You stay here while Conrad and I search for those two other shafts."

Yeats could see a flash of fury in Serena's eyes. She clearly had trouble taking orders. No wonder she was such a pain in the ass for the Vatican. She pressed against his arm toward the doorway, but Conrad gripped her shoulder and pulled her back.

"It's all right, Serena," Conrad said. "When we find the other shafts, we'll come back for you."

That'll be the day, Yeats thought. "Of course we'll come back for you," he told her. "As soon as we find something."

"Promise," added Conrad earnestly, which bothered Yeats. Conrad didn't have the right to promise anybody anything.

The look on Serena's face told Yeats that she didn't believe Conrad for a second. "Fine," she said. "Go."

Yeats nodded to Marcus and Kreigel, who took up

positions at the doorway, and then he followed Conrad out of the chamber and down a low, square tunnel.

As they proceeded through the dark, Yeats worried that he had badly miscalculated in allowing Mother Earth to join the team. Not because there was anything wrong with her, but because something clearly was wrong with Conrad whenever she was around.

A little space, Yeats hoped, would clear the kid's head.

The strategy paid off several minutes later when they reached a solid horizontal platform. It looked like some kind of altar. Conrad suddenly stopped.

"What is it?" Yeats asked.

"This lies exactly along the east-west axis of the pyramid," Conrad explained. "It marks the point of transition between the northern and southern halves of the monument."

"So?" Yeats was about to take another step when Conrad braced him with his arm. It was stronger than Yeats expected.

"Look." Conrad aimed his flashlight into the darkness, revealing what looked like a gigantic subway tunnel plunging toward the center of the earth. Running down the middle of the shiny floor was a sunken channel about forty feet wide and twenty feet deep. It mirrored precisely the design of the vaulted ceiling at its apex three hundred feet overhead. "This is the main corridor or Great Gallery."

"Goddamn it, son." Yeats stepped back from the ledge.

"You certainly know your way around this place. You sure you've never been here before?"

"Only in my dreams."

"Looks like a nightmare to me," Yeats said as he peered over the ledge. "Where does it go?"

"Only one way to find out." Conrad unraveled rope from his pack. "The slope is about twenty-six degrees and the floors are slick. We'll need to use lines. Just stick to the ramparts and try not to slide into the channel."

They had descended about a thousand feet when Yeats suddenly lost all sense of direction. It was the same sort of vertigo he sometimes felt back at Ice Base Orion on the surface. He couldn't tell which end of the tunnel was up or which was the floor or ceiling. Yeats rubbed his eyes, which stung from the salt of his cold sweat, and continued down the Great Gallery.

Conrad said, "You didn't really bring Serena as an observer, did you?"

Yeats sensed that Conrad actually missed the nun. Good grief, he thought, they had only just left her. "Hell, no," Yeats said. "I want to see how much she knows about this thing. It's more than she's letting on."

Conrad asked, "What makes you so suspicious?"

"My job description."

"Then maybe Serena shouldn't be alone."

"I've got three good officers standing guard."

"I just don't think we needed to leave her behind."

"Yes, we did. And now you can tell me whatever you couldn't tell the good sister. Namely, what you're really thinking."

"It's probably nothing," Conrad said. "Pure coincidence."

"No such thing in this place," Yeats replied. "Talk."

"Look around." Conrad gestured across the vast, gleaming gallery. "No inscriptions, religious iconography, or any discernible symbolism in this gallery or the pyramid."

"So?"

"So this isn't a tomb. It's not even a puzzle for initiates to wander through and solve like I proposed earlier."

"Then what the hell is it?"

"It feels like we're inside some enormous machine."

Yeats felt a deep and disturbing jolt inside his bowels. The news was like some sort of prophecy, both expected and alarming. "Machine?"

"I think it's supposed to do something."

There was a heaviness in the air. Yeats cleared his throat. "Do what?"

"I don't know. Maybe disaster struck the builders before they ever got a chance to turn it on."

"Maybe."

"Or maybe," Conrad went on, "this machine caused the disaster."

Yeats nodded slowly as the words sunk in. Somehow he had felt it all along. He wanted to tell Conrad more. But now was not the time. Conrad would hopefully figure it out on his own anyway.

Descending to the Great Gallery, Conrad was sorry he had left Serena behind in the upper chamber. And not just because he wanted her to see for herself how right he was about P4. He could tell from her eyes how put out and excluded she felt. He knew the sensation well and felt a twinge of guilt for not sticking up for her with Yeats. But he wasn't about to blow his own chance to explore the lower levels and lead the way to the greatest archaeological discovery in human history.

As soon as he reached the bottom of the gallery, however, Conrad's mental map of the pyramid's interior began to unravel. He faced a fork branching off into two smaller tunnels. There should have been three.

He could hear Yeats's heavy breathing behind him. "Well?" Yeats demanded impatiently. "Which way?"

Conrad studied the two "smaller" tunnels. Each was more than thirty feet high. One continued along the twenty-six-degree slope of the gallery. The other dropped ninety degrees into a vertical shaft. Neither satisfied him.

Conrad instinctively turned around and began to search for a third tunnel that would double back beneath the gallery. But he couldn't find it.

"What are you doing?" Yeats asked.

Conrad patted the cold wall and said nothing. He was positive the central chamber he was looking for was on this level. And if the Great Pyramid in Giza was indeed modeled after P4, then the corridor leading to that central chamber should have been there at the bottom of the gallery.

But it wasn't.

Perhaps he was assuming too much to think the ancient Egyptians got it right from the Atlanteans. Even if his initial hypothesis was correct, that didn't mean the Egyptians had the knowledge or means to fashion an accurate copy of P4.

"The chamber we're looking for is on this level," he said. "But we'll have to access it from below."

"Fine," Yeats said. "Which tunnel?"

"Theoretically, both corridors should lead to the burial chamber," Conrad said, hesitating.

Yeats said, "As long as it isn't ours."

"You don't understand," Conrad said. "The burial chamber at the bottom of the pyramid serves as a kind of cosmic dressing chamber where the king can dance and celebrate the completion of life. At the top of the pyramid is the phoenix or benben stone, symbolizing resurrection. There's an ascension to all this."

"I get it," said Yeats. "And somewhere in between, the hocus-pocus happens."

"At the central chamber," Conrad said. "That's where we can expect to find a repository of texts or technology to unlock the meaning of P4." Conrad took another look around. "Since the access corridor isn't here, I suspect the burial chamber will point the way."

"So which tunnel leads to the burial chamber?"

Conrad could feel Yeats's brooding stare. The reality was that he was still getting used to attacking this pyramid from the top down, when every previous experience in his life was from the bottom up.

Conrad looked down the first tunnel. It would be natural to continue along the slope of the gallery they had just passed through. But he suspected that tunnel led to the main entrance of P4. It was probably blocked at some point to keep outsiders from entering P4 at the ground level.

"Make up my mind, son."

"Door number two," Conrad said. "We'll take the vertical shaft."

"OK." Yeats leaned over the shaft and dropped a new line.

Conrad emerged from the bottom of the vertical shaft a half hour later, dropping into a lower north-south corridor. This, too, was more than thirty feet high. Yeats had just landed behind him when the alarm on Conrad's watch started beeping.

"You've got an appointment somewhere?" Yeats asked.

"We're under the base of P4." Conrad pulled back his left glove and tilted his wrist to reveal the blue electroluminescent backlight of his multisensor watch face. In addition to a built-in digital compass, barometer, thermometer, and GPS, it included an altimeter graph. "We've descended almost a mile and a half. I set the alarm for my target altitude."

Yeats pulled out his own USAF standard-issue altimeter. "You were off by more than a quarter mile," Yeats said. "We're barely a mile down."

Conrad looked at his altimeter doubtfully. His father wasn't cutting him any slack now. Not an inch. Much less a quarter mile. This might as well be the first human landing on Mars as far as Yeats was concerned, Conrad realized, and NASA allowed no margin for error. As Conrad rolled it over in his head, he concluded Yeats was right. If anything, P4 was more significant to humanity than Mars. It was certainly closer. Palpably so.

"So which way now?" Yeats pressed. "North or south?"

Conrad cut his line and instinctively turned to the north. "This way."

After about 1,200 feet, the floor sloped suddenly and almost doubled the height of the ceiling. Fifty yards ahead was the entrance Conrad was looking for. He could feel his blood starting to really pump.

"This is it," he said.

They entered a vastly larger space. The beams of their headtorches disintegrated into nothingness as the floor beneath their boots sloped at a slight grade. Engulfed in darkness, and feeling very cold, Conrad sensed that this cavity was in some ways many times larger than the upper chamber they had left at the top of the Great Gallery. Yet the emptiness beyond the torchlight beams also felt compressed in some way. This was definitely uncharted territory, he realized, and could feel the tension in his gut.

"I'm tossing out a flare—thirty-second delay," Yeats said. "Three, two, one."

Conrad could hear Yeats heave the stick into the dark. Mentally he counted down as he pulled out his digital camera to capture whatever image would burst forth. A few seconds later the chamber exploded with light.

Conrad shielded his eyes as he panned what fleetingly resembled a stone crater with his camera. As his eyes adjusted to the light, he began to see that's exactly what they were standing in. They were on the rim of a titanic crater almost a mile in diameter. But it was only two hundred feet high.

The flare sputtered and died. Once again Conrad and Yeats were in darkness.

Yeats said, "Show me what you've got."

"Right here."

Conrad replayed the footage on the flat display screen on the back of his camera. It glowed bright in the darkness.

"Stop," said Yeats.

Conrad paused the screen. There was something in the center of the crater. A circle or hub of some sort.

"Can you zoom?"

"A little."

Conrad, fingers tingling with adrenaline, magnified the image until it filled the display. But the picture was still too blurred to make it out clearly.

"Let's go," he said.

Conrad and Yeats marched in unison toward the center, careful not to lose their balance on the sloping floor. Conrad could feel his heart pounding. He'd never experienced any sort of chamber like this in Egypt or the Americas, nothing even remotely similar in size or configuration.

At the half-mile mark Yeats called a halt.

Conrad lowered his flashlight beam to the floor and found something about ten yards in front of them. Carved across the polished stone floor were four rings radiating from an oval cartouche in the center, like some magnificent seal.

Yeats let out a low whistle. "Finally, inscriptions for Mother Earth."

"Not quite," said Conrad, breathing hard. Part of him wanted to run back and get her. Another part refused to admit he couldn't figure this out by himself. "It's an icon or symbol."

"Then even you should be able to decipher it."

Conrad walked to the center of the floor, where a familiar-looking hieroglyphic was inscribed inside the oval cartouche. It was of a god or king seated inside some sort of mechanical device. He resembled a bearded Caucasian and wore what looked like an elaborate head ornament known as an Atef crown. And he held some sort of scepter in his hand. It looked like a small obelisk.

"This figure looks familiar," Conrad heard himself saying, "but I can't put my finger on why."

Conrad looked again at the cartouche on the floor. The image inscribed inside was similar to the symbols he had seen depicting the gods of Viracocha in the Andes and Quetzalcoatl in Central America. But this other-worldly symbol awakened something primeval and terrifying inside him, and suddenly he knew why.

"This pyramid is dedicated to Osiris." Conrad's voice wavered.

"So what?" said Yeats. "I thought most of these pyramids were dedicated to some god."

"You don't understand," Conrad said excitedly. "This seal suggests P4 was built by the King of Eternity himself, the Lord of First Time."

"First Time?"

"The Genesis epoch I told you about back at Ice Base Orion, the time when humanity emerged from the primordial darkness and was offered the gifts of civilization from the gods," Conrad said. "Ancient Egyptian texts say these gifts or technologies were introduced through intermediaries or lesser divinities known as 'The Watchers' or *Urshu*."

Yeats paused. "So you think the *Urshu* were the Atlanteans who built P4?"

"Maybe," Conrad said. "I'm sure Serena has her own interpretation. But there's no denying that we've found the mother lode." Conrad could hear the triumph in his voice. "The Mother Culture."

"First Time," Yeats said.

"First Time," Conrad echoed and spoke the phrase in his best Ancient Egyptian: *"Zep Tepi."*

As soon as the words fell out of his mouth, they seemed to swirl around the chamber, spinning out from the center of the crater floor like some centrifugal force. The floor started to shake.

Suddenly the cartouche split open and Conrad stumbled backward as a pillar of fire shot up from the floor and through a circular shaft in the ceiling.

"Whoa!" he shouted and slipped flat on his back. He started to slide across the bottom of the crater floor toward the fiery hole.

Yeats grabbed his arm and held him back. "Easy, easy, easy."

Then the fire burst disappeared and the rumbling stopped. All that remained was a craterlike shaft where the cartouche had split open.

Conrad felt a tug as Yeats pulled him up on his feet. "Now where on earth do you think that goes, son?"

Conrad leaned over and peered down the fiery shaft. For a flickering second he glimpsed a glowing tunnel that seemed to descend to the very bowels of the earth. But the residual heat from the blast burned his forehead and he quickly pulled away.

"From the looks of it," Conrad said, gingerly touching his forehead to see if it was still there, "I'd say the pit of hell."

16
DESCENT HOUR SIX

IT WAS THE VODKA.

It had to be the vodka, Colonel Ivan Kovich swore, when he first beheld the pyramid at the bottom of the ice chasm. That or some experimental hallucinogenics the Americans had slipped into his drink at their base on the surface.

Whatever it was, he decided, it was part of an American plot to drive the Russian people insane. It had started with the imperialist capitalist bankrolling of the Communist revolution in 1917. It had moved into full gear with the installation of Stalin and the gulags, and then the slaughter of twenty million during World War II. It culminated in the humiliating disintegration of the Soviet Union in 1991 and rise of the golden arches of American hamburger stands in Moscow.

Now that the United States was the world's undisputed superpower, Kovich was convinced, the Americans were simply keeping the Russians alive for their own cruel pleasure, starving their bodies of nutrients with Big Macs and their souls with TV shows like *Baywatch*.

It was from this hell that Kovich had sought refuge in

the spare, unspoiled beauty of Antarctica, only to stumble across a veritable Four Seasons Resort in the snow in the form of Ice Base Orion. With state-of-the-art computers, plush sleeping quarters, toilets that flushed, and a stockpile of food, the only thing lacking was a swimming pool and health spa.

The concierge of Hotel Orion, Colonel O'Dell, was pleasant enough during the inspection. But the American grew increasingly nervous when Russian dosimeters detected radiation, and Kovich suggested a survey of the gigantic ice chasm over which the base was perched.

Kovich was convinced he was on the verge of discovering a rogue nuclear testing facility, mostly because Russia itself had one at the other end of the planet in the Arctic Circle.

Only after reaching the bottom of the abyss and beholding the protruding summit of a pyramid did Kovich realize that the Americans had pushed him and his twenty Russian comrades over the brink. And how could he ever forget the horror on his men's faces when they saw the hundreds of human bodies frozen in the walls of this ice tomb?

Truly their commanding officer had finally led them down to hell.

The shiny white exterior of the pyramid didn't even show up on their radio-echo scans from a few feet away. It was obvious the Americans had developed a super-secret, indestructible stealth material that could render their fleets and bombers both invisible and invincible.

As if that were not enough, a message played in Kovich's head over and over again: "Wait, there's more!"

the voice repeated, like some terrible American infomercial. "Much, much more!" As a special bonus at the bottom of hell, the Americans had left what looked like an RV parked atop the pyramid summit along with another hole that beckoned them farther.

Here at this "habitat" Kovich left the two American observers who had accompanied them down, along with five of his men. He and the rest of his team proceeded down the seven-foot-tall shaft and didn't reach the other end for a good half hour.

They emerged inside what seemed to be a massive stone oven the size of an Olympic stadium. And inside this chamber were four American soldiers—two men and two women—who surrendered their weapons but refused to say a word.

As a final bonus, there seemed to be no way out of this tomb. When attempts to reach Vlad and the rest of the crew at Ice Base Orion on the surface failed, Kovich feared the worst.

He had been duped, he concluded. This was a trap. They had been lured into this mass grave so they could be killed. Meanwhile, the Americans would monitor their slow descent into madness with hidden cameras and use the results in their training videos for new recruits.

Finally, one of his men found an open passageway.

Kovich left a few men to guard the Americans and took the rest down a low, square tunnel to a plateau overlooking what looked like a gigantic Moscow metro tunnel plunging toward the center of the earth. It was at least one hundred meters tall, he guessed, and could swallow Russia's GUM retail mall, the biggest in the world. Running along its shiny walls and floor and ceiling were sunken channels about forty feet wide and twenty feet deep.

"Look, sir!" shouted one of his soldiers, pointing into the abyss. "There's more!"

Peering over the ledge, Kovich could only rub his disbelieving eyes. For inside one of the channels were two lines daring him to descend even farther.

Something rose up inside Kovich's bubbling psyche, bursting through the swirling images of fast food, bikinis, Ginsu knives, and self-improvement CDs. That something was the stark realization that he and his men were going to die. They would never make it back to the surface again.

With chilling clarity, Kovich made the last strategic decision of his life: if they weren't leaving this tomb, then neither were the Americans.

17
DESCENT HOUR SEVEN

INSIDE THE SUBTERRANEAN boiler room beneath P4, Conrad applied a cold canteen to his scalded forehead as a dull glow from the shaft crept across the crater floor. Still smarting from the burn, he removed the canteen and noticed some singed eyebrow hairs clinging to the condensation on the outside.

"Things are certainly heating up," Yeats was telling him. "We better move out before another blast fries both of us. Between frostbite on your hand and second-degree burns on your face, you've already got two strikes against you."

"Let's at least get a reading," Conrad said. "You've got a remote heat sensor, don't you?"

Yeats produced a small ball from his backpack. "The shell is made of the same stuff NASA uses on the outer tiles of the space shuttle," Yeats said. "Stand back."

Conrad watched Yeats toss it into the shaft. A minute later the numbers showed up on Yeats's handheld computer. Conrad looked it over.

"Before your little heat-shielded sensor melted during its descent," Conrad said, "it plunged four miles and recorded a temperature of almost nine thousand degrees Fahrenheit."

"Mother of God," Yeats said. "That's as hot as the surface of the sun."

"Or the molten core of the earth," Conrad said. "I think this is a geothermal vent."

"A geothermal vent?" Yeats narrowed his eyes. "Like the kind found in oceans?"

Conrad nodded. "One of my old professors discovered a hot spot like this west of Ecuador, about five hundred miles out in the water and eight thousand feet down," he said. "There's very little life at the bottom of the ocean because there's no light and the temperatures are below freezing. But where there are cracks in the earth's crust, the heat from the core escapes to warm the water. That's how some forms of ocean life—earth-heated crabs, clams, ten-foot-long worms—survive down there."

Conrad looked around. This geothermal chamber had to be the same kind of thing. The only question was whether the Atlanteans built P4 over an existing vent to harness its heat or possessed such advanced technology that they could tap Earth's core—or any planet's, for that matter—for unlimited power.

"According to Plato, Atlantis was destroyed by a great volcanic explosion," Yeats said. "Maybe this was the cause of it."

"Or maybe this is the legendary power source of Atlantis," said Conrad. "The Atlanteans allegedly had harnessed the power of the sun. Most scientists naturally assumed this meant solar power. But this geothermal vent taps into Earth's core—which is as hot as the surface of the sun. So this could be the so-called power of the sun that Atlantis possessed."

"Could be," said Yeats.

But Conrad could tell Yeats had another purpose in mind for P4, and it probably had little to do with its archaeological or even technological value. "You have another theory?"

Yeats nodded. "What you're really saying is that P4 is essentially a giant geothermal machine that can channel heat from Earth's core to melt the ice over Antarctica."

Conrad grew very still. He hadn't thought about it in terms quite so catastrophic. In his mind that kind of thinking was the domain of environmental alarmists like Serena. But a slow-growing angst crept over him as he remembered the bodies in the ice chasm above P4 and Hapgood's earth-crust displacement theory. He hadn't entertained the possibility that a natural disaster on the scale of a global shift of the earth's crust—the culmina-tion of a forty-one-thousand-year-old geological cycle—could be triggered by design. Yeats, on the other hand, seemed to have given this scenario some serious thought. At the very least, Conrad had to agree that there was enough heat bottled up beneath P4 to melt so much ice that rising sea levels would certainly wipe out coastal cities on every continent.

"Yes, I suppose this machinery could warm Antarctica," Conrad said slowly. "But to what end?"

"Maybe to make the continent or planet more habitable for their species," Yeats went on. "Who the hell cares? The point is that there must be a control room somewhere, and we've got to find it. Before anybody else does."

"Right," Conrad said, wondering why he should be so surprised that Yeats was as practical a man as he was. "That would be the central chamber we've been looking for, the one with the two hidden celestial shafts."

"Then let's get the hell out of here and go for it," Yeats said. "Before this thing goes off again—for real."

As they made their way back up to the gallery, Conrad was haunted by fear that he had just done what he denied ever doing—destroyed the integrity of a find. Worse, he may have destroyed himself and others with it. He could almost hear the whispers that had haunted him his entire career now chasing him up the tunnel: "Tomb Raider" . . . "Raper of Virgin Digs" . . . "Conrad the Destroyer." Now, more than ever, they had to get back to Serena, find P4's secret chamber, and make sure this cosmic heat valve was shut off.

Upon reaching the fork at the bottom of the Great Gallery, Conrad wasn't surprised to find three tunnels now instead of two.

"Now don't tell me you saw that one before too," Yeats said.

"No, it definitely wasn't there before," Conrad said. "Maybe something we did in the lower chamber opened a door."

Conrad looked up the gallery toward the upper chamber and saw several figures rappeling down.

Yeats saw them too and gripped his arm. "Fall back," he whispered. "That's an order."

They cut their headtorches and retreated to the new access tunnel, where they took cover on either side of the entry. Pressing his back against the wall, Conrad looked across at Yeats. His father's silhouette was blackened by the dim glow radiating out from the bottom of the gallery.

"Team Phoenix, copy," Yeats spoke into his radio microphone. But there was no response. "Copy me, Team Phoenix." Again, nothing. "Goddamn it."

Conrad pulled out his nightscope and peered around the corner. Two figures dropped down onto the landing at the bottom of the gallery. Their green eyes—night-vision goggles—bobbed up and down in the dark. Conrad pulled back and looked at his father.

"Who are they?" Conrad whispered.

"Can't say," Yeats said. "But they sure as hell aren't mine. Move."

They started down the long, dark access tunnel. This corridor was thirty-five feet tall, but it felt much smaller after the grandeur of the Great Gallery they had descended. After about 1,200 feet due south, the floor sloped sharply into a larger tunnel with a ceiling twice as high.

"Over there." Yeats pointed his flashlight beam to the floor.

About a hundred yards ahead was either a doorway or the end of the tunnel. It was hard to tell. But then Conrad felt a blast of air. He looked up and found a shaft in the ceiling of the tunnel. There was another one in the floor, angled at the same slope.

"That could be one of those two extra star shafts that lead into the secret chamber," he said. "I think it cuts through this corridor. I'll have to drop a line down to be sure."

Yeats said, "I'm going to follow this corridor for another hundred yards or so to see what's at the end. Then I'll come back and you can tell me what you found."

Conrad watched Yeats disappear while he uncoiled a line down the shaft. He was peering over the edge cautiously when he heard the scrape of a boot behind him and he swung around to see a pair of green eyes glowing in the passageway.

"And who the hell are you?" Conrad asked.

The figure in the night-vision goggles raised an AK-47 machine gun. "Your worst nightmare," he said with a thick Russian accent and fingered his radio. "This is Leonid calling Colonel Kovich. I've captured an American."

"The hell you have." Conrad kicked the AK-47 out of Leonid's hands and picked up the broken laser sight from the floor. Leonid whipped out a Yarygin PY 9 mm Grach pistol just as Conrad painted his forehead with a red dot from the laser sight. Conrad hoped Leonid couldn't see there was no gun attached to it. "Drop it. Now."

The Russian dropped his gun and Conrad exhaled.

"Very good."

A bone-handled hunter's knife slid out of the Russian's right sleeve and dropped into the palm of his hand. There was a click as his thumb found the button, and his arm swept up, the blade streaking for the soft flesh beneath Conrad's chin.

Conrad, anticipating such a move the second he heard the click of the knife, blocked the arm and grabbed for the wrist with both hands, twisting it so that the Russian dropped the knife and cried out in pain. Conrad wrenched the arm around and up, still keeping that excruciating hold in place. This time the Russian screamed as muscles tore, and Conrad ran him headfirst into the wall and then plunged him into the floor shaft.

Conrad was peering into the darkness below when he heard footsteps. He grabbed the Russian's AK-47 from the floor and looked up to see Yeats running toward him.

"Dead end," Yeats said. "What the hell happened here?"

Conrad was about to tell him when he felt a yank at his ankle. He looked down and saw his nylon line tightening like a noose around his boot, realizing a second too late that the Russian had somehow snagged it on his way down and was taking Conrad with him.

"Hold this!" Conrad tossed Yeats the other end of the line as he plunged down the shaft in the tunnel floor. "Don't let go!"

Tumbling through the darkness, Conrad struggled to clip his line to his harness. He could sense himself falling through one level after another, with no end in sight. He tensed up as he braced himself for something to break his fall.

Soon the line around his boot slacked off while the line around his harness stiffened. Finally, he burst into some large space. His line snapped tight and caught him in midair. He dangled helplessly.

"Dad!" he called. "Can you hear me?"

There was nothing at first, then the faintest, "Barely!"

Conrad fingered his belt for a flashlight and switched it on. The shock of what he saw took a few seconds to sink in.

He was swinging like a pendulum inside a magnificent chamber in the shape of a geodesic dome. His fingers tingled with adrenaline as he scanned the ceiling with his beam. The apex of the dome was about two hundred feet above him. Scattered across the four merging walls were numerous constellations. It looked like some kind of cosmic observatory.

He lowered his beam. Some kind of altar with a two-foot-tall obelisk in the center rose from the stone floor. And impaled on it was the Russian.

"Dad!" Conrad shouted. "I found it!"

18
DESCENT HOUR EIGHT

CONRAD CUT HIS LINE and dropped twenty feet to the floor of the geodesic chamber. He looked up at the star carvings scattered across the domed ceiling almost two hundred feet above him. There was no other entrance into this chamber that he could see. Only the overhead shaft. This was a virgin find. His find. He was the first human to set foot in this chamber in more than twelve thousand years. For all he knew, he was the first human ever.

Except, that is, for the Russian impaled on the obelisk in the center of the chamber. Conrad had to push hard to lift the corpse off the obelisk and onto the floor, so that he could drag it off to the side.

Conrad wiped the Russian's blood off his hands and slowly circled the altar with the obelisk while he waited for Yeats to find his own way into the chamber. Tingling with anticipation, he pointed his torchbeam at the four rings radiating out from the altar. Then he lifted the beam until it splashed the obelisk with light.

It looked like a classical obelisk. Its height was ten times its width. Except for its rotundalike base, it resembled a two-foot-tall scale model of the Washington Monument. On every side were technical inscriptions, the only inscriptions so far inside the entire pyramid.

He'd eventually need Serena's help to crack their meaning, he realized as he pulled out his digital camera and took pictures. For now he took special note of a series of six rings on one of the obelisk's four sides and a sequence of four constellations—Scorpio, Sagittarius, Capricorn, and Aquarius—on another.

Most important, the obelisk looked exactly like the scepter held by Osiris in that royal seal he had seen on the floor of the geothermal chamber. Historically the king's scepter connoted awesome power, the very power his father the general was looking for and afraid somebody else would capture.

This is the Scepter of Osiris, he thought. *This is the key to P4, the geothermal vent and everything else.*

Conrad leaned forward to take the obelisk when a hidden door began to rumble open—a series of doors, really. Four great granite slabs began to part from the bottom up.

Conrad stepped back as the last door opened to reveal a lone figure standing in a corridor that seemed to lead to the Great Gallery.

"Conrad."

He knew it was Serena before she stepped into the chamber. Behind her emerged a big Russian, holding an AK-47, its laser sight glowing.

"Doctor Yeats, I presume?" The voice carried a thick Russian accent. "My name is Colonel Kovich. Where is Leonid?"

Kovich shoved Serena toward him, and Conrad caught her in his arms.

"Thank God you're OK," he breathed as he pulled her close.

But her business-only stare froze him. Then she glanced at the obelisk. She also took in the corpse on the floor and, much to his horror, connected it with the blood on his hands.

"Eureka, Conrad," she told him. "You've found it. I hope it was worth the price."

He said, "I can explain."

"You killed Leonid," Kovich said.

"Actually, he tried to kill me," Conrad said. "That was just before he fell down a shaft without a line. In case you hadn't noticed, your officers aren't the best-equipped in the world."

At that moment a gruff voice from behind the Russian said, "You can say that again."

Conrad turned to see Yeats march into the chamber pointing an AK-47 at Kovich. "Damn piece of shit jammed on me twice. Now drop your rod, Kovich."

Kovich frowned and placed his AK-47 on the floor next to Leonid's corpse. "Please, General Yeats," Kovich chided. "We are soldiers."

Yeats walked over to Kovich and gave him a good swift knee to the groin. The Russian doubled over in agony. "Put your ass on the floor," Yeats ordered. "Then cross your legs. Don't screw up unless you want to look like your comrade here."

Kovich stared at the massive hole in Leonid's chest, then slid down the wall like Humpty-Dumpty. Yeats whipped the butt of his gun against the Russian's skull. Conrad heard a crack and Kovich crumpled to the floor, moaning in pain.

"He'll live," Yeats said. "But we've got dozens of armed Ivans crawling all over this place, so we don't have much time. What have you found?"

"This obelisk," Conrad said. "It's the key to the pyramid."

Yeats looked at the inscriptions on the sides of the obelisk. "You know what these mean, Doctor Serghetti?"

"They say that Osiris built this thing," Serena said, surprising Conrad by how easily she could translate the writings. "The obelisk is his scepter. It belongs in the Shrine of the First Sun."

"What's that?" Yeats demanded.

"The 'Place of First Time' I was telling you about back at Ice Base Orion," Conrad said excitedly. All of which made sense to Conrad, because the figure of Osiris he had seen in the geothermal chamber was sitting on some kind of seat or throne. The Seat of Osiris was obviously located in this Shrine of the First Sun—along with the Secret of First Time itself.

"So then we'll grab this Scepter of Osiris and put it where it belongs, in this so-called Shrine of the First Sun," Yeats said.

"Not a good idea, General." Serena pointed to the markings on the south face of the obelisk, which included a series of six rings. "The inscriptions under the six rings say the machinery controlled by the pyramid was set in motion by Osiris in order to keep a check on humanity— a sort of cosmic 'reset' mechanism designed to wipe the slate clean six times before the end of time."

"A check on humanity?" Yeats said. "What's that supposed to mean?"

"It means the Atlanteans built this thing to prevent us from getting too advanced," Serena said. "Kind of like the Tower of Babel in Genesis. The idea is that technological advancement is meaningless without moral advancement. So humanity is constantly tested to prove its goodness or nobility."

"Six times," Conrad said. "You said humanity gets six chances before the end of history. Where did you get that?"

"The six Suns, Conrad." She read the inscriptions within each ring on the south face of the obelisk. "The First Sun was destroyed by water. The Second Sun ended when the terrestrial globe toppled from its axis and everything was covered with ice. The Third Sun was destroyed as a punishment for human misdemeanors by an all-consuming fire that came from above and below. This pyramid was built at the dawn of the Fourth Sun, which ended in a universal flood."

"So we're the children of the Fifth Sun, just like the Mayan and Aztec myths?" Conrad asked. "Is that what you're saying? That we're condemned to repeat the sins of the ancients?"

"No, that's what your precious obelisk says," Serena said. "And as for repeating the sins of the ancients, if the past century of human history is any guide, then we already have—in spades."

Conrad was quiet for a moment. She had a point. Finally, he said, "And just when exactly does the Fifth Sun end and the Sixth Sun begin?"

"Just as soon as you remove the Scepter of Osiris from its stand."

"Seriously?" Conrad said.

"Seriously."

"She's lying," Yeats said.

"No, I'm not." She glared at Yeats. "It says here that only 'he who stands before the Shining Ones in the time and place of the most worthy can remove the Scepter of Osiris without tearing Heaven and Earth apart.' Anybody other than the most worthy will trigger unimaginable consequences."

"Shining Ones?" Yeats said. "Who the hell are they?"

"Stars," Conrad said. "The Shining Ones are stars. The builders could read the stars, which foretell a specific moment in the space-time continuum, a 'most noble' moment. This is humanity's 'escape clause,' so to speak, the secret that breaks the curse of the ancients once and for all."

"How convenient for you, Conrad," Serena said. "The answer is written in the stars, and you can interpret those however you want."

"You mean like the wise men and the birth of Christ?"

Serena wasn't biting. "That's completely different."

Conrad pressed her. "Or the fish symbol of the early Christians, which just happened to coincide with the dawn of the Age of Pisces and which, coincidentally, is about to end with the dawn of a new Age of Aquarius."

"Meaning what, Conrad?" Serena demanded.

"Meaning the age of the Church is over, and that's what's got you and your friends at the Vatican in a tizzy."

"You're wrong, Conrad."

"The stars say I'm right."

Yeats pointed to one side of the obelisk. "You mean stars like those four constellations on the scepter?"

"No, the ones up there." Conrad pointed up at the engravings on the domed ceiling. "This chamber is a kind of celestial clock. Watch."

He put his hand to the obelisk and heard Serena gasp as he twisted it like a joystick, moving it one way and then another. As he did, a dull rumble began and the geodesic dome overhead began to move in sync.

"If we want to set the skies for a certain time, we begin with the cosmic 'hour hand' or age, which corresponds to the zodiac," he said. "We're at the dawn of Aquarius, so that constellation is locked over there to the east."

As he spoke it, the dome reverted to its original position.

"The 'minute hand' of the clock comes from a location, such as the Southern or Northern hemispheres."

Here Conrad moved the obelisk, and an entirely new pattern of stars rotated up from beneath the chamber floor. He rotated the dome farther, however, until he could lock the original pattern overhead.

"A third, more precise setting comes with the various equinoxes of the year."

Conrad made his final adjustment and completed his demonstration by locking everything as it was before he started. The rumbling ceased.

"So you see, Serena, the obelisk and altar around which we stand represent the earth at a fixed location.

The constellations on the dome above us are the heavens. Together they 'lock' at a fixed point in time."

Serena, apparently still shaken by what she obviously perceived to be his reckless meddling with an artifact, said, "And how are the stars in the chamber aligned right now?"

"They're aligned to the obelisk like the heavens over Antarctica in the present day," he said conclusively, as if there could be no debate.

"Which I suppose must surely be the most worthy moment in human history," she said, "because the great Conrad Yeats is alive and he discovered it."

Conrad smiled. "Finally, we agree on something."

Serena looked at him with scorn. "Has it dawned on you that maybe you're the biggest jackass of all time and that this is humanity's most ignoble moment if you remove that obelisk?"

It had indeed dawned on Conrad, and now he was getting annoyed with her.

"Think about it, Serena," he told her. "If what you're saying is true, then P4's builders knew that only an advanced civilization with sophisticated technology could even locate this pyramid, much less penetrate it. It's our advancement that makes us noble. So this moment simply must be the most worthy time, and this obelisk is the key to the knowledge of the origins of human civilization."

"Or maybe it's a Trojan horse," she said. "Maybe that obelisk is like the hour hand of a clock, the pin in a grenade. You remove it and our day is over, Conrad."

"Or maybe you're afraid the Church is going to lose

its place as the arbiter of Genesis," he said, having heard enough of her hysterics. "Maybe it's time to let go of ignorance and fear and make way for a new day of enlightenment."

Conrad looked at Yeats, who gestured to the obelisk.

"Just pick up the goddamn scepter, son. Because if you don't, there are dozens of armed Russians outside this chamber who might, and God knows how many more UNACOMers on the ice."

Conrad glanced at Serena and approached the Scepter of Osiris. He could feel her fear as he placed his hands on the obelisk. It felt smooth, as if the inscriptions were beneath its surface.

"You're dreaming, Conrad, if you think your father is going to let you walk out of P4 with that scepter," she said. "At least within the context of the United Nations, there's a chance the rest of the world will know about your find."

Conrad hesitated. He felt a weird floating sensation inside, something he couldn't explain. Reaching for the obelisk, he could feel tiny vibrations radiating from it. But then he pulled back.

"What in God's name are you waiting for?" Yeats demanded.

Conrad wasn't sure. This was a once-in-a-millennium chance to make his mark in the sands of time and turn history on its head with a spectacular discovery. It was his one shot at immortality.

"I'm telling you, Conrad, don't rush into this," Serena urged him. "You might unleash something you can't undo."

"You don't know what you're talking about, Sister," Yeats said. "Somebody is going to remove this obelisk, and it had better be Conrad. Because he's the only one who can do it. If anybody is worthy, it's him."

"Allow me to be a character witness and tell you that you're completely wrong," Serena said. "Just because he's your son doesn't mean—"

"Conrad's not my son."

Conrad stopped cold. So did Serena. Even the Russian held his breath. A heavy silence filled the chamber.

"Fine, you're his adoptive father," Serena said quietly, apparently sympathetic to Conrad's sensitivity to the subject.

"Not even that." Yeats shed his supply pack and started to rummage through it.

Conrad stared at his father, wondering what sort of revelation he was about to produce. Why now, of all times? Conrad thought. Why here, of all places?

"He is." Yeats held up a digital camera.

"You have his picture?" Conrad looked at the digital image in the viewing screen. It was a picture of the Seal of Osiris from the floor of the geothermal chamber.

"This is your father," Yeats said.

Conrad stared at the figure of the bearded man inside the mechanical-looking throne and felt something stir deep inside him, from a place he never knew existed.

"What are you saying?"

"I found you in a capsule buried in the ice more than thirty-five years ago," Yeats said in a grim voice that rattled Conrad to the bone. "You couldn't have been more than four."

Conrad was silent. Then he heard a giggle. It was Serena.

"My God, Yeats," she said. "How dumb do you think we are?"

But Yeats wasn't laughing, and Conrad had never seen the look in his father's eyes that he did right now.

"You don't need anyone to tell you what's true, son," Yeats said. "You know it."

Conrad's mind was racing. Yeats had to be lying. After all, Conrad had his DNA tested in search of his parentage, and there was nothing that would suggest he wasn't a red-blooded American male. On the other hand, setting aside its utter implausibility, it explained everything about his lost early years.

"If this is a lie, then you're one sick son of a bitch," Conrad told Yeats. "But if it's the truth, then everything else is a lie, and I've never been anything more to you than a science project. I'm damned either way."

"Then save yourself now, Conrad," Yeats said. "I was the same age you are when Uncle Sam scrubbed the Mars mission and took my dream away from me. I never had a choice. You do. Don't be like me and regret losing this opportunity for the rest of your life."

The dirty trick worked. As Conrad stared at Yeats, he could behold a cracked reflection of his future self should he fail now. It was a visage that made him shudder.

Serena seemed to sense she had lost the battle. "Conrad, please," she begged.

"I'm sorry, Serena," he said slowly as he began to twist

the obelisk in its socket. As he did, the curved walls of the geodesic chamber began to spin and the constellations above them changed. With a dull rumble, the floor itself began to rotate.

"We need more time to figure this out," Serena screamed, lunging for him. "You just can't make a decision for the rest of the world. You've got to wait."

But Yeats stopped her cold with the barrel of a Glock in her face. "Like Eisenhower stopping on the banks of the Elbe when he should have beat the Russians to Berlin in 1945?" he said. "Or Nixon pulling the plug on the Mars mission in 1969? I don't think so. Decisive force was required then, and it is now. I'm not stopping anywhere short of my mission's objective."

Conrad glanced at Serena trying to squirm out of Yeats's arms. "Don't do it, Conrad. I swear—"

"Stop swearing, Serena," he told her. "You'll only break another vow."

Reaching for the obelisk with both hands, he told himself that this opportunity was simply too irresistible to pass up. And if he let this moment go, then he might as well count his life as over.

"Please, Conrad . . ."

Conrad could feel the obelisk easing away from the altar as he lifted it free and clear. He smiled in triumph at Serena.

"There," he said with a trace of relief. "That wasn't so—"

But the rest of his sentence was cut off by an ear-splitting crack.

"Oh, my God," Serena breathed as a great rumbling overhead grew deafening.

The domed walls of the chamber spun at fantastic speeds like some cosmic coil ready to snap. Then, suddenly, the spinning stopped. The constellations locked, and an explosive shock wave rocked the pyramid.

19

DESCENT HOUR NINE
ICE BASE ORION

INSIDE ICE BASE ORION ON THE SURFACE, Colonel O'Dell was playing poker with Vlad Lenin and two other Russians in the mess hall module when their plastic cups of vodka began to shake and the Klaxon sounded.

O'Dell looked at the puzzled Vlad. Whatever it was, it wasn't the Russians. He darted out of the mess module, Vlad right behind him.

A group of Americans and Russians were already huddled around the main monitor screen inside the command center when O'Dell ran in. The display was blinking SOLAR EVENT.

"That can't be right," said O'Dell, stepping into the circle of concerned faces.

A lieutenant called up the computer display for CELSS, the Controlled Environmental Life Support System that kept the crew alive in space and in Antarctica. He located the sensor that was giving the abnormal reading.

"The readings are coming from below, sir," he said, holding on to the console as the shaking intensified. "The only other explanation I can think of is the SP-100."

O'Dell cast an involuntary, nervous glance at Vlad, who did not seem to comprehend what the lieutenant had said. The SP-100 was Ice Base Orion's compact nuclear power plant, a hundred-kilowatt system buried a hundred yards away behind a snow dune.

"My God." O'Dell took a deep breath. "Dosimeter readings?"

"I've got penetration of the outer wardrooms at two hundred seventy rems, sir. I'm recording sixty-five rems here in the command center, with each of the crew absorbing fifteen rems. We're still below the safety threshold."

But it was the shaking that was scaring the daylights out of O'Dell and the Russians. "Now what?"

"No choice, sir," the lieutenant said. "We've got to retreat to the doghouse."

The doghouse was an Earth capture vehicle under the command center and supply tanks, shielded from the SP-100's high-energy protons by the command center's aeroshell.

"Get as many of the crew inside as possible," he ordered.

The American crew quickly obeyed and ditched the command center in orderly fashion. The Russians, however, looked around the empty command center, then dashed in the opposite direction to the outer air lock and their Kharkovchankas.

"Wait!" O'Dell called as he ran after them.

But they had cracked open the inner and outer doors and escaped by the time he reached the air lock. A blast of snow slapped O'Dell's face as he grabbed a freezer suit, goggles, and gloves from the nearest storage compartment and ran outside.

The Russians were starting up their Kharkovchankas. O'Dell raced toward the row of Hagglunds transports and grabbed the door of the nearest forward cab.

"Where the hell do they think they're going?" he said out loud, intending to hail them from the Hagglunds. The last thing he needed was Yeats or Kovich or the U.N. blaming him for more Russian deaths.

He was about to scramble aboard his Hagglunds when he felt a jolt. He looked down as a crack in the ice shot past his feet. His mouth opened in horror, and then he felt something sharp clamp down on his glove. It was Nimrod, Yeats's dog, frantically pulling him with his teeth.

"Get out of here!" he yelled as he opened the door, but Nimrod jumped into the cab.

O'Dell heard what sounded like a series of thunderous explosions and looked back to see the base break away like an iceberg. Then he felt a rumble and watched in horror as the ice beneath him began to spiderweb.

The ice was melting!

He jumped into the cab with Nimrod. As soon as he closed the door, the Hagglunds lurched forward and back. Cracks radiated out on the ice below. My life is over, he thought, when the fiberglass cab dropped into the swirling, freezing water and was washed away. Then, feeling the transport bob up and down, he nearly choked with elation. "Goddamn, it does float!" he screamed to Nimrod, who was leaping from seat to seat in a frenzy.

The Russian Kharkovchankas, however, were dropping like stones beneath the bubbling surface of the icy waters.

O'Dell frantically switched on the windshield wipers. As the sheets of water were temporarily whisked away, he glimpsed a churning landscape. There was no Ice Base Orion, only what looked like a mushroom cloud forming in the air. For a wild moment he thought the reactor had blown, but the SP-100 didn't possess the destructive power he was witnessing.

Another shock wave sent his head to the floor beneath the dashboard. He heard his skull crack against something sharp as the cab spun wildly away, Nimrod barking incessantly.

20
DESCENT HOUR NINE

THE RUMBLING INSIDE P4's obelisk chamber grew so loud that Serena could barely hear herself shouting at Conrad, who stood frozen like a statue, the Scepter of Osiris tightly gripped in his hand.

"Put it back!" she screamed.

Conrad stepped toward the altar when suddenly the floor beneath his feet split open and a blazing pillar of fire shot up and turned Colonel Kovich into embers.

Conrad leapt back from the gaping hole as the altar disappeared down a fiery shaft. What was left of the Russian exploded in a cloud of dust. The obelisk fell to the floor.

Serena reached down to grab it but lunged too far and teetered over the edge. For a horrific few seconds she hovered above the hell hole and could feel its searing heat burning her cheeks. Then Conrad, coming up from behind, yanked her back from the brink.

For a moment she was safe in his arms, looking up into his concerned eyes with gratitude. But before she could catch her breath a shock wave rocked the chamber and threw them off their feet. The obelisk slid across the floor.

"The scepter!" she shouted.

Yeats dashed to retrieve it. But as the vibrations grew more violent, his right leg gave way, and he tumbled back into the floor shaft. He managed to catch the ledge at the last second. Serena could see his fingers sticking up above the shaft, clawing at the stone floor.

Conrad picked up the obelisk from the floor and grabbed Serena. "See if you can reach him!"

With Conrad firmly clasping her hand, she peered over the edge of the shaft and was surprised to see Yeats swinging above the infernal abyss.

She knew she didn't have the strength to pull him up, but she shouted to Conrad, "I think I can give him a tug and he can climb out himself."

She stretched out her hand when another jolt hit, sending Leonid's corpse sliding into the shaft. The corpse struck Yeats on the way down. Yeats's fingers disappeared and Serena heard Conrad cry out.

"Dad!" Conrad shouted.

Then she felt Conrad pulling her away so he could look down into the shaft. He stood there, paralyzed, trying to comprehend that his father was really gone.

Serena looked around the chamber as everything shook. She didn't want to leave. But she didn't want to stay behind and melt either. So she put her hand on Conrad's shoulder and said, "There's no time to mourn for those we're about to follow."

Her words were enough to bring Conrad back.

"This chamber is going to turn into a furnace in a few seconds," he said, picking up the pack Yeats had left behind and slinging it over his shoulder. "Back to the gallery!"

They ran to the outer corridor. The rumbling wasn't so loud here, she thought, following Conrad down the long tunnel. But when they emerged into the Great Gallery, Conrad stopped and looked up.

"Now might be a good time for you to say a brief prayer," he said.

"Conrad, what's happening?"

"I think P4 is releasing a burst of heat through the shafts, melting the ice outside," he said. "And the water is being processed through this machinery."

She followed Conrad's gaze up the gallery and squinted her eyes. There was a shadow swirling in the distance at the top. Then she felt the first droplets of water splash against her cheek and realized what was coming.

"Oh, my God!" she screamed as the cascades of a gigantic waterfall began to tumble down the gallery behind them. "We've got to take cover!"

Now she was pulling him back to the chamber.

"Not yet," he told her, "or we'll fry."

Already the water was knee-deep in the tunnel. By the time they were halfway back to the chamber, it was up to their waists. In seconds the current swelled to a torrent and swept them off their feet.

Serena reached for Conrad but couldn't feel him anymore. She panicked and splashed desperately, taking in water, gasping for breath. She was going to drown, she realized. They were going to be flushed away and drown. Surely this is not what God intended for her life, she thought. But then she remembered the little girl in the ice and realized she had seen too many faces just like hers around the world to know for sure what God intended for her. All she knew was that she wanted to live, and she wanted Conrad to live too.

Oh, God, she prayed, help us.

A shadow fell across her, and she looked up to see Conrad standing in the entry of the tunnel to the star chamber, water swirling around his knees. He held the obelisk in one hand.

"Grab the other end!" he yelled above the rushing waters.

She reached up and clasped the obelisk and let Conrad pull her up. But she felt a tug at her ankle and looked down to see a bloody face emerge from the water.

It screamed something unintelligible, and she tried to shake it off. But it pulled still harder. Suddenly she recognized the disfigured face of one of Kovich's men from the upper chamber.

"Hold on!" Serena yelled and let Conrad pull her up.

Once over the ledge, she turned to help the Russian. The soldier's burned legs had barely cleared the ledge when Serena heard Conrad's shout.

"Hurry!"

Then she saw the door to the star chamber closing down behind Conrad, a great granite slab dropping from the ceiling. Conrad, obelisk in hand, ducked into the chamber, which had apparently cooled back down, and started waving them in.

Serena was still dragging the Russian across the entrance to the chamber when a massive crash behind her rocked the tunnel. She glanced back to see that the door had closed, sealing off the water. Pausing to catch her breath, she heard Conrad cry out her name. He was pointing to the ceiling. Three more great doors were dropping, the second one right over her head.

She lurched forward, her soaked parka weighing her down like a cement tomb as she struggled to drag the Russian, whose limbs had stopped moving.

"Serena!" Conrad shouted.

The third door was dropping.

She fell to her hands and knees and dragged the Russian across the floor. Then she felt Conrad's hands clasp her ankles like leg irons and start to pull. Her knees slipped and she fell flat on her stomach.

"Let him go!" he shouted.

"No!" Serena gripped the Russian's cold hands tightly, even as Conrad towed her inside.

The Russian was halfway through when the slab door sliced him in two. Suddenly Serena realized she was dragging only half a body. And still she found it hard to let go, to accept that there was nobody left for her to save.

With a massive scraping sound, the fourth and final door started to drop. She struggled to free herself from the cold grip of the legless corpse. Finally, the hand fell away, and at the last moment something whisked her inside as the final granite slab sank with a sickening thud.

Serena turned to thank Conrad but saw him sprawled on the floor, his hair matted with blood. He must have struck the back of his head against the falling door when he pulled her in.

"Conrad!" she called. "Conrad!"

She scrambled to his limp body. But there was no

movement. And the chamber was shaking too violently for her to take a pulse. She saw the obelisk on the floor next to his pack—Yeats's pack—and picked it up.

Another temblor hit, and she backed herself up against the shaking walls until they began to burn with tremendous heat. She moved away, stumbling across the floor, her body shaking uncontrollably as she tried to keep her balance.

She was alone now, she realized, and fell to her knees with the obelisk cradled in her arms, praying to God that the quaking would stop, all the while trying not to think about the little girl in the ice. There was a loud blast and she looked up as the whole chamber seemed to turn upside down.

21
DESCENT HOUR NINE
U.S.S. CONSTELLATION

THE BOOM OF THE HUGE GLACIER collapsing into the water was like a bomb blast, knocking Admiral Warren off his feet and shattering the glass of the bridge on the U.S.S. *Constellation.*

Another boom followed seconds later, and then he heard more still as the massive waves crashed over the bow. Glass fragments were scattered across the flight deck, where seventy-six attack jets were straining at their chains.

"Admiral?"

Warren turned. It was a signalman.

"FLASH traffic." The petty officer handed over the clipboard and held a red-covered flashlight over the dispatch so Warren could read it.

"God Almighty," said Warren as he started reading. "U.S. Geological Survey sensors at McMurdo just registered an eleven-point-one shock wave."

"Admiral!" shouted a lieutenant.

Warren looked up in time to glimpse a towering, muddy green wall of water descend on the bow and wash over the flight deck, scattering the attack jets like toys and crashing into the superstructure where he stood. A deafening crack split his ears as the crush of water demolished the bridge. Desperately he searched for something to hang on to.

Water filled the compartment. Warren held the bar of a console and braced his back against the wall to stay upright. On calm waters, the 86,000-ton carrier rose 201 feet above the waterline. But these swells were lifting the aircraft carrier like an empty Cuban cigar box.

Warren coughed up some water and yelled to anyone who could hear him. "Turn us into the wave or we'll capsize!"

He strained to hear his command received with an "Aye, sir!" from a helmsman, but there was no sound beside the crash of water.

When the wave broke, he looked around the bridge and saw two floating bodies. The rest had been swept to sea. He ran down the stairs to the wheelhouse, gripping the rail tightly. The wheelhouse was empty.

He turned toward the coast to see another towering gray mass, a cliff-size wave. He grabbed a chain reserved for one of his 55,000-pound planes and hoisted it on his broad shoulders and headed down to the flight deck.

Men and planes were thrashing about the tilting deck. Then a new wave lifted the carrier toward the sky. As he fell through the air, still clutching the chain, Warren saw a rail. Water crashed over the deck again, knocking him to his knees. But he saw his salvation. If he could just reach the rail in between waves, he could chain himself down.

The next wave split the twin-finned JSF attack jet in front of him, and Warren ducked to avoid being sliced in half by a broken wing. He willed himself to stand, his numb legs wobbling beneath him, and broke into a run, splashing through the shallows toward the rail.

Part of him wanted to slip and fall so he could just stop fighting and die, but he stayed on his feet until he rammed into the rail. He reached up and grabbed the heavy chain on his shoulders with both hands and lashed himself to the rail before the next wave crashed.

The winds and spray swept the deck as he clung for his life. The wave broke over the bow, and just as Warren could feel the force lift his body off the deck and sweep him aside, his chain caught and held.

For more than a minute he stayed that way, sure his arm would be torn off and he would be washed away like the remaining planes on deck. But God help him, he swore, he was going to survive this cataclysm if only to pay back Yeats. Then, slowly, he felt the carrier shifting and heard the creak of the massive steel buckling. He looked up and saw that the entire ship was on the verge of capsizing before the giant swell had passed.

"Goddamn you, Yeats!"

PART THREE

DAWN

22
DAWN MINUS FIFTEEN HOURS

INSIDE P4'S STAR CHAMBER, Conrad coughed as the whiskey stung the back of his throat. He looked up at Serena sitting next to him. Her wet hair was wiped back, her face pale.

"Jack Daniel's?" he asked hoarsely.

"Found it in Yeats's pack." She reached over and touched his face. The feeling of her hand on his face brought him back to life. "You're warm."

"This whole place feels warm." Conrad sat up and felt a terrific pain at the base of his skull. He groaned. "Where's the obelisk?"

"I don't know," Serena said.

"It was right here." Conrad quickly scanned the star chamber. He saw the empty altar standing in the middle of the cartouche. Something in his gut churned and he remembered a nightmare about the floor splitting open. "Where's Yeats?"

"Disappeared down the floor shaft."

Conrad looked for the shaft, but it had closed up again beneath the altar. He's dead, thought Conrad. He felt himself shake, his heart beating rapidly.

"I'm so sorry about your father, Conrad."

He looked into her eyes. She was indeed sorry, he thought. But there was something peculiar about the way she looked at him now. Something different. He wouldn't call it fear, but there was something else in her eyes that put distance between them. Surely she didn't believe Yeats's bizarre revelation about his origins, did she? It was obviously a psychological ploy.

"You don't actually believe—"

"Whatever else you may be, Conrad, you're clearly not on anybody's 'most worthy' list—not God's, not the Atlanteans' and not mine," she said. "You're still going to die for your sins. Only this time it looks like you're going to take the rest of us with you straight to hell. That's what I believe."

Conrad could only stare at her. "You never stop, do you? You always have to have the last word."

"Yes."

Then Conrad saw something gleaming on the floor. He reached out to touch it. Was it sunlight? He looked up at the ceiling and blinked his eyes. The two concealed shafts he suspected had been there all along were now wide open, and a beam of sunlight strained through the southern shaft and touched the center of the floor where the obelisk had been.

Had the ice chasm overhead collapsed? he wondered with alarm. What about Ice Base Orion? The horrific thought that P4's geothermal vent might have melted the ice or even shifted the earth's crust briefly drifted across his consciousness, but he quickly suppressed it. Had something so catastrophic happened, he and Serena would be dead.

"What time is it?" Conrad asked Serena.

"Three in the afternoon," she said. "Antarctica has equal hours of daylight and darkness in September. So we only have a few hours until dusk."

Conrad craned his neck at the shafts on the sloping north and south walls of the chamber. He could crawl out one to check. It was the only way out. But the angles of the shafts looked steep, and it was at least a thousand feet up to God knows what.

"I'll need to have a look outside," he told her.

She nodded slowly, as if she had reached the same conclusion long before he had regained consciousness. "You'll need these to climb up the shaft."

She was holding pressurized suction-cup pads for the knees and hands.

"Where did you get those?" he asked.

"Your father's pack," she said. "He seemed to have prepared for everything."

Conrad looked at the altar in the center of the room covering the shaft that had swallowed his father. "Not quite everything."

Conrad rose to his feet, took the suction gear from Serena, and crossed the floor to the southern shaft. He stared up at the sun and blinked. "Looks like the polar storm cleared."

"That's what it looks like." Serena didn't sound so sure. She didn't even look like she wanted to know.

"If there are any search parties looking for us, we

need to send a signal or flare," he told her, strapping the suction pads on. "I'll have to crawl up through the shaft. And I'll carry up a line with me, just in case it's our only way out and you'll need to join me. Meanwhile, you try to raise Ice Base Orion on Yeats's radio and tell them what happened."

He could feel her searching his eyes for clues. "What did happen, Conrad?"

He wanted to hold her in his arms, if she'd let him, and tell her everything was going to be OK. But they both knew that would be a lie. "I'm going to find out," he told her. "I promise."

The square of light overhead grew larger as Conrad neared the top of the shaft. It had been a steeper climb than he expected, slowed by the suction pads he needed for traction, and he was out of breath. The wind whistled as he gripped the outer edge of the shaft and pulled himself up to the light of day.

The brightness was harsh and he blinked rapidly, allowing several seconds for his eyes to adjust. When they did, he blinked again in disbelief.

Spread out a mile below him were the ruins of an ancient city. Temples, ziggurats, and broken obelisks lay strewn amid what had been—could be—a tropical paradise. He noticed a series of concentric, circular waterways radiating out from the base of the pyramid complex, which he deduced was the center of town. It was an advanced, otherworldly city grid hidden for twelve thousand years under two miles of ice.

Until now.

Conrad shaded his eyes. The subglacial terrain stretched out in a six-mile radius from the pyramid—a tropical island in a sea of ice. In the distance he could see the snowcapped Transantarctic Mountains.

The air smelled crisp and fresh, and he could hear the distant rumble of waterfalls. Somehow his fears and doubts and petty ambitions were swept away by the majesty of it all. But as he gazed out across the new world, he suddenly wondered what had happened to the old.

23
DAWN MINUS FIFTEEN HOURS
U.S.S. CONSTELLATION

ADMIRAL WARREN SPLASHED across the inside hangar deck of the U.S.S. *Constellation,* surveying the damage. The ship hadn't capsized after all, but the deck had taken on enough water to sink the *Titanic* twice. And yet the old girl was still afloat, limping along on emergency power.

Initial reports coming in from the U.S. Geological Survey in Golden, Colorado, and some earthquake-forecasting agency in Japan blamed the tidal wave on a major quake in East Antarctica—11.1 on the Richter scale. But Warren couldn't confirm it with McMurdo or Amundsen-Scott. All communications with American bases on the continent had been cut off by a burst of EMP.

All of which seemed to validate reports coming out of Moscow and Beijing that the "seismic event" in Antarctica was really a secret U.S.-sponsored nuclear explosion—a flagrant violation of the international Antarctic Treaty.

The electromagnetic pulse, or EMP, had also blinded spy satellites overhead. Warren was told that if he couldn't get a bird up in the air to fly reconn over the epicenter, it was going to take at least sixteen hours before any U.S. forces could reach the target to either prove the nuke accusations false or cover up Yeats's dirty work.

"Goddamn you, Yeats," Warren muttered as he stepped around the floating pieces of a broken wing. Looked like one of their F/A-18 Hornets. The rest was mangled with what used to be an S-3B Viking.

Warren shook his head. Twenty-six wounded, three in critical condition and nine missing. And that was just the *Constellation*. News reports said one-third of the island of Male, the Maldives's capital, was underwater. Even a small rise in sea levels at this point could wipe out the island nation—all 1,180 islands. The entire population of 263,000 inhabitants was at risk.

The only positive news Warren could report back to Washington was that his crew had managed to rescue the Greenpeace protesters from their now-sunken ship. The meddlers were helping out with the wounded and serving up some of the best damned coffee Warren had ever tasted.

He was on his fourth cup when one of his radio officers splashed over. "EAM coming over Milstar, sir."

Warren watched a sock float past him on the hangar deck. Milstar was the president's communications link to senior military commanders. The $17 billion Military Commanders' Voice Conference Network was designed to enable commanders to discuss whether a ballistic-missile launch threatened North America and, if so, to determine the appropriate response.

"Priority one, sir."

"I'm coming."

Warren took a final gulp as he eyed the rad-hardened Black Hawk chopper that several of his maintenance crew were working on in the corner—at his orders. He then crumpled the Styrofoam coffee cup and tossed it on the hangar floor, where it floated away.

Inside the *Constellation*'s war suite, the water was only ankle deep. Warren walked in to find his senior officer, McBride, seated at the conference table. Next to McBride, to Warren's surprise and dismay, was the scruffy Greenpeace geek from the *Arctic Sunrise* whom CNN had featured. He was fiddling with some candy-colored laptop computer that looked like a toy.

Warren frowned. "What's this civilian doing here, McBride?"

"This is Thornton Larson, a Ph.D. in geophysics from MIT," McBride said. "He reviewed the Milstar downloads and has a presentation for you."

"Couldn't your officers figure it out, McBride?"

McBride said, "The data is so off the charts, sir, we felt we needed a second opinion. Dr. Larson has some valuable insights."

Warren sat down and studied the disheveled Larson. The smart-ass hasn't even discovered the razor blade, he thought to himself, and McBride was sharing national security secrets with him. "Enlighten me, Larson."

"I was able to retrieve one final image from a satellite overhead before its innards were fried by that EMP," Larson said excitedly. "I cleaned it up and here it is."

Warren looked up at the large wall screen. A blue-tinted image of Antarctica, all too familiar to Warren these days, came into view. But in the middle of it, or rather just off center in East Antarctica, was a brown-yellow dot.

"Is that awesome, dude, or what?" Larson could only marvel at his work.

"God almighty, tell me that's some storm and not ground zero," Warren said.

Larson addressed the image on the wall screen. "Well, hello Mr. Ground Zero, are you ready for your close-up?"

The brown-yellow dot on-screen started to magnify, frame by frame, until Warren found himself looking at a crater in the ice, and at the bottom of it was a complex of pyramids, temples, and waterways. The kid was obviously playing them all for fools, Warren decided.

"You think you're pretty funny, Larson, don't you?" Warren said, starting to get up. "Let's see how hilarious the brig can be."

"Please, sir," McBride said. "We checked it out and this guy hasn't doctored anything."

Warren slowly sat down, his thoughts immediately turning to Yeats. The SOB must have known all along. "So you're telling me what I'm seeing on that screen is for real?"

"What you're seeing is a localized event, like a garage band on the verge of stardom," Larson said. "This is just the first single off an album I'll call *Mother Nature's Cacophony in Doomsday Major*."

Warren gave McBride his "your ass is on the line here" stare, which his executive officer acknowledged.

Larson said, "Your attention, class."

Warren looked up at the large wall screen. The image

208   Thomas Greanias

of an ancient city surrounded by ice was gone. In its place, spinning in the center, flickering with each power drain of the carrier's electrical system, was what looked like a thermal image of the sun in space.

"Tell me what I'm looking at on the screen, Larson."

"Earth's core, baby," Larson said. "The *core!* A new technique similar to a medical sonogram enables us to generate an image of the inner planet. I've used the latest version of PowerPoint on my G5 to generate—"

Warren waved his hand impatiently. "Get to the point."

"Earth is an onion, man, made up of layers," Larson said. "And it's a rotating onion too, churning up hurricanes and storms in the atmosphere. But the core spins independently, and changes there can trigger significant consequences near and at the planet's surface. I'm talking *consequences.*"

"You mean earthquakes and tidal waves?" Warren said.

"Big time," Larson said. "Albert Einstein, Dr. Relativity himself, even theorized that the outer crust, the lithosphere, periodically shifts over the asthenosphere due to ice buildup in the polar regions."

"What are you saying?"

"What I'm saying, baby, is that we seem to be witnessing what is known as an earth-crust displacement. You dudes in the military-industrial complex prefer the perverse little acronym ECD."

Warren didn't know what this kid was smoking, but he had to know where this theory was going. "And what's this ECD going to do?"

"Well, here's where it gets really nasty," Larson said. "Antarctica is going to get pushed toward the equator and North America into the Arctic Circle."

Another computer image appeared on-screen, this one of Earth. Warren felt his own temperature rise as Antarctica moved up toward the center of the globe, ice free, and North America was pushed to the top of the globe.

Warren said, "So you're saying we're better off staying here and sunning on the beaches of Antarctica rather than freezing our asses off in the USA, which is going to get buried under two miles of ice."

"Bingo!" Larson said. "Bingo! An ECD would cause extinctions to occur on different continents at different rates, based on varying changes in the world's latitudes. I've mapped the projected lines of destruction. We'll call them PLDs. Hey, I made up a new acronym! Well, these PLDs are pretty damn awesome, I've got to tell you."

On-screen Larson drew a circle around the globe, through the North and South poles. "The line of greatest displacement runs through North America, west of South America, bisects Antarctica, travels through Southeast Asia, goes on to Siberia, and then back to North America. All the continents along the line of greatest displacement—or LGD—are about to experience mass extinctions."

"Nobody knows the future," Warren said, uncomfortable with this green alarmist's certainty. "If you ever read old five-year budget projections from the Pentagon, you'd know that. How long will it take for this alleged ring of death to make us all extinct?"

"It's only an estimate, but my models project an ECD taking place over the next couple of days and running itself out within a week."

Warren was stunned. "All that destruction in a few days?"

"Dude, it took God only six days to create the universe, according to Genesis," Larson said. "Why should an ECD take any longer to destroy it? It's like a coil that can unwind with unstoppable, devastating speed once it reaches threshold."

Warren leaned forward. "This has happened before?"

"Several times."

"And I suppose you were there to measure them all?"

"I wish," Larson said. "The last one was roughly eleven thousand six hundred years ago, about 9600 B.C. That's when the geological record says vast climatic changes swept the planet. Massive ice sheets melted, ocean levels rose. Huge mammals perished in great numbers. A sudden influx of people flowed into the Americas. It was *party* time, you know?"

"And this happens every twelve thousand years or so?"

"No, every forty-one thousand years," Larson said, who had suddenly hit his own threshold and run out of gas. He plopped down on a seat. "We aren't due for an ECD for another thirty thousand years. Somehow the cycle has been accelerated. I don't know how."

Neither did Warren. But he was pretty damn sure who was responsible. "And how soon until we reach threshold?" Warren demanded. "What kind of countdown are we talking about here?"

"The ECD should reach threshold by dawn tomorrow morning." Larson started counting on his fingers with a glazed look in his eyes. "Damn, that's less than fifteen hours. One last night to get lucky before it all goes poof."

Admiral Warren could only stare at the kid in the hope that his Ph.D. stood for Piled Higher and Deeper. Otherwise, they were all out of luck.

24
DAWN MINUS FOURTEEN HOURS

SERENA PACED BACK AND FORTH across the floor of the geodesic star chamber while she waited for Conrad to return.

Something had gone horribly wrong. She could smell it in the air and feel it in her bones. Something on a large scale, something very profound, had occurred. Her stomach felt terribly unsettled, like it did when she didn't eat or drink anything for hours except one cup of espresso after another. If only she had acted on her doubts earlier, or been more persuasive with Conrad, or stalled Yeats longer.

As she paced and pondered, she eyed the empty altar in the center of the room uneasily. In one terrifying moment it had opened up like the pit of hell and incinerated Kovich and swallowed Yeats.

Perhaps it was a geothermal vent of sorts, something that could tap the heat of Earth's interior and harness its power. After all, the most advanced fuel cells ever devised by human engineers generated the by-products of heat and water. P4 certainly had plenty of both.

In any case, she concluded, P4 was following the preprogrammed instructions of its builders, whoever they were. And it was clearly intended to create some kind of global extinction event unless humanity could come up with some kind of "most noble" moment to justify its existence.

Looking to her left and her right, she reached into her pack and pulled out the Scepter of Osiris. She held the gleaming obelisk in her hands. For some intuitive reason she had lied and failed to tell Conrad she had it.

She moved over to the empty altar and eased the scepter into its rotundalike base. There was a rumbling as the geodesic star ceiling whirled. She tried to reset the heavens as they appeared before Conrad removed the obelisk. The whirling stopped and she waited. Nothing happened. Whatever Conrad did could not be reversed. So much for her virginity. Clearly she was no more "worthy" than he was.

She removed the obelisk from the altar and felt a shudder from the wall behind her. She turned to see the four chamber doors open in a row.

For a long minute she stood there, frozen, wondering what to do. Then she looked at the obelisk in her hands. Something about it seemed different. The side with the four suns had changed. Now there were six, the sixth sun being the largest. Her worst fears had been realized: a new age was dawning, which could only spell the end for the old age.

What had not changed was the inscription that said the Scepter of Osiris belonged in the Shrine of the First Sun. Somewhere nearby, she realized, was a structure like P4, a monument to an epoch in time. If P4 was the

Pyramid of the Fourth Sun, then the Shrine of the First Sun must have been built during the First Time or Genesis. If Conrad was right, then Genesis simply had to be the "most worthy time," since in the beginning God looked upon creation and said it was "good."

She had to find this Shrine of the First Sun and its secret, she resolved. Then she could reset the star chamber to the most worthy time and stop whatever was happening.

But where was this shrine and how would she even recognize it?

Conrad would know. She walked over to the square patch of sunlight beneath the southern shaft and with her eyes followed Conrad's line up the shaft. There was a flicker of daylight at the other end. What was taking him so long?

Serena turned from the shaft and surveyed the empty chamber. There on the floor was Yeats's backpack. She had already rummaged through it once, but now she noticed that the lining in back didn't look right. Upon closer inspection she realized there was something flat sewn inside.

She pulled out a military knife from the same pack and used it to slash through the lining. Inside she found a folded blueprint of some sort. It appeared to be a technical schematic of some kind of pillar. Then, all of a sudden, she recognized the "pillar" as the obelisk in her hand, complete with the rotunda at its base.

As she suspected, the Americans knew far more about this place than Yeats admitted. Clearly Yeats had this blueprint before they even entered P4, much less found the obelisk. Somehow Yeats knew the Scepter of Osiris was down here before he ever saw it.

Surely Yeats's crazy story about finding Conrad in the ice wasn't true, she told herself. It was simply a ploy to play on Conrad's emotions during a crisis situation. Even Conrad thought as much.

But there was something Conrad had mumbled before he woke up, something she had been pondering ever since. It had sounded like a moan made in pain. But there was something about the structure and syntax and accent of the sound that rang familiar. And now as she thought about it, she realized Conrad had been repeating the word *Mama* in some kind of pre-Aymaran form. But there was no way Conrad could know that.

A chill shot up her spine. Maybe Conrad was an Atlantean after all. Or maybe she was crazy. She picked up the obelisk and compared it to the blueprint. They looked identical, except for the markings, which, as she had just seen, possessed the ability to change.

Serena opened her pack and removed her coffee thermos. She twisted the outer shell until it unlocked and then slid it off like a sheath. She then rolled the blueprint around the outside of the inner tube and slid the outer shell back on, twisting it until it locked. It was a hiding place she had learned to rely on more than once in her journeys. Then she placed the thermos back into her pack.

She looked up at the southern shaft, thinking she shouldn't leave without Conrad. But he had been gone too long, she told herself as she glanced at the open doorway. She couldn't wait forever. And who knew where Conrad's path of self-discovery would take his loy-alties? She, on the other hand, knew exactly what she had to do. She had to take the Scepter to the Shrine of the First Sun. There she would find, she hoped, the so-called Secret of First Time that would somehow enable her to stop whatever was happening.

As for Conrad, it was clear she could not trust him, just like she could not trust Yeats. For all she knew she couldn't trust the pope or even God. How could he let this happen—again? She thought of the girl in the ice. She couldn't get the expression on her face out of her mind. This had happened once before, so clearly God could let it happen again. But she couldn't.

She put the obelisk back in her pack, slung the pack over her shoulder, and stepped out of the chamber through the open door. The tunnel led her to a fork at the bottom of the great gallery, and she took the middle tunnel down and out through P4's entrance.

When Serena emerged from the dark interior of P4 into the light of day, it seemed to her that the sun was more brilliant than ever. It was hot, but it was the dry kind of heat that she liked. Antarctica was a desert climate with or without the ice, she thought as she shaded her eyes. More likely, however, the heat originated from the vast geothermal machinery underground.

A minute later, after her eyes had adjusted, she real-ized that she was standing in the center of a city at the bottom of some great crater. Walls of ice lifted up in the distance, forming a spectacular backdrop for this desert

landscape of pyramids, obelisks, temples, and waterways. She could hear the roar of a distant waterfall.

She closed her eyes and took a deep breath. The rush
of fresh, oxygen-rich air overwhelmed her senses. So did
the realization that there were probably centuries of
research down here, and if she lived a thousand lifetimes
she still would just be getting started at unraveling the
city's mysteries.

Whatever else, she realized, this discovery changed
everything about human history.

Eyes still closed, she thought she heard a dog barking.
Ridiculous, she thought, and realized she should be
praying, listening for some inner prompting from the
Holy Spirit or direction from God. But all she heard was
that barking, and it was getting louder and more annoy-
ing. Then she blinked her eyes open to see Yeats's husky,
Nimrod, trotting toward her.

She was surprised by the joy she felt and called out to
him, "Here, boy!"

Nimrod ran into her arms and started licking her face.

"Are you OK?" she asked him. "Is everybody else OK?"

Nimrod immediately turned and started running in
the other direction, pausing to look back.

"You want me to follow, boy?"

Nimrod barked and kept running and this time did
not look back.

Serena followed the canine for a half hour along what
appeared to be the main waterway of the empty city. But
the longer they walked, the less it felt like a city. There
was nothing to suggest anybody ever actually lived here
on the plateau. No streets, just waterways. Some cours-

ing with glistening water, others dry. And the ground between the pavilions was barren. No plant life, nothing. Maybe that would change in a few days.

Perhaps the dwellings were on the outskirts, she wondered, still buried under ice. But these monuments, however coldly magnificent, reminded her of a city of abandoned oil rigs she once toured along the Caspian Sea in the former Soviet Union: miles of rusted pipes you could drive a truck through and ghostly refineries that stretched like heaps of filth across the horizon.

She also had the uneasy feeling of being watched, although she knew that was absurd. There was nobody around to watch her. Then again, Nimrod was here. Maybe there were others. She occasionally lost sight of the dog but always remained within earshot of his barks. Then the barks grew louder, and she realized he was waiting to show her something.

From a distance she could see the object glisten in the sun. Soon she came upon a smashed Hagglunds tractor on the banks of the water channel. The rear cab was crushed to bits, fragments of fiberglass gleaming across the ground. But the front cab seemed intact.

Serena walked over to the driver's side door, which was ajar, and opened it. She gasped as the body of Colonel O'Dell crumpled to the ground at her feet, his head a bloody mess with bits of the dashboard matted in his hair. Nimrod sniffed the corpse with a whimper.

Poor O'Dell, she thought, realizing she would have to bury his body. It would be only proper. But first she had to see if the tractor's transmitter was working and if there was any food or water. She hated to admit it, with

O'Dell lying there on the ground, but she was famished.

She climbed inside the cab and searched methodically for any SAT phones, weapons, food packs, anything. But the cab had been stripped of everything save for a single meal-ready-to-eat and a shortwave radio.

She tore open the MRE. Nimrod made it clear that he expected a share of the food, nuzzling his way into the cab.

"Oh, OK," she said. "Come on in."

Together they split the meal. But the longer she chewed, the more she realized what she was really hungry for was news. She eyed the shortwave radio, wondering if it worked, but perversely almost hoping it didn't.

Unable to bear it any longer, she turned the radio on. It worked. The static grew louder as she turned up the volume and then searched the band of frequencies to find the BBC. When she did, the announcer's voice was filled with tension.

"Mass evacuations of U.S. coastal cities are under way," the announcer said. "The federal government reports that it is opening up the nearly six hundred fifty million acres of public land it owns—almost thirty percent of the United States—for refugees."

Bit by bit, the details began to fill in: the massive "seismic event" in Antarctica that split off a glacier the size of Texas, the swamping of the Maldives and other Pacific Islands, the meetings of the U.N. Security Council in New York, and accusations of secret American nuclear weapons tests in Antarctica.

Dear Lord, she thought. What have we done? Serena

looked at her food and suddenly lost her appetite. She didn't stop Nimrod from finishing the meal.

Various commentators, analysts, and scientists of the international sort soon weighed in, some expressing fears that the ice cap was breaking up, others that rising sea levels would wipe out coastal cities and sink low-lying lands such as Florida. Those with access to the corridors of power confessed to hearing whispers of a potential shift in Earth's crust and global geological catastrophe.

She turned off the radio and removed the Scepter of Osiris from her backpack. Staring at it, thinking about all that it had wrought thus far, she felt her stomach churn.

She opened the passenger door of the cab. Nimrod jumped out and ran to the river's edge and began lapping up water. She walked over and squatted next to him and looked across to the other side. It was about five hundred feet away.

Seeing that Nimrod was no worse for his drink, she removed an empty water bottle from her pack and dipped it into the water. The current was so strong it ripped the bottle away in an instant, so she cupped a hand into the water and sipped. She was splashing some water on her oily, dusty face when she heard a yelp.

She looked over to see Nimrod lying on his side, panting heavily, eyes in shock. She spit the water out of her mouth and looked him over.

"What's wrong, boy?" she asked, suddenly worried as she stroked his ear. "Please don't tell me it's the water."

It wasn't. There was blood coming from Nimrod's thigh. She looked closer. It looked like a bullet hole.

"Oh, God," she began to say when a bright red dot

appeared on Nimrod's furry chest. A second later blood spurted out. She jumped back and screamed.

A dozen soldiers in UNACOM uniforms emerged from the horizon and closed in around her with their AK-47s at the ready. Their commanding officer stepped forward from the circle around her and spoke into his radio.

"This is Jamil," the man said in Arabic. "We have one survivor, sir. A woman."

The accent sounded Egyptian to Serena, and this was confirmed when she heard the reply on the radio: "Bring her to me."

"Yes, sir."

Before Serena could move, Jamil motioned to one of his men, and the grunt flung her across the ground, holding her down with one hand and considerable strength. He ripped open her fatigues, slipped a hand inside, and felt her up and down.

"What is this?" the soldier said with a Saudi accent, yanking away a switchblade knife.

The Saudi held up the knife and sprang the blade, eliciting howls of laughter from his comrades. Then he flipped the knife across the air to bury itself in the dirt. His eyes sparked fire as he stood over Serena, hands on his hips.

Serena had had enough. The Saudi was about to step away when she kicked him in the groin. As he doubled over in pain she jumped up and prepared to knee his bowed face. But suddenly a half-dozen red dots painted her chest and she looked up to see the barrels of a dozen AK-47s pointed at her.

Serena put her hands up in surrender and looked at the Saudi she had kicked. He was groveling in the dirt. Another Arab came behind her, this one an Afghan by the sound of his accent, and marched her outside the circle to stand before the commanding officer, Jamil.

Jamil seemed delighted by her performance. "Ah, what have we here?"

"I'll show you," said Serena in Arabic, and with her elbow spiked the face of the Afghan behind her. He let out a cry and dropped his AK-47. Serena took it and pointed it at the wounded soldier.

"Let me go," Serena ordered Jamil, digging the AK-47 into the back of the Afghan. "Or I'll kill your man here."

"You couldn't hurt a butterfly, mademoiselle."

Jamil took out a pearl-handled Colt, aimed it at Serena's hostage, and shot him dead himself. Serena watched in stunned silence as the Afghan fell to the ground, leaving her standing alone and exposed to Jamil's pistol.

"Hand over the Scepter of Osiris, mademoiselle, or I'll kill you too."

"You know about the scepter?"

"Shoot her," another soldier told Jamil.

Jamil smiled. "Not before she tells me what she knows."

The wind picked up and Serena looked up to see a chopper flying in. It was one of those French jobs she had flown a couple of times herself, a Z-9A, and it apparently belonged to the UNACOMers, because Jamil wasn't terribly concerned with its arrival.

"The scepter, I said."

"I've hidden it in a safe place," she said. "Let me go and I'll show you."

But one of Jamil's men, who was ransacking Serena's pack, suddenly called out and produced the obelisk.

Jamil took the obelisk in his hands, examined it for a moment, and then looked at her and laughed. "Tell Colonel Zawas we have found the Scepter of Osiris."

25
DAWN MINUS THIRTEEN HOURS

FROM HIS PERCH NEAR the summit of P4, Conrad had a bird's-eye view of the lost city in the late afternoon. If only Dad could see this, he thought, gazing out from the mouth of the exterior shaft.

The city was comprised of concentric waterways laid over a grid. Wide avenues flanked by temples and pavilions radiated outward from the central P4 compound. This layout reminded him of the Avenue of the Dead in Teotihuacán, Mexico, and even the National Mall in Washington, D.C.

About a mile long, the necropolis was anchored by P4 in the center, a Sphinx-like structure at the east end, and at the west end a step-pyramid with working waterfalls that churned brightly in the sunlight. The dimensions were spectacular.

Most astounding of all, Conrad could see the various rings of pavilions slowly shifting and locking into place. Or was it P4 that was slowly rotating? He couldn't tell. At any rate, the builders did more than construct a city aligned to the stars before an ancient earth-crust displacement shifted the continent. They constructed a city

in which the monuments could somehow realign themselves, perhaps through the hydraulic pressure of the
water that coursed through its very veins.

Conrad tried to let this otherworldly landscape sink
in, to burn this image into his memory so he'd never forget it. The magnitude of its scale, however, defied comprehension. There were probably ten square miles of
city to explore inside a crater of ice whose walls rose two
miles into the sky along the city outskirts. And that was
only the part of the city that was visible. Conrad could
only assume what he saw was part of a bigger metropolis.

He was tempted to slide back down the shaft that
instant to tell Serena what he had found, if only to convince himself. But he knew he must first capture a picture. He pulled out his pocket digital camera and
panned the valley below. Whatever else he took away
from this city, he could at least have this, proof that he
was the first person in twelve thousand years to glimpse
humanity's earliest epoch. Perhaps he was the first
human to glimpse an entirely alien civilization. Maybe
even his own, if Yeats was to be believed.

Yeats's revelation raised more questions than it
answered. It certainly raised a wall between him and
Serena. He had seen the uncertainty in her eyes as she
studied him back in the star chamber. He couldn't tell if
it was for who he was or what he had done. But the
pangs of guilt for an obsession that cost the life of the
only man who might have answers for them—Yeats—
refused to subside.

The reality was that the only father he had ever
known was dead.

He loved me, Conrad thought. He did the best he could. He even tried to tell me that in his own way. Now Yeats was gone, and they'd never have the father-son reconciliation Yeats deserved.

Conrad suddenly felt nauseated. But he took a deep breath of fresh Antarctic air and asked himself what Yeats would say. And the answer that came to mind was clear.

Yeats would no doubt quote some military figure like Admiral Mahan of the American Navy during the Revolution and say: "Whenever you set out to accomplish anything, make up your mind at the outset about your ultimate objective. Once you have decided on it, take care never to lose sight of it."

For Conrad, the objective was clear: he had to map the city and find its Shrine of the First Sun, which was clearly a memorial to the epoch of First Time. Inside the shrine would be the Seat of Osiris, just like the one on the royal seal he had seen. If he could bring the scepter from the star chamber into the shrine and sit in the Seat of Osiris he would unlock the Secret of First Time— surely the "time and place of the most worthy."

Holding his camera up, Conrad panned to his right and to his left, up to the sky and down to the ground. Then he zoomed in on various structures, starting with the Sphinx-like landmark in the east and working his way toward the step-pyramid with the waterfalls in the west.

Satisfied he had captured everything he could, he replayed some of the images on the viewfinder screen to make sure once again that he wasn't dreaming. As he did, however, he saw a dot moving across the ground. It was over by the great waterway that cut through the heart of the city.

Heart surging with fear and excitement, Conrad pointed the camera in the dot's direction, slowly boosting the magnification. There it was, a blurry image, definitely moving. No, there were two blurry figures. He focused further. Suddenly the first one jumped into view.

It was Nimrod, the husky from Ice Base Orion. And walking beside him was Serena. A few moments later the dog dropped in his tracks and a dozen figures surrounded Serena before a chopper landed next to the group. The encounter did not look friendly.

Conrad lowered his camera only to see a swarm of military choppers buzz overhead. Before he could wave, a burst of machine gun fire came his way, raking the side of the pyramid.

He slid down the shaft as fast as he could to the star chamber, which was completely empty. Serena was gone, Yeats's pack was gone, and the sequence of doors leading out to the gallery was wide open.

Something rattled overhead, and as Conrad looked up the shaft he had just slid down, a smoking canister dropped to the floor. Conrad's eyes started to burn and he realized it was tear gas. He ran out of the chamber.

Once at the fork at the bottom of the gallery, he looked down the tunnel Serena must have taken to P4's entrance. A dozen pairs of glowing green eyes were coming his way. His only choice was to drop down the shaft toward the boiler room. He landed in a torrent of water washing down the subterranean channel away from P4.

He was racing down the channel now, caught in a current of such power that there was nothing he could do except keep his head above water. What the hell had he gotten himself into now? he wondered. Then he saw the mouth of a tunnel closing in on him, and a second later he was swallowed up by the darkness.

Deep beneath the ancient city, Conrad splashed in the darkness, gasping for air as he was swept through the underground canals. The freezing water disoriented him, and all he could hear were furious sucking sounds all around.

He bounced off a wall and spun in circles as the canal merged with another, larger tunnel. The overwhelming push of the new stream churned the raging river into a whirlpool. He glanced over his shoulder as a white curl of foam bore down on him in the darkness. He thought it would kill him, but instead the wave lifted him over a stone bank to a walkway.

Out of the water, he paused to catch his breath when another wave flooded in, the water grasping at his knees, trying to suck him back in. But it receded quickly and he was up on his feet, moving down the walkway. A cursory glance told him this tunnel was at least twice as high as those inside P4.

As he made his way through the labyrinth that crisscrossed beneath the city, Conrad was both awed and angered by the extent of the builders' subterranean infrastructure. He could spend an eternity studying this city, he thought, and if he didn't find a way out of here very soon he just might.

He also was angry at Serena, another one of life's mysteries he'd felt he would never understand. She obviously didn't trust him. Why else would she have left him back at P4 to venture off on her own? She had gone into her survivor mode and for all he knew considered him the enemy. And yet he was anxious about her safety after witnessing her capture.

A few minutes later he came to a fork in the tunnel and stopped. Two smaller aqueducts, each about forty feet high and twenty feet wide, presented themselves. Then he heard a faint rumble coming from the right aqueduct. He stared into the darkness and saw a glimmer of light. It was growing larger as the rumble grew louder. It was another surge of water coming down the pike, and in a few seconds the force would slam him against the tunnel walls and kill him.

His only way out, he realized, was to run into the left aqueduct. He dove in before a wall of water from the right pipe flooded the larger tunnel. From inside the left aqueduct, knee-deep in water, he watched the deluge roar for a full three minutes before it emptied itself out.

When it was over, he realized he was shaking. Too close, he thought as he rose to his feet. He took his first step down the aqueduct when he heard a distant splash. For a second he expected another torrent of water to wipe him out. But none came. He cocked his ear. This splashing had a rhythm to it.

He peered into the darkness. Someone in the distance was walking toward him. More than one, actually, because now he could hear the coarse murmur of conversation growing louder. They were speaking Arabic.

Conrad took a step back toward the large tunnel. The

splash of his boot was louder than he intended. He froze. For a second he heard nothing. Then the sound of splashing footsteps picked up its pace.

"Stop!" called one of the figures in English.

Conrad glanced over his shoulder to see two pairs of glowing green eyes bobbing in the blackness. He ran back into the large tunnel. Then a shot rang out and he ducked as a bullet ricocheted off a wall. He froze at the fork before the two aqueducts. Slowly he turned around and saw the red dot on his chest. No, two dots.

Conrad grew very still as the pair emerged from the left aqueduct in night-vision goggles. They were wearing UNACOM uniforms, their AK-47s still trained on his chest. But these didn't look like U.N. weapons inspectors to him.

"Radio Zawas, Abdul," said the one on the right.

The one called Abdul tried to make the call but only got static. "We have to surface," he said, sounding frustrated. "These walls are blocking the signal."

Abdul's partner started toward Conrad when another rumble began in the distance. Conrad edged toward the right aqueduct.

"Stop!" Abdul demanded. "Where do you think you are going?"

"To the surface like you said," Conrad replied without looking back. As he approached the mouth of the right aqueduct he could feel a cool wet breeze on his face. The distant roar grew louder. Then a bullet whizzed past his ear and he stopped and turned around.

Abdul and his companion were almost twenty yards away in the large tunnel, staring beyond him with growing curiosity. They were saying something, but the rumble from behind was too loud for Conrad to hear them. Then, just as Conrad could feel the first drops of water spraying his back, he saw them lower their weapons and start running away.

Conrad dove into the left tunnel as a wall of water blasted out of the aqueduct behind him and flushed the soldiers away. And then the mighty flow thinned into a tiny stream, as if some automatic timer had turned off the faucet. They were gone.

Conrad stood still, listening to the trickle of water and his heavy breathing, when he heard a splash from behind. He spun around and saw a hulking figure walking toward him in the dark, growing larger and more menacing until he emerged from the shadows and ripped off his night goggles.

"I've been looking for you," said Yeats.

"Dad!" Conrad wanted to throw his arms around his father.

But Yeats instead bent down and picked up something shiny floating in the water. Conrad could see it was an Egyptian ankh from the neck of one of the soldiers. The crosslike necklace with a circle at the top was a symbol of life, but it meant little to the dead soldier now. Yeats held the ankh up to the light of his headtorch.

"At least you're starting to screw things up for somebody else now, Conrad," he said.

26
DAWN MINUS TWELVE HOURS

SERENA FELT HOT AND UNCOMFORTABLE inside the Z-9A jet helicopter as it jerked haphazardly across the plateau. The Egyptian pilot was having some trouble keeping the overloaded chopper steady, and each dip brought spews of profanity from the UNACOM soldiers in back. Meanwhile, Jamil's stench was offensive in the cramped space. She could feel his cruel eyes fixed on her breasts with each lurch of the chopper.

"You are enjoying the ride, no?" he asked in Arabic.

"Not so much as you," she said. "Maybe if your pilot lets me take the stick."

Jamil looked at her, eyes burning with rage. "You dare talk back to me?"

She said nothing. She focused on the spectacular views of the city and waterways below, wondering what had happened to Conrad and who these UNACOM soldiers really were and what they wanted.

She had known that Colonel Ali Zawas was in Antarctica on behalf of the United Nations, and these men clearly reported to him and were no doubt taking her to him now. Perhaps their UNACOM assignments were merely covers to position themselves. Perhaps these soldiers had been lying in wait all along to relieve the Americans of whatever they found beneath the ice. Jamil seemed to know about the Scepter of Osiris. How?

The few answers she had gleaned thus far were grim: the Americans at Ice Base Orion were dead, along with the Russian weapons inspectors, and now Zawas and his arsenal controlled the city, until American reinforcements arrived. By then, however, it would be too late to stop Zawas from accomplishing his mission, whatever that might be, much less the impending worldwide geological cataclysm.

The chopper banked right, and in a flash she saw the great water channel below and beyond it, at the end of an acropolis, a gigantic step-pyramid looming like a dark fortress. The Temple of the Water Bearer is how Jamil referred to it as he spoke to the pilot, and indeed it lived up to its name. Two Niagara-like waterfalls tumbled down its sides, and some sort of encampment was set up in the promontory in between.

They descended along the temple's flattened eastern face between the two huge waterfalls and touched down on a landing pad on the promontory below. Those waterfalls, Serena realized as the door slid open and the soldiers emptied out, had been responsible for the low rumble she had been hearing ever since she emerged from P4 into the city. It was the power of those vibrations that made her feel uneasy and provided a constant sense of foreboding.

She climbed out and surveyed her surroundings. Two ramparts of narrow steps wound to the ground on either side. In the center sat crates of equipment. In back was an iron gate, before some sort of entrance to the temple. Meanwhile, a tower and antiaircraft gun stood atop the summit overhead. There must have been a second helipad up there, because she could make out the blades of another chopper hanging over the side. She looked over the ledge. Down below were dune buggies, and even a Navy SEAL–type of rubber raft with an outboard motor tied at the base of the falls. Whoever these people were, they were well financed and well prepared.

The makeshift iron gate opened, and a man sauntered across the promontory. Like the other soldiers, he wore a camouflaged United Nations uniform. The only difference was that he was bareheaded and wore no badges or rank, yet she recognized him immediately.

He was Colonel Ali Zawas, an Egyptian air force colonel and scion of Egypt's most prominent family of diplomats. He was born and raised in New York City until he graduated from the U.S. Air Force Academy and moved back to Cairo. More American than Egyptian. She had seen him several times before at the United Nations, once at the American University in Cairo. But he was always in dress uniform at formal functions, not in the menacing field fatigues he now sported. He also normally had dark, wavy hair, which was now shaved off.

Zawas paused in the center of the promontory before the group of soldiers. Jamil moved in smartly and saluted. Zawas waved it off. He was a handsome man with deep-set eyes. There was a brief exchange in Arabic. Serena couldn't quite catch all of it, but the contempt on Zawas's face was enough.

His eyes traveled over the men casually, and fixed on her. He stood there staring at her in the silence, then said something to Jamil, who walked over, grabbed Serena by the arm, and propelled her in front of him. She fought to control the panic that surged inside her, for fear would not help her now, and schooled herself to play it cool.

She kept her head down, but Zawas lifted her chin, and she looked into the dark eyes. "If you're an Atlantean," he said in English, "then this is indeed paradise. But I take it you are an American."

She shook her head and said in a low voice, "No, Colonel, I'm from Rome."

It took a moment for her Australian accent to register, and then she saw the shock of recognition. Then a broad, genuine smile crossed his face. "Sister Serghetti, it is you," he said. "What on earth are you doing here?"

"It's Doctor Serghetti, Colonel, and I was going to ask you the same question," she said, looking around at his troops. "You don't really expect me to believe you are acting on behalf of the United Nations?"

Zawas smiled. She realized he was amused that she was the one demanding answers. "Consider us representatives of certain Arab oil producers who have the most to lose from the discovery of alternative energy sources." He took her arm and said casually over his shoulder, "Get to work, Jamil."

Jamil gave them enough time to get clear then shouted something unintelligible that was drowned out in the immediate uproar as the soldiers began to break out equipment. Drills, seismic meters, metal detectors, explosives.

They reached the steps leading up to the iron gate and the entrance to the temple, and Zawas paused, turning to look at her, a slightly quizzical frown on his face.

"I didn't recognize you at first," he told her. "It's been so long, and you're usually not so dirty on those magazine covers."

"Sorry to have disappointed you."

"Not at all. I find it quite becoming."

She studied him closely. Handsome, shrewd, even gentle if he wanted to be, she was sure of that.

"And why is that?"

"It brings you down to earth." He smiled faintly, opened the front gate, and led her inside.

The chamber was sparsely furnished. Table, chairs, computers, a cot. As he closed the door, he took her backpack from her and dropped it on a chair.

"Please, sit down."

He politely pulled out a chair for her, and she sat down. He seated himself on the opposite side of the table.

She wasted no time. "So that's what you think you'll find down here?" she asked him. "An alternative energy source?"

"Not just any source, Doctor Serghetti, but *the* source," he told her. "The legendary power of the sun itself that the Atlanteans are said to have harnessed. What else did you think General Yeats and Doctor Yeats were after?"

Serena couldn't say, her eyes involuntarily glancing at her pack on the chair. She considered the blueprints of the obelisk that she had hidden inside her thermos. What she really wanted to know was why Zawas seemed to believe Antarctica was Atlantis, let alone that there was some all-powerful "source" behind its power.

"So you're here because you're just as power hungry as the rest of them," she said. "That's not your reputation at the United Nations."

"On the contrary," he said. "I'm concerned that faltering economies in the Middle East will permit increasingly influential mullahs to sow unrest and seize power. That I must use animals like Jamil to stop the rest of his kind is but one of geopolitics' many ironies."

"I've got it all wrong then," she said. "You're not a terrorist. You're really a patriot who's simply been misunderstood."

"You worry too much about the souls of men like me and Doctor Yeats," he said. "Oh, yes, I know all about him. More than you even, perhaps. If he's still alive, we'll find him. You, however, should be asking yourself why you're down here. Clearly, it's not to protect the environment, which as you can see has altered significantly since your arrival."

"All right then," she said, folding her arms. "Tell me why I'm here."

"You're here because I sent for you."

Her mouth went dry. "You sent for me?"

"Well, maybe not you exactly, but somebody like you," Zawas said. "I knew I would need a translator to help me find the Shrine of the First Sun. Why else do you think I tipped off the Vatican about Yeats's expedition?"

Serena's heart skipped a beat. What was Zawas implying? What did he know that she didn't? "Just what exactly do you want me to translate?"

"A map."

Zawas unrolled an old parchment across the table.

Serena looked at it and realized it was a map of the city. The inscriptions were some sort of pre-Egyptian hieroglyphics. She could see the Temple of the Water Bearer clearly marked, along with other pavilions. It was a terrestrial map that mirrored the celestial map Conrad recognized from the Scepter.

"We found it some years ago in a secret chamber beneath the Great Sphinx at Giza," Zawas said. "Drawn by the ancient Egyptian priest Sonchis, the primary source for Plato's story of Atlantis. Of course, we had no way of knowing whether the map depicted a real place, let alone its location, until the American discovery of P4 in Antarctica."

She said, "So how did the Americans know the location of P4?"

"They didn't, as far as I know," Zawas said. "It was the seismic activity that brought them to East Antarctica. Only after they found something under the ice was the Vatican brought on board."

"The Vatican?" Serena arched an eyebrow. "I don't think so."

"The Vatican has its own map of Atlantis," Zawas said. "It originally had been stored in the Library of Alexandria during the time of Alexander the Great. Then the Romans stole it during their occupation of Egypt. Later, after the fall of the Roman Empire, it was moved to Constantinople. When Constantinople was sacked during the Fourth Crusade, the map was smuggled to Venice. There it was rediscovered in the seventeenth century by a Jesuit priest."

Serena felt shaky, the fury building inside her. But was she angry at Zawas for telling her this, or at the pope for telling her nothing? "I don't believe you."

"Why else would Rome be so eager to send you?" Zawas asked. "You didn't really think it was to save the virginal ecosystem of Antarctica?"

"Then what for?" she asked.

"Surely it was to protect itself, its power. The Church is no more noble than the secular, imperialist American republic. It fears any sort of real divine revelation that might undermine its influence in the course of human events. And that's what this is, Doctor Serghetti. Something older than Islam, Christianity, and even Judaism. Your superiors have every reason to be scared. And you have no reason to trust them or anybody else—only the man who bothered to tell you the truth. So come now, you will help me find the Shrine of the First Sun which contains the source."

"And if I don't?"

"Suffer like the rest of the world," he replied.

"The rest?"

"Ah, you haven't heard the news," he told her. "McMurdo Station has lost its ice runway. And the U.S. carrier group off the continent is recovering from that tidal wave and is running at half power. My intelligence tells me American forces are at least sixteen hours away. Until they get here, I am the ultimate power in Atlantis."

"And when they do get here?"

"It will be too late." Zawas's dark eyes flashed with determination. "I will have captured the technology housed in the Shrine of the First Sun, and the world's balance of power will be shifted. The United States will be wiped out, a victim of the earth-crust displacement it unleashed itself. Atlantis, on the other hand, will be ours."

"You're a fortune-teller too?"

"It's our destiny." He leaned forward and smiled. "You see, Doctor Serghetti, this is my people's Promised Land."

27
DAWN MINUS ELEVEN HOURS

CONRAD ZIPPED UP A UNACOM weapons inspector's uniform and grimly noted the CAPT. HASSEIN tag over his left breast pocket. Yeats had a couple of these uniforms, sans bodies. Conrad could only guess how he had obtained them. He looked around the chamber Yeats had brought them to. It was stockpiled with computer equipment, M-16s, and explosives.

Conrad asked, "What is this place?"

"A weapons cache I found." Yeats was busy stashing bricks of C-4 plastique into a backpack. "I ended up down here after you flushed me down that shaft in P4 like a piece of shit. Crawled out, got my bearings, and got to work hauling whatever I could find."

"And this cache wasn't guarded by those goons outside?"

"No goons," Yeats said. "Not anymore."

Yeats's survival instincts were astounding even to Conrad, who had already fought hard to stay alive himself in the last several hours. How in the world did he survive that fall? Conrad wondered. He didn't know whether to give his father a medal or a kick in the groin. The man had yet to express relief at seeing his only son alive, nor had he uttered another word about his origins.

"How do you know all this won't get flushed away again?"

"I don't." Yeats checked the timers for the C-4. "But this alcove is separated from the corridors below. Anyway, we won't be sticking around much longer."

"So I see." Conrad eyed the bulging pack of C-4 that Yeats slung over his shoulder. "So you know who these guys are?"

"I trained their leader, Colonel Zawas."

Conrad stared at Yeats. "You trained him?"

"At the U.S. Air Force Academy in Colorado Springs under a U.S.-Egyptian military exchange program in the late eighties," Yeats said. "Came in handy a few years later during the Allied bombing of Iraq in the Persian Gulf War. An Arab pilot taking out two Iraqi jets proved to be priceless PR and legitimized the bombing campaign as a multinational effort."

"So that's what you taught him to do—kill other Arabs?"

"In my dreams," Yeats said. "No, I trained him in the Decisive Force school of warfare. The idea is to use overwhelming force to either annihilate an enemy or intimidate him into surrender."

"So the U.N. weapons inspection team was only a cover?" Conrad asked.

Yeats nodded. "Obviously, Zawas stacked the team with his own men. Probably offed the other internationals and plans to say we did it. I wouldn't be surprised if he put the Russians on us back at P4 and was just waiting for us to do all the hard work."

Conrad said, "So you're saying Zawas came with friends."

"And firepower," Yeats said. "In the real world, a few terrorists are no match against the world's lone super-power. But Antarctica is a different theater of war. It doesn't take much to overwhelm a small team of Americans on an otherwise empty continent."

"Well, his lieutenant killed your dog and abducted Serena."

Conrad could see the veins in Yeats's neck bulge. "So where's the obelisk?"

Conrad said nothing.

Yeats shot him one of those rare, withering glares that used to make Conrad crumble as a boy. "Goddamn it. Are you telling me that Zawas not only shot my dog but also has the Scepter of Osiris?"

"No, I said he has Serena."

"Same difference. Open your eyes. You heard Ms. Save-the-Earth back at P4. The Scepter of Osiris belongs in the Shrine of the First Sun. That's where she's going to lead Zawas."

"You're selling her short."

"You're thinking with the wrong head," Yeats said. "Our mission is to deny Zawas any advanced weapon or alien technology that could shift the world's balance of power. Asymmetrical force. Got that? Burn it into your brain."

"Gee, and I thought we were going to settle who I am and where I really came from, Dad," Conrad shot back.

Yeats paused, and Conrad could practically hear the

whir of the hard drive behind Yeats's eyes as his father searched for an appropriate response.

"We do that by beating Zawas to the Shrine of the First Sun and setting a trap for him if and when Serena finally leads him there." Yeats patted his pack full of C-4 and moved on as if he had disclosed everything. "The problem, of course, is going to be finding it without them finding us first. Which is about the time between now and when Zawas discovers that several of his men are missing. They control the skies and everything on the surface. We're going to have to stay underground until dark."

"We'll need the stars, anyway," Conrad said, pulling out his handheld device with the images of the obelisk he had captured. "Because the scepter instructs the would-be sun king to put heaven and earth together. Only then will the 'Shining One' reveal the location of the Shrine of the First Sun."

"Serena never said that."

"I know," Conrad said. "The scepter did."

"I thought you couldn't read the inscriptions."

"Let's just say some things are feeling a little more familiar."

"So you believe me now?" Yeats asked. "About finding you in the capsule and everything?"

"I'll never believe everything you tell me," Conrad said. "And I reserve judgment on some things. But this inscription beneath the four constellations on one side of the obelisk is almost identical to the inscription Serena read for us."

"What's the difference?"

"The inscription Serena read to us warns against

removing the scepter unless you're the most worthy, according to the Shining Ones, or else you'll tear Heaven and Earth apart," Conrad said.

"Which seems to be happening right now," Yeats said.

"So it seems," Conrad said. "But this inscription under the four zodiac signs tells the would-be Sun King how to find the Shrine of the First Sun with the help of a Shining One and bring Heaven and Earth together again."

"And what on earth is the Shining One?" Yeats asked.

"It's not of this earth. It's probably some kind of astronomical phenomenon. I'll know it when I see it."

"Hot damn, Conrad, looks like you really are the Sun King." Yeats slapped him on the back for the first time in years, and Conrad couldn't deny it felt good. "But where exactly are we supposed to consult this Shining One? There are millions of stars out there."

Conrad said, "We'll follow the map on the scepter."

"What map?"

"The four constellations." Conrad showed Yeats the 360-degree digital scan he had taken of the obelisk. "See? The zodiac signs of Scorpio, Sagittarius, Capricorn, and Aquarius."

Yeats looked at the image. "So?"

Conrad tapped his device. "So if this city is astronomically aligned, then maybe these celestial coordinates might have terrestrial counterparts."

"Maybe?" Yeats said. "You'll have to do better than that."

"We already know P4 is aligned with the middle belt star of Orion, Al Nitak," Conrad said, and Yeats nodded.

"In the same way we might find strategically positioned shrines in the city that are aligned to Scorpio, Sagittarius, Capricorn, and Aquarius."

Yeats furrowed his brow. "Meaning we follow the pavilions or temples that correspond to these signs like some kind of heavenly treasure trail?"

"Exactly."

"So these celestial markers will lead us to Aquarius," Yeats said. "And then we find its terrestrial double."

"That's right," said Conrad. "It's dusk outside now. Soon the stars will be out. They'll serve as our map and lead us to some kind of monument dedicated to the Water Bearer. That's where the Shining One will be, to lead us to the Shrine of the First Sun."

Yeats nodded. "And everything we've spent our lives searching for."

28
DAWN MINUS SIX HOURS

INSIDE THE TEMPLE OF THE WATER BEARER, starlight seeped into the chamber where Serena stood tied to a post. It was her punishment for refusing to help Colonel Zawas translate his map of Atlantis. To help Zawas locate the Shrine of the First Sun would be to betray Conrad, she reasoned, having concluded that Conrad, for all his faults, was still her best hope in stopping a global cataclysm. But even if Conrad could reach the shrine first, Zawas still had the scepter. Somehow she had to hold on long enough to figure out a way to steal it.

She could hear voices outside, and three dark silhouettes filled the doorway, blotting out the heavens. It was Jamil, flanked by two Egyptians. Serena stiffened as he unfurled a towel with assorted knives and needles across a small table.

"Colonel Zawas was disappointed he couldn't persuade you to cooperate, Doctor Serghetti," he said. "Now it's my turn."

"So I see," she said, staring at the cruel instruments on the table. "Isn't this a bit over the top? I already told

Zawas that I don't know where the shrine is. Honest. If I did, I'd tell you."

"A brave front, Doctor Serghetti, really." Jamil looked over his wares, stocked mostly with syringes, knives of various shapes, and shock rods. "Ah, the tricks your Inquisition taught us."

He picked up a two-foot-long black club. Suddenly it came to life like lightning. It was an electric shock baton.

"This is my favorite," he said, waving it in front of her. A bolt of blue electricity sizzled between two metal prongs. "Each jolt delivers seventy-five thousand volts. A few pokes would leave you unconscious. A few more, dead."

"Is this what you intended your life to become, Jamil?"

Jamil cursed and tried to force her jaw open. She turned away. But he shoved the baton into her mouth. She choked on the metal rod as he dug it deeper.

"The Chinese like to shove this down a prisoner's throat and charge it up," he said as she gagged. "The current that races through your body will leave you crumpled on the floor in a pool of blood and excrement and in extreme pain."

She could feel the hot metal prongs at the back of her throat and moaned. But Jamil pulled it away and pushed the button again so she could see the blue electric charges flash between the prongs.

"There are other places I could ram this," he told her, and she unconsciously squeezed her thighs together. "Good," he said with a smile and set the shock rod down on the table. "I see you understand." He then picked up a syringe and with the back of his finger flicked the hypodermic needle. A yellowish fluid spurt out. "Now we can begin."

A few hours later, Serena regained consciousness and found herself in the dark, staring at a makeshift lantern Jamil had hung from the ceiling—his shock rod swinging on a rope, making grotesque zapping sounds as it flashed. She tried closing her eyes, but the zap-zap of the shock rod only seemed to grow louder. Or maybe it was the drugs injected into her bloodstream that made her feel so sloshed.

Somehow she sensed another presence in the chamber and opened her eyes to see a long shadow on the wall. Her eyes drifted to the doorway, where a fuzzy figure stepped inside.

"Conrad?" she said.

"It's nice to have dreams, Doctor Serghetti."

It was Zawas. Serena hung her head again as he walked over to the small table where Jamil had left his tools of torture.

"I'm told you haven't been terribly cooperative," Zawas said, examining Jamil's toys. "It was all I could do to keep Jamil from permanently erasing your memory with those chemicals of his. But he is an animal. He gives Arabs everywhere a bad name. You know that most of us are not at all like him. You must understand this. Your Church has priests who molest children. Yet you aren't about to abandon your mission. Neither am I."

She said nothing as he looked around the chamber.

Her pack on the floor caught his eye. He circled round it and watched her face. Then he lifted it to the table and unzipped it. He began to rifle through its contents, examining her personal belongings—water purification tablets, hot water bottles, a flare, and the like.

Then he came to her green thermos. Her chest constricted as he began to unscrew the top. She prayed he wouldn't find the blueprint inside the secret shell. For all she knew, that blueprint contained enough information for him to find or deploy this unlimited power source he was searching for in the Shrine of the First Sun.

"You remind me of Pharaoh, Zawas," Serena said. "You know, from the Bible."

He seemed amused and put the thermos down on the table. "Then you know my authority comes from the gods themselves and you must answer to me."

"The gods of Egypt were defeated once before," she said. "They can be defeated again."

"History is about to be rewritten, Doctor Serghetti. But first I must find the Shrine of the First Sun. So far, its location has eluded me. As has Doctor Yeats. Oh, yes, he's alive. I know this because several of my men are missing," he said. "He killed them, just like he's killed so many others in Atlantis thus far in his selfish quest for the origins of human civilization. I know all about this man. He cares little for the consequences of his actions on governments, people, even the very sites he excavates. It's a good thing I saved you and the Scepter of Osiris from him."

Serena said nothing, because there was no defense against Zawas's accusations. They were true.

"Unlike the reckless Doctor Yeats, however," Zawas went on, "I appreciate and want to preserve natural beauty in all its forms, especially the feminine. I would hate to see a monster like Jamil mar you in any way."

That was a lie, she knew. "So you're a gentleman among the barbarians."

He looked at her carefully. "I see we understand each other well. It's not as if the Catholic Church hasn't wrapped itself up in nobility and social mercy only to make pacts with the devil at convenient points in history."

"Then you're a hero, really," she told him. "You just happen to be on the wrong side of history."

"Exactly," Zawas said. "Like Pharaoh during the Exodus. It was his bad luck that the eruption of the volcano at Thíra in the Mediterranean should produce the plagues you eagerly attribute to the God of Moses. There was no parting of the Red Sea. The Israelites crossed at the Sea of Reeds in only six inches of water. But it was enough to bog down the wheels of Pharaoh's chariots."

"Then it was a greater miracle than I thought," Serena said. "That all of Pharaoh's soldiers and horses should drown in six inches of water."

Zawas was not amused by her argument, she could see, and his face grew more stern in the flashing light. "History is written by the victor," he told her. "How else can you explain Judeo-Christian exaltation of an allegedly merciful and loving God who goes around killing the firstborn of the ancient Egyptians?"

"He could have killed them all," she said.

Zawas was put out. "So it was Pharaoh's fault?"

She tried to focus. Even in her somewhat shaky state she recognized this could be a pivotal moment in persuading Zawas. "You know that at certain points of history, everything rests on one man or one woman," she told him. "Noah and the ark. Pharaoh and the Israelites. God offered Pharaoh the divine opportunity to be the greatest emancipator in history. But his heart was stubborn and arrogant. Now is such a time. You may be such a man."

"Or you that woman," he said. "Where is the Shrine of the First Sun?"

"I honestly don't know."

"Then I honestly must give you to Jamil to finish the job," he said. "It's out of my control now. I wash my hands clean of this."

"Says Pontius Pilate."

"And I thought I was Pharaoh." He shook his head and threw up his hands. "Am I to be compared to every villain in your Scriptures? Have you ever considered the possibility that these leaders are history's true heroes and your saints the revisionist authors of fiction?"

He was about to turn and leave when his eyes once again drifted to the coffee thermos on the table.

"Why are you still carrying around your thermos?"

Serena said nothing, pretending not to hear.

But he was already untwisting the outer shell. He smelled the coffee and made a face. "I prefer tea myself."

He emptied the coffee onto the stone floor and then tried to screw the lid back on. As he did, the blueprint fell to the floor.

Serena caught her breath.

Zawas picked up the blueprint and let out a hearty laugh. Then he showed it to her and said, "Do you know what these schematics are?"

She hung her shoulders in defeat. "The blueprint to the Scepter of Osiris."

"No," he told her. "This is the blueprint to the Shrine of the First Sun."

She just stared at him, head rushing with dizziness.

"Yes," Zawas said. "Now I have three things Doctor Yeats wants. And if he won't lead me to the Shrine of the First Sun, then you will. I'll tell Jamil he has more work to do."

29
DAWN MINUS TWO HOURS

SCORPIO. SAGITTARIUS. CAPRICORN. For several hours
Conrad led Yeats across the dark city, following each
celestial coordinate to its terrestrial counterpart, and
then moving on from one astronomically aligned monument to another. Each temple, pavilion, or landmark
would in itself be the archaeological prize of the ages,
but time and the buzz of choppers and searchlights overhead kept them marching forward. Finally, the heavenly
treasure trail ended at the terrestrial counterpart to the
constellation Aquarius, a spectacular temple dedicated
to the Water Bearer.

The Sphinx-like pavilion loomed like a skull against
the heavens, its silvery waterfalls glistening in the moon-
light. Beyond it lurked the dark, towering peak of P4.

"That's it," Conrad said as he handed the nightscope
to Yeats. They were crouched along the banks of the
city's largest water channel, which flowed directly from
the monument. "The Temple of the Water Bearer."

Yeats took a look. "That's not all you found. Look
again."

Conrad scanned the Temple of the Water Bearer and

suddenly saw lights around the base and promontory. "Zawas?"

"Looks like he's turned it into his base camp."

Conrad lowered the nightscope. "How the hell did they know?"

Yeats shrugged. "Maybe Mother Earth is helping him."

"Or maybe they have some sort of map."

"Doubtful," Yeats said. "You said yourself that the map is in the stars." Yeats paused. "Now you're absolutely sure you need to get in there? Because it's both our asses if Zawas catches us."

Conrad nodded. "Only by standing in the right place at the right time will the Shining One pinpoint the location of the Shrine of the First Sun," he said.

Yeats narrowed his eyes. "And where exactly are we supposed to consult this 'Shining One'?"

Conrad hesitated to break the bad news. "I suspect it's between the waterfalls at the Temple of the Water Bearer. In the middle of Zawas's base."

Yeats flipped his wrist and glanced at the luminous dial of his watch. "It's already zero four hundred hours. Almost dawn. The sun is going to be coming up. We don't have much time."

Conrad spent the next half hour surveying the temple from a distance while Yeats drew up a plan.

"You'll see the promontory on the east face is about a hundred and fifty feet high," Yeats told him. "Two narrow stairways on either side go to the base of the falls. Because of that, I doubt Zawas posts more than one guard at the bottom of each flight of steps. That and the fact he needs as many warm bodies as possible looking for the Shrine of the First Sun."

Conrad scanned the east face down the falls to the ground. Suddenly the sentries at the north end of the east face came into sharp focus. So did an inflatable attack boat moored beneath the falls. The upturned bow and stern cones told him it was a Zodiac Futura Commando, a favorite of special forces around the world.

"I see the guards," he said. "They've got a Zodiac inflatable tied up."

"Just one?"

"The others are probably patrolling the waterways, looking for us."

"Let me see." Yeats took the nightscope. "Zawas rotates his guards every three hours. At least that's the way he used to do things during U.N. peacekeeping jobs. This shift looks about done by the body language." Yeats handed the nightscope back to Conrad. "So we simply relieve the present shift a few minutes early. Then, after I make sure you're covered, we split."

"And just how do we do that?"

Yeats flicked on an old cigarette lighter to illuminate the drawing he had made in the dark.

"You find this so-called Shining One who's going to lead us to the Shrine of the First Sun," Yeats said, tracing a line toward the promontory with his finger. "I'll go to the summit where Zawas keeps his choppers and secure one for the getaway. You'll have six minutes to get from the promontory to the summit. Then we fly away."

"Just like that?" Conrad said.

"Just like that," Yeats said. "I'll rig the other choppers

to blow so Zawas can't tail us in the air. It will buy us the time we need to beat him to the shrine."

Conrad stared at the lighter Yeats was using to illuminate his drawing. It was an old Zippo with a NASA emblem and an engraving to Yeats from Captain Rick Conrad, one of the crew who died in Antarctica in 1969 and the man Conrad was told was his biological father. That was back in the days when astronauts smoked. He had often snuck into Yeats's study to play with it. Once he almost burned down the house. He had hoped Yeats would finally figure out how badly he wanted something of his father's and just give the damn thing to him. But Yeats never did.

"I thought you quit smoking."

"I never quit anything in my life, son." Yeats flicked off the lighter and gave it to Conrad.

Surprised, Conrad felt the old, familiar weight of the Zippo in his hand for a moment and then flicked it on and off.

"What about Serena?" Conrad asked. "What about the obelisk?"

"If Zawas finds either one missing before you find the location of the Shrine of the First Sun, he'll be on to us and our mission is over," Yeats said. "And after we take off without the obelisk or the sister, he'll figure we failed. By the time he figures out we got what we really wanted, we'll already be inside the Shrine of the First Sun, have taken what we needed, and set a trap for him. Zawas will then bring us both the obelisk and Serena."

"If he doesn't kill her first."

"Will you listen to me for once," Yeats said angrily. "She's the one who's going to lead him to us. Trust me, Zawas is counting on her. He's not going to kill her until she's lost her usefulness."

"That's reassuring." Conrad offered the lighter back to Yeats, but to his amazement Yeats refused. "Let's go."

There were lights up above, the roar of churning water drifting from the falls all around. As he turned the final corner, Conrad could see the black cutout of a sentry at the base of the steps, and beyond him the Zodiac attack boat bobbing in the water. The Egyptian was smoking a cigarette. Conrad was about to step forward when his boot scraped the stone.

The sentry spun around. "Yasser?"

Conrad nodded and tapped his watch.

The sentry spat out a rebuke in Arabic and turned and left.

Conrad watched him march up the steps and took a quick look around. It would only be a few minutes before the sentry went back and found the real Yasser. Satisfied nobody was near, Conrad ascended the stone steps to the promontory.

The steps were narrow and water-slicked from the falls, but he reached the top quickly. Stepping onto the promontory, Conrad looked across to see another figure walk toward him.

"Yeats, is that you?" he whispered into his radio.

"I'm making a circle with my hand," Yeats said.

Conrad could barely hear him over the roar of the

falls. But he could see the figure on the other side making a circle. "OK," Conrad said.

"Get to work," Yeats said. "And no matter what happens, stick to the plan and rendezvous in six minutes." Then he disappeared into the darkness.

Conrad walked up to the edge of the promontory between the falls and positioned himself. The tremendous vibrations of the falls rumbled beneath his feet, and he had to steady himself.

He gazed out and found what he was looking for. There, in the predawn of the spring equinox, the constellation of Aquarius was rising in the east. It was a perfect lock with the monument he was standing on. The Water Bearer on earth was staring at the Water Bearer in heaven. And the predawn sun—the Shining One—marked the spot.

He quickly pulled out the digital surveyor Yeats had packed for him and made his calculations. From what he could make out, the Shrine of the First Sun was buried ninety degrees to the south. That placed the X directly under the river, at a depth he guessed to be about a thousand feet. He scanned the horizon with his digital camera to mark it.

Conrad looked again at the skies. The first stain of dawn was glimmering. Soon Aquarius would be fully risen, a water bearer in the sky with its jar resting on the horizon. At the same moment, the sun—marking the vernal point—would lie somewhere beneath the last star pouring out from the jar.

Conrad glanced at his watch. It was almost 5 A.M. He had to move quickly, he thought, when he turned to see an Egyptian emerge from the temple and walk toward him.

"Why aren't you at your post, Yasser?" he barked.

"Why aren't you at yours?" Conrad grumbled back in passable Arabic. His Arabic was a jumble of odds and ends he had picked up over the years.

The man calmed down. "Taking a break," he said, or at least that's what Conrad thought he said. "These nuns, they do not break easily. They are trained to be martyrs. I have to be careful where I hurt this one. She can still be of use to me after she's dead."

Conrad noticed something in his hand. It was a fistful of hair. Serena's hair. Conrad wanted to kill him then and there and rescue Serena. But he knew he couldn't let the soldier see his face. So he simply laughed at his sick joke and turned around and looked ahead over the falls. Then he felt the barrel of an AK-47 digging into his back.

"So you've found the shrine, Doctor Yeats?"

He turned to him and looked into his smoldering eyes.

He smiled in triumph. "No need for the nun now," he said. "Where is it?"

"Over there," Conrad said, playing along. "See the constellation of Aquarius?"

He pointed with his left hand and the soldier couldn't help but follow. In that instant Conrad's right hand swept across his neck with the bone-handled knife he had lifted from the Russian back at P4 and had held in his sleeve. The blade left a thin red line.

He tried to call out but could only gurgle in shock as he staggered back over the promontory edge and disappeared into darkness. Conrad watched the body take two bounces off the monument and splash into the river.

Conrad turned to find the steps leading to the upper promontory and the flight deck, where he was supposed to rendezvous with Yeats. But then another Egyptian emerged from inside the temple and started walking toward him, and Conrad froze. The way the man carried himself told Conrad it was Colonel Zawas. And this time, he knew, there would be no escape.

30
DAWN MINUS ONE HOUR

IT WAS A FEW MINUTES past five in the morning when Zawas stepped out of his chambers to have a smoke on the promontory and take another look at the blueprints of the Shrine of the First Sun he had obtained from Serena. Now that he knew what he was looking for, he only needed to know where to look.

Sucking on his unlit Havana under the stars, he noticed the skies were lightening. Soon the sun would be up and his window of opportunity to find the Shrine of the First Sun gone. He then saw one of his guards—it looked like Yasser—by one of the falls and walked over. Yasser stiffened to attention in the dim light as he approached.

"At ease, lieutenant," Zawas said, and Yasser relaxed. "We don't see a sunrise like that often, do we?"

Yasser grumbled something that Zawas took to be a no. He realized most of his men were showing the effects of exhaustion and stress.

Zawas sighed and patted his pockets in search of some matches when Yasser's hand came up with an old-fashioned Zippo lighter. Zawas touched the tip of his

Cuban cigar to the flame and inhaled. It felt wonderful.

"Carry on," Zawas said and walked back to his command quarters.

Halfway back, however, he realized there was something familiar about his hand-rolled cigar. No, it wasn't the cigar. It was the old silver Zippo lighter Yasser flashed. It was just like the one his grandfather had. Only Zawas wasn't aware of Yasser or any of his other men possessing such an artifact. He would have to ask Yasser where he found it.

But when Zawas turned to find Yasser, the guard was missing from his post. Zawas swore softly to himself and walked back to the promontory. Peering over the ledge down the falls, he could see nothing. It was as if Yasser had disappeared into thin air. Could he have actually fallen? Yasser was no such fool.

Zawas grabbed his radio from his belt. "Jamil!" he barked. "Round up your men. Conrad is here!"

But Jamil wasn't answering.

"Jamil," Zawas repeated when he heard a blast behind him.

Debris rained down, and Zawas looked up to see flashes of light from the top of the step-pyramid. Suddenly the flaming shell of a Z-9A chopper came tumbling down the east face, steel scraping against stone in an ear-splitting scream. Zawas dove back inside as it crashed onto the promontory and exploded in a ball of fire.

"The scepter!" he cursed.

He ran inside to the chamber where the obelisk was kept under guard. But the two guards were on the floor, dead, and the scepter was gone.

• • •

Conrad hit the water at the base of the Temple of the Water Bearer with such force that he thought he died. But a minute later he surfaced for air with a gasp and realized his splash from space went unnoticed by the guards below, thanks to the roar of the falls.

He swam over through the dark to the Zodiac inflatable, cut it loose, climbed on board and hit the motor. By the time the guards saw what was happening and started shooting, he was a hundred yards down the channel and racing away.

He glanced back over his shoulder to see the distant explosions coming from the top of the Temple of the Water Bearer. He also saw a big shadow coming down on him fast—one of Zawas's choppers. Its lights were out and it was flying low, practically on top of him, blocking out the stars. Conrad kicked the onboard motor into high gear but couldn't shake it.

The chopper then moved overhead and passed him by, landing a few hundred yards ahead on the banks of the water channel. As Conrad neared the bank, he could see a figure waving him down.

It was Yeats. And in his hand was the Scepter of Osiris.

"How did you get here?" Conrad asked as he pulled up to the bank.

"Followed the gunfire," Yeats said, stepping into the Zodiac. "You find the location of the shrine?"

Conrad looked in amazement at the helicopter. "Whatever happened to slipping in and out undetected?"

"I had to create a diversion and leave Zawas a clue at the same time."

Conrad felt the familiar pang of betrayal from his childhood. "You took the scepter and left Serena behind?"

"I didn't have much of a choice once I saw you and that goon, son," Yeats said matter-of-factly, in clipped military speed. "I knew the plan was blown. I grabbed what I could and took off. Now did you find the shrine or not? Zawas is pissed as hell and coming after us."

Conrad wiped a wet flop of hair from his forehead. "I found it. It's just ahead."

"That's my boy," Yeats said with an approving nod. "Let's go."

They followed the waterway into a tunnel. Conrad's GPS marker took them to a small dark corridor that branched off the subterranean waterway. At the end of it was some kind of stone grating.

"That's the door to the Shrine of the First Sun," Conrad said. "It's down there. About a thousand feet."

They ditched the Zodiac, sending it on its way down the tunnel as a decoy.

Conrad watched the boat disappear into the dark and then checked his GPS watch. They were running out of time. It was almost 5:15 A.M., and the first faint hint of dawn was falling across the city above.

They dug out the grating to find a manhole-size shaft. They slid down into another labyrinth of subterranean corridors, going deeper and deeper into the earth. A half hour later they reached a long dark tunnel that ended in a blue light.

"That's it," Conrad said.

Yeats pulled out his flashlight. Its beam revealed a

door. As soon as they passed under the blue light, the door slid open, and they stepped inside a dark cavern. This chamber felt like the largest they had stood in yet.

"I'm sending out a flare," Yeats said. "Thirty-second delay."

Conrad shielded his eyes as Yeats flung the little cylinder into the chamber. He counted down to two seconds when everything exploded with light. For an instant he saw the unbelievable spectacle of a towering obelisk much like the one from P4. Only this one was cradled in some fantastic cylinder and stood at least five hundred feet tall. And at its base was some sort of great rotunda that had to be its entrance.

All around them, the terraced slopes of the cylinder rose up until they merged into a domelike ceiling. And Conrad realized they stood only halfway down this cavity by the time the light went out.

"Incredible!" he said, his voice echoing loudly.

They descended the steps that spiraled alongside the interior of the cylinder to the bottom and stood at the base of the giant obelisk and looked up. He could see no more than twenty feet overhead, except the blinking of red lights around the cylinder—the remote switches to the C-4 bricks Yeats had set on the way down.

"What the hell are you doing?" Conrad said.

"Setting a trap for Zawas," Yeats said.

"Who's got Serena, remember?"

"Don't worry, they're not on timers. I've got the detonator right here."

If that was supposed to comfort Conrad, it didn't. But he was too engrossed with their discovery to be distracted by an argument he couldn't win. Instead he followed Yeats through the rotunda to what appeared to be a doorway at the base of the giant obelisk.

Conrad wondered if it was even possible to enter at this point. Then he noticed a square shaft next to the door. It looked about the size of the base of the Scepter of Osiris.

"We might need the scepter to open this."

"Here you go, son," Yeats said, handing it over.

Conrad inserted the scepter into the square display and felt a small vibration. The door opened, and they stepped inside the giant obelisk.

Zawas clenched his jaw as he surveyed the wreckage outside. He cursed the name of Conrad Yeats, a man whose face he'd never even seen but who had managed to steal the Scepter of Osiris from under his nose.

Zawas shook his head as he looked down the waterfall to the burned-out shell of the Z-9A jammed into the basin, breaking off into bits as the water carried it down the river. With the other one gone too, he now had only one bird left to fly.

Zawas followed a chunk of windshield as it floated down the canal out toward the horizon, where the first rays of dawn were breaking as the stars began to fade. Something about the pattern of those stars caught his eye. And then he jumped back as he found himself staring at the constellation of Aquarius. Suddenly everything about the map made sense.

He ran into his quarters and looked at the Sonchis

map. He stared at the Temple of the Water Bearer, his present location. Then he looked at the "key" symbols in the corner—the constellations of Aquarius, Capricorn, and Sagittarius. He was sweating slightly as he picked up the Sonchis map with shaking hands and stared at it as if for the first time.

He then rushed over to Serena's chamber and began to untie her.

"Things going awry, Zawas?"

"*Au contraire,* Doctor Serghetti," he said and pushed her outside to the promontory.

As they neared the ledge, she resisted, fearing he would throw her over. But instead he told her to follow the water canal with her eyes to the horizon with its first glint of dawn. And then she found herself staring face-to-face with the constellation of Aquarius.

"I've found the Shrine of the First Sun," he told her, "and that means I've found Conrad Yeats."

PART FOUR
DOOMSDAY

31
DAWN MINUS
FORTY-FIVE MINUTES

INSIDE THE GREAT OBELISK, Conrad and Yeats stood on a circular platform five feet wide suspended in darkness. Conrad heard a low hum and could feel a greasy draft against his cheek. He flicked on his halogen flashlight. The beam shot out fifty feet before it struck a towering column and in less than a second ricocheted off three other metallic columns that surrounded them. Each bounce intensified the blinding light. Conrad closed his eyes.

"Shut it off!" Yeats shouted, his voice echoing in the darkness.

Conrad, eyes pressed shut, felt for a switch and turned off the halogen lamp. After a minute he blinked but couldn't shake the blinding afterglow. "Those columns of light," Yeats said, still rubbing his eyes. "What are they?"

"They're not made of light," Conrad said. "They just reflect and magnify any light that hits them. Hold on." Conrad reached into his pocket and pulled out the Zippo lighter. "This is low wattage. Ready?"

"For you to blind us?"

"It won't be so bad this time," Conrad said. "Put your shades on and relax."

Conrad put on his sunglasses and waited for Yeats to do likewise before Conrad flicked on the lighter. The effect was like a single candle burning in a cavernous cathedral. Surrounding them in the dim light were four glowing, translucent pillars, each about twenty feet in diameter, rising two hundred feet into the darkness above and two hundred feet into the abyss below.

"So here's your so-called Shrine of the First Sun," Yeats said, staring straight up.

"It's like being inside a bronze coffee filter," Conrad said, looking around and feeling very small. A halo of mist clung to the glowing pillars, which seemed to come together like a funnel at their apex high above. And the air definitely smelled greasy. Conrad looked down and wondered just how deep into the earth this Shrine of the First Sun descended, and how much farther must they go to discover the Secret of First Time. He was in awe of how much there was for him to absorb and painfully aware of the limited time.

"Look at this." Yeats guided the lighter close to a smooth, shiny pillar. The mirrorlike surface not only seemed to magnify the brightness a hundredfold but also seemed to tremble. "I bet this surface has a reflectance of greater than a hundred percent."

"That's significant?"

"The best we've been able to come up with is eighty-eight percent using aluminum."

"These columns aren't made of aluminum."

"No." Yeats ran his hand over the surface of the column. "They're made of something much lighter."

"Lighter?" Conrad touched the column. The surface was slick, almost liquid. Yet he could sense some kind of indefinable texture to it. "It feels as soft as a cobweb and as strong as steel. Like some sort of lighter-than-air silk."

"That's because the fabric is perforated with holes smaller than the wavelength of light." Yeats sounded almost excited. "I'd say somewhere between one-micron or four hundredths of a mil thick. So what now? Do we go up or down this thing?"

Fabric. That's just the word he was looking for, Conrad realized. The surprise was that it was Yeats who came up with it. But he was right. These columns were like giant rolls of some thin, lightweight, and mirrorlike fabric so shiny they could be mistaken for the light they so brilliantly reflected.

"Up or down, son?" Yeats repeated.

"Up," Conrad said, surprising himself. Because in reality he didn't know. He had never come across anything like this shrine in the ancient pyramid texts of the Egyptians or in the tales of Meso-American lore. And he couldn't recall it from any childhood nightmares or memories. Its sole significance, so far as he could tell, was to serve as a live-scale projection of the obelisk he had taken from P4. But somewhere in this obelisk was the so-called Seat of Osiris, the final resting place of the scepter and the Secret of First Time. The only question was whether he would recognize it when he saw it, much less know what to do. "We're going up."

And so they were. The platform they were standing

on began to lift like an elevator, carrying them up between the columns of light. Conrad looked up to see the columns funnel toward an apex.

"Hang tight," he said, tense but determined. He realized he had never been more excited about anything in his life.

They must have passed through several levels of compartments, Conrad figured, when he looked up to see a pinprick of light at the end. A minute later they emerged into a cool chamber. Suddenly the platform locked with a thud. Conrad stumbled backward toward the edge of the platform. Yeats caught his arm with a viselike grip.

"End of the line," he said.

Conrad paused to get his bearings. It felt cramped up here compared to the soaring spaces below. Their voices had stopped echoing, and the air felt cooler. Conrad removed his sunglasses and switched on his halogen lamp. This time there was no blinding reflection. The beam stabbed out and bathed the nearest wall in light.

A quick survey revealed one corridor on either side of them. Conrad entered the corridor to their right.

"This way," he said, his impatience hanging thick in the air, pushing them forward.

"Now how would you know?"

"According to you, I'm an Atlantean, remember?"

Conrad led him along the dark tunnel for a minute. At the end was a cryptlike door, about six feet tall. Next to it was a square pad much like the one at the outside entrance. Conrad focused his light on the door. Carved into its metallic surface were unusual engravings that at first defied comprehension. Only when Conrad ran his fingers across them did their meaning register.

"It's a constellation," he said flatly.

Yeats nodded. "That star right there is Sirius."

"The goddess Isis in her astral form." Conrad placed his hand on the cold metallic door, overcome with awe. His throat constricted and his heart beat faster. He could barely manage a whisper. "We found the queen's crypt."

"I was looking for the king's." Yeats sounded detached, businesslike. "How much you want to bet we'll find that bastard Osiris down the opposite corridor?"

And the Seat of Osiris and the Secret of First Time, Conrad thought, when he saw a red dot on the back of his hand and spun around. Yeats was pointing his AK-47 at the door, the laser-sighting on.

Conrad jumped back. "What the hell are you doing?"

"You're going to open this door so we can see if the bitch is still in there."

Conrad, his pulse pounding, put his hand on the square pad, and he could feel a surge of energy. He pulled his hand back and the door slid open. A cool mist escaped from the chamber.

"You didn't even need the obelisk for that," Yeats said, almost in awe.

"Maybe once you use it, the system remembers," Conrad said.

"Or maybe your ID is already in the system."

They stepped through the cloud and into the small chamber. The red beam from Yeats's laser sight criss-crossed the cell and locked onto an intricate alcove of some kind. It was contoured for a human being no taller than two meters. Based on the shape, it was clearly a woman. She had two arms, two legs, ten fingers and ten toes, and an hourglass figure.

"Mama." Conrad looked at the display and let out a whistle. "Are you happy now, Yeats? You've met the enemy and she looks like us. Maybe it's not just me. Maybe we're all Atlanteans."

"Let's hope not. Not unless you want us to suffer the same fate. Now let's check out Papa."

Down the hall, the door to the Osiris crypt bore the markings of the Orion constellation on its surface. And this time Conrad didn't hesitate. He put his hand on the door and it split open. Again, a fine cool mist escaped. Yeats climbed through with his AK-47 with Conrad close behind. Conrad shined his light up on the far wall and caught his breath.

"Say hello to Daddy, Conrad," said Yeats.

This crypt was clearly contoured for a vertically standing creature that stood much taller than a human. Inside was an impressive harness or exoskeleton that appeared as mysteriously complex as the being it was designed for. A translucent bandolier crisscrossed the center ring and boasted an awesome array of instruments, gear, and, perhaps, weapons.

"Holy God," Conrad murmured.

"Not so holy if Mother Earth is right," Yeats said. "This one's about three meters high."

Conrad flicked on the Zippo and held it close to the edge of the harness. Whatever it was made of was fireproof and perhaps even indestructible for all intents and purposes. But it clearly supplied its bearer with only partial protection. Judging by the size of it, Conrad could only assume the rest of such a creature required little else.

Creature, he thought. Is that what his true father was? Is that what he was? He had more in common with the man next to him than whatever creature used that harness.

"There is no way in hell I'm related to the thing that belongs here," Conrad told Yeats. "It would have shown up in my DNA tests or something."

"If Serena is right and the Atlanteans are the so-called sons of God from Genesis," Yeats said, "then your biological father was a generation or two removed from the first coupling and more or less human."

"More or less human?" Conrad repeated. "That sounds even more—"

"Show me the goddamn Seat of Osiris, son. We're running out of time."

Conrad nodded. "It's got to be somewhere in here, closer than we think," he said. "If we split up, we'll double our coverage in half the time."

"Then you can hold on to this."

Yeats tossed over the Scepter of Osiris, which Conrad caught in one hand. The thing was practically vibrating with raw energy.

"Now switch your headset to our backup frequency," Yeats said. "It's marked with that little blue tape on the back. Blue is for backup."

"I get it. I get it." Conrad switched to frequency B. "Check."

"Check."

For a minute or two Conrad could hear Yeats's gravelly voice in his right ear as they continued exploring. But it didn't take long for Yeats to move out of range. By the time Conrad was satisfied he had explored every surface of the top story of the obelisk and returned to the central platform, Yeats had disappeared. Conrad was alone and disappointed. He had found nothing and wondered where Yeats went and what he had found.

Conrad stood there on the platform, inside the top chamber of the obelisk, and pondered the alien nature of the obelisk's interior. For all its strangeness there was something about this place that persuaded him to believe he had been here before. Or somewhere like here. An inner urge prompted him to look up at the ceiling. Something about it had bothered him. Now as he flashed his light on it he could see what he had missed before: a small square pad, just like the earlier one.

There was one more, hidden chamber above him, he realized with a surge of excitement.

It was also two meters beyond his reach.

Conrad managed to use the control lever to nudge the platform up half a level, careful not to squash himself against the ceiling, and placed his hand on the square pad. Suddenly the outer ring of some sort of hatch appeared before it split open to reveal another chamber above him with a cathedral ceiling—clearly the very top chamber of the shrine.

Conrad rode the platform up to the top level. His light scanned the chamber, revealing a large high-backed seat that lay horizontally on a kind of altar and pointed to the apex of the cathedral ceiling overhead.

Eureka, Conrad thought. The Seat of Osiris.

"Yes!" Conrad exclaimed out loud. He fumbled anxiously for his radio. "Yeats, I found it."

But there was no response. Where the hell was he?

"Yeats." The silence was eerie, unsettling.

He cranked his ear full of static until it hurt and still he heard nothing. So he switched it off. He wondered what Yeats could be up to, if he was OK. He felt a sick knot forming in his stomach. Well, he couldn't wait.

Slowly he circled the empty chair and surveyed the scene. His flashlight showed nothing else in the chamber. No artifacts, markings, or any evidence this room had ever been used before. But it all felt very familiar.

It was as if he had stepped into an ancient hieroglyph come to life. Ancient Egyptian reliefs of Osiris often showed the Lord of Eternity sitting in his chair and wearing his Atef crown, like the one inside the Seti I Temple at Abydos. Conrad also recalled the Man in the Serpent sculpture from the ancient Olmec site of La Venta, Mexico, which depicted a man seated inside a mechanical-looking device much like the chair before him. Then there was the sarcophagus lid inside the Temple of the Inscriptions at the Mayan site of Palenque in Chiapas, Mexico. That, too, revealed a mechanical design involving a man who appeared to be seated inside some kind of device.

Yes, he had been here before, he thought, feeling sweat begin to bead on his forehead. His hands felt heavy and clammy. Only this time the chair was real, the very Seat of Osiris. And so was the small altarlike base next to it, clearly the receptacle for the Scepter of Osiris.

The only thing left to the imagination was for him to take the scepter, sit in that seat, and behold the Secret of First Time.

Conrad ran his hand over the smooth contours of the chair. It was like an empty eggshell. Conrad pressed the surface, felt it bend to his touch. He wanted to sit in it. But he remembered what had happened with the scepter in P4 and paused.

This time was different, he rationalized. The first time was a mistake. He knew that all too well. This time he was trying to correct that mistake, and if he didn't try, billions of lives could perish. Yes, he concluded, whatever his own shortcomings, however unworthy, he had to sit in the chair, if not for himself, then for humanity.

Conrad slipped into the Seat of Osiris, inserted the Scepter of Osiris into its receptacle, and looked straight up at the pyramidlike ceiling. This is interesting, he thought, feeling like one of his students on the Nazca Lines tour, waiting for some great revelation to materialize that never does.

"Sure, Conrad," he said out loud, just to hear the sound of his voice. "You've finally made something of yourself. You've self-actualized yourself and become your astral projection. You are the Sun King."

He laughed nervously. If Mercedes could see him now, she'd be taping everything. He could picture the ads on TV: "Live from the Shrine of the First Sun! The Secrets of Atlantis Revealed! Witness the End of the World!" The way things were going, unfortunately, he soon would.

A wave of depression suddenly washed over Conrad as he sat in the Seat of Osiris. Had he traveled so far, and would humanity have to suffer so much, only to discover this was all some cosmic joke? What if the Secret of First Time was that there was no secret?

No, Conrad decided. Somebody went to too much trouble to build all this. And there were clearly some astronomical correlations he was missing. There must be a way to stop the earth-crust displacement. Perhaps he was simply the wrong man to find that way. He felt overwhelmed by a sense of helplessness. He had failed Serena. He had failed humanity. He had failed himself, period. What more could he do? This was indeed the end of the line.

Conrad leaned back in the seat, closed his eyes, and prayed: God of Noah, Moses, Jesus, and Serena. If you're there, if you care at all for Serena and all she cares for, then help me figure this thing out before Osiris and his kind screw your kind over for good.

Conrad opened his eyes. Nothing happened.

Again Conrad leaned back in the seat, and as soon as he did, he realized it had settled into a pocket and locked in with a click. Conrad tried to lean forward to look. But the egglike capsule, while comfortable, held him back.

He felt a sequence of vibrations shoot up his spine.

The chair was squeezing him, tightening around his waist and pushing down on his shoulders, devouring him. A metallic console telescoped itself beyond his forehead.

"Yeats!"

Suddenly the console overhead came to life with a beep. It glowed an eerie blue and a panel of instruments lit up. A tremendous shudder reverberated throughout the obelisk and Conrad could feel vibrations building in the back of his chair.

"Yeats!"

A single shaft of intense white light from above blinded him.

"Yeats!"

Then another flash shot up from below, imbuing the entire chamber in light. Conrad realized it was sunlight through two shafts above and below his reclined seat. Just like the star shaft in P4. Sunlight? Where did that come from?

Conrad managed to put on his sunglasses and gaze out the shafts. They were windows and framed a lightening sky. He had opened the doors of the silo.

Another shudder, and suddenly all became clear.

This obelisk isn't a shrine, he thought. It's a ship. A starship.

"Dad!"

Conrad tried to pull himself out of the seat. It wouldn't give. He tried twisting to the right. No. To the left. Yes. Now he hurled himself forward with everything he had and came out with a spark like an electrical cord from a socket. The console went dead and disappeared into the chair, the vibrations stopped, and the chair snapped forward and released its grip on him. Conrad, breathing heavily, collected himself.

For several moments he sat there on the floor, numb. But his mind was racing. He had no references for this experience in his past. Or did he? Ancient Egyptian funeral texts referred to a number of cosmic vessels intended to take the dead on celestial voyages to heaven.

There was the "bark of Osiris," for example, and the "boat of millions of years." Egyptologists dubbed them "solar boats." There was also Kamal el-Mallakh's 1954 discovery of a 143-foot cedarwood boat buried in a pit on the south side of the Great Pyramid. Subsequent digging turned up similar boats in the same area—symbolic of the solar boats in which the souls of deceased kings could sail into the afterlife.

This silo, he realized, was on the south face of P4.

He remembered the markings of the three zodiac signs on the obelisk. He recalled the pyramid texts in Giza said the Sun King would ride his "Solar Bark" across the Milky Way toward First Time. To astro-archaeologists such as Conrad, the "solar bark" was a metaphor for the sun, specifically its ecliptic path through the twelve constellations of the zodiac in the course of a year. But what if it was more than a metaphor?

This is the actual Solar Bark, Conrad thought, the celestial ship built to take the would-be Sun King across the stars to First Time. He felt a shock wave of euphoria exploding within him.

But then the stark reality of his discovery suddenly sapped his hope: the Secret of First Time lay waiting at the end of the Solar Bark's intended destination. Yet the earth-crust displacement was only hours if not minutes away. There was no way to reset the star chamber in P4 to the date of First Time without completing the journey. The best he could do was guess the date of First Time based on the estimated light-years it would take to get to the Solar Bark's destination. And that information was beyond his grasp.

His radio headset squawked. Conrad said, "Yeats. Where the hell have you been?"

The voice that came over was Serena's. "Conrad."

"Serena?" he said. "Where are you?"

"Look out your cockpit window."

Conrad looked up and saw the silhouettes of Egyptian soldiers circled along the rim of the silo, guns and SAMs pointed in his direction. But what caught his eye was the outstretched arm of Zawas holding a gun to Serena's head.

Serena said, "Colonel Zawas wants you to know that unless you meet us at the base of the shrine in ten minutes and hand over the scepter, he's going to kill me. I told him you wouldn't do it. I'm not worth it and you're not that stupid."

Conrad spoke into the radio. "Tell Zawas I'm coming down."

32
DAWN MINUS TWENTY-FIVE MINUTES

CONRAD HEADED DOWN THROUGH the vast ship to the rotunda base. Along the way, it all made sense—the crypts were some sort of cryogenic chambers for the long interstellar flight, the towers of light some sort of propulsion system.

Conrad emerged from the Solar Bark to find the entire silo imbued with the first rays of dawn. Then he looked up and noted that the dome had split open. He shaded his eyes and felt a sharp poke at his back.

"Move it," said a voice from behind with an Arab accent.

Conrad, still blinking in the brightness, craned his neck to take a look. His curiosity was rewarded by a knock on the side of his head with the butt of an AK-47.

"Idiot!"

His head throbbing, Conrad stumbled forward beyond the rotunda.

Serena and Zawas were waiting for him. As Zawas took the scepter from his hands, Conrad looked over at

Serena and swallowed hard. There was sadness in her eyes, but everything else about her was cool as ice.

"Tell me what these bastards did to you," Conrad said.

Serena said, "Not much compared to what the world is going to suffer, thanks to you."

"Doctor Yeats." Zawas studied him carefully. "Your reputation is well deserved. You've led us to the Shrine of the First Sun."

"A lot of good it will do you."

"I will be the judge of that." Zawas then held up the Scepter of Osiris before his men like some idol. There were no oohs and aahhs. These were professional soldiers Zawas had brought along for backup, Conrad thought, not mere fanatics. To them the obelisk might as well have been the head of an assassinated enemy, or a torched American flag, or a nuclear warhead. Their possession of such a symbol only confirmed their power in their own eyes.

Zawas then looked at him and said, "Now you will tell me the Secret of First Time, Doctor Yeats."

"I don't know. It's not there. And it may be impossible for us to discover."

Zawas narrowed his eyes. "Why is that?"

"The shrine, as you call it, is really a starship, intended to take the seeker to the place of First Time— the actual First Sun, as far as the Atlanteans are concerned."

"A starship?" Zawas repeated.

"Which is why we'll probably never know the Secret of First Time." He stole a glance at Serena, whose sad eyes told him she had concluded as much. "The existence of the Solar Bark implies the secret is not of this earth but at its intended destination, which from what I've gathered is somewhere beyond the constellation of Orion."

Serena's voice was scarcely stronger than a whisper. "So there's no way to stop the earth-crust displacement."

Conrad shook his head but fixed his eyes on hers. "Nothing I can come up with."

Zawas stepped up to Conrad and put his face within an inch of his. "You say this shrine is a starship, Doctor Yeats. You say there is no hope for the world. Then why didn't you take off?"

Conrad looked over Zawas's shoulder at Serena.

Serena could only shake her head in disbelief. "You're such a fool, Conrad."

A voice said, "Well, we finally agree on something, Sister."

Conrad turned around as Yeats emerged from behind a pillar in the rotunda, as grim as Conrad had ever seen him.

"Give me the obelisk, and the girl, Zawas," Yeats demanded. "And we'll be on our way."

Conrad, dumbfounded, stared at Yeats. "On our way where? You're just going to hop on a spaceship and go?"

"Damn straight I am."

Conrad realized that Yeats didn't necessarily care where he was going so long as he went somewhere. He was hellbent on completing the space mission he had been denied in his youth.

"Look, if we don't go, son, then we'll just perish with the rest of them," Yeats said.

"You can rationalize it all you want, but I'm not biting."

Zawas tightened his grip on the scepter and gave a cool nod to his men, who circled Yeats with their AK-47s.

"You destroyed much of my base and cost me many good men," Zawas said. "Now you insult my intelligence."

Conrad shifted his gaze back and forth between Yeats and Zawas, their eyes locked on each other.

"You were never interested in finding a weapon or disabling some alien booby trap, Yeats, were you?" Conrad said, incensed at Yeats's desertion. "And you weren't interested in helping me find my destiny. You pulled that Captain Ahab routine all these years because you knew this thing was down here."

"I suspected it, son," Yeats said. "Now we know. This is the happy ending we've been working for ever since I found you. You're going home."

Home? Conrad thought. It was the first time in years he had ever even considered that he had a real home anywhere, much less not of this Earth.

Zawas cut in, "Surely you don't expect me to let you take off with the Solar Bark, do you?"

"As a matter of fact, I do," Yeats said.

Yeats's left arm swung up, holding a small remote control. He looked at Zawas with the coldest pair of pale blue eyes Conrad had ever seen. "I go or we all go," Yeats said. "I've got enough C-4 in here to blow us all to First Time without any starship."

Zawas's eyes darkened. "You're bluffing."

"Oh?" Yeats flicked one of the buttons, and a stereophonic beeping filled the silo as a circle of red lights in the shadows began to blink. "Go ahead, take a closer look."

Conrad watched as Zawas walked over to the nearest blinking box, bent over, and froze. Slowly he straightened and returned to his men. "Let Doctor Serghetti go."

"And the scepter, Colonel. Give it to her."

Conrad watched Zawas hand her the Scepter of Osiris and nudge her toward Yeats. "I'm sorry, my flower," Zawas said.

Yeats immediately grabbed her and pulled her toward the rotunda at the base of the Solar Bark. "Come on, Conrad."

But Conrad didn't move. He looked at Yeats and Serena and said, "I think I've just figured out the way to stop the earth-crust displacement. But the answer is back at the star chamber. Not there." He was pointing at the Solar Bark.

A bewildered look crossed Yeats's face. "It's too late. Let's go."

"No. I'm staying." He looked at Serena. "But I need the scepter and Serena."

Yeats shook his head. "I'm sorry, son. We need the scepter to take off."

Conrad could feel the fury building inside. "And what the hell do you want Serena for?"

"An incentive for you to reconsider," Yeats said, dragging her away toward the Solar Bark. "You want her, then come get her."

Conrad, desperate to run after her, looked on as she shot a quick glance back at him, her eyes filled with uncertainty. Then she disappeared inside the giant starship.

A moment later the ground started to rumble as the launch sequence began. Zawas could only watch in furious admiration at his former teacher before shouting to his soldiers to evacuate the silo.

"What about you?" Conrad shouted to Zawas. "Where are you going?"

"For cover," Zawas said. "If this alleged disaster should strike the planet, we are in the safest place of all. We can find survivors and rule a new world. If nothing happens, we have captured an unlimited energy source and will rule the world anyway."

"What about me?" Conrad asked.

"You can go to hell, Doctor Yeats," Zawas told him as two Egyptians tied Conrad to a pillar near the Solar Bark base. "Either the prospect of your death will force your father to abort his plans, or you'll depart this life in a blaze of glory when this Solar Bark of yours lifts off and its fires consume you."

Conrad watched as Zawas led his men out of the silo, leaving him alone. He strained at the ties that bound his hands. And he burned with desperation as he watched the Solar Bark rumble to life and prepare to lift off with Serena and the obelisk.

Inside the Solar Bark, Serena found herself with Yeats on a circular platform surrounded by four magnificent golden columns of light. Each column throbbed with energy. Yeats, still holding the remote to the C-4 in one hand, set the scepter down with the other. Suddenly the platform began to take them up.

"Yeats, if we don't reset the star chamber the whole earth will shift," she said, her voice spiked with anger and desperation. "Billions will die. You can't just take off."

"It's futile to go back," he said dismissively. His gaze was locked on the chamber above them. "You heard Conrad. Whatever the Secret of First Time is, it sure as hell ain't on earth. The survival of the human race dictates that we launch."

She looked at him. He wore the expression of a cocky warrior, pleased with himself and sure that nobody could stop him. His jaw was set and his eyes glinted in the dim glow of four light-filled columns. It made her furious—his complete unconcern for people who were about to lose their lives.

She said, "How do you know we'll even get off the ground?"

"What you see all around you is some kind of heliogyro system," Yeats said. "Those massive columns are an array of four unbelievably long heliogyro blades, like a helicopter's but on a massive scale. As soon as we leave Earth's orbit on an escape trajectory into space, they'll fan out and unfurl the solar sail."

Clearly she was in Yeats's world now, and however crazy the former astronaut was, he was the native in the terrain and she was the alien.

"Once deployed," Yeats went on, "the sail will function like a highly reflective mirror. When photons hit the surface, they impart pressure on it, creating a force to push the sail. The bigger the sail, the greater the force. And by tilting the mirror in different directions, we can direct the force wherever we choose."

"Don't tell me you actually think you can fly this thing."

"Like Columbus sailed the *Pinta*," he said. "I'm sure all measurements, orbit determinations, equations of motion, and velocity corrections have been factored into the ship's navigation system."

She said nothing as the platform locked. Yeats shoved her with the tip of the obelisk down a long corridor that ended in a metallic door with strange carvings.

"Why would they build the ship like this?" she heard herself asking. She had to keep him talking, had to buy time so she could figure out a way to stop him.

"You'll have to ask them when we get there," Yeats said. "But I'm assuming this ship was built as a lifeboat and designed to travel long distances with minimal power. That's the beauty of this baby: it may be low thrust, but it has infinite exhaust velocity, since it uses no propellant. The solar sail is the perfect vehicle for interstellar travel."

"Except that it requires sunlight," Serena observed, "which we'll run out of as soon as we leave the solar system. Just like a sailboat on a windless ocean."

Yeats stopped at the door and said, "Gravity assist."

"Excuse me?"

"That's how we'll coast without light," he explained. He spoke so calmly and rationally it both frightened and infuriated her. "We'll fly around Jupiter close enough to use its gravity to boost ourselves into a faster trajectory toward the sun. Then we'll slingshot around the sun and pick up even more speed as we exit the solar system. At any rate, I'm sure this thing is packing an array of masers and lasers whose microwaves can generate huge accelerations and speeds in the sails."

"You seem to have convinced yourself, Yeats," she said. "How long will it take?"

Yeats paused. "At conventional speed, probably a year."

A year? Serena thought. "At that speed we wouldn't reach the next star for . . ."

"Anywhere between two hundred fifty to six thousand six hundred years."

Serena didn't even want to think how long it would be until they reached the target star. Or who would be there to greet them. "Any plans on staying alive in the meantime?"

"Yes."

Yeats stabbed the scepter into the wall and the door split open to reveal a chamber filled with cool mist. Serena stared inside and could make out what looked like an open coffin in the rear. The mold was of a shapely woman about Serena's size.

"Seems the builders thought of everything," Yeats said. "Welcome to your cryocrypt."

An alarm went off inside Serena's head as it dawned on her that Yeats expected her to lie inside that machine. She stiffened at the door and refused to go in. Then she felt a clammy hand on her neck. There was no way in hell she was stepping into that chamber.

"You first," she said, stomping the heel of her boot onto Yeats's toe and jabbing him in the stomach with her elbow.

He groaned and she spun around and kneed him in the groin and clasped her hands together to deliver a crashing blow to his hunched-over back. She rose to catch her breath, but then Yeats whipped his head up, nabbing her in the jaw and splitting her lip. She staggered back into the chamber as he straightened up. He lifted his head to reveal cold, dead eyes in the dim light. His arm came up pointing his gun at her.

"Say your bedtime prayers, Sister."

Yeats raised his boot and slammed it full force into her chest, driving her back into the crypt, which molded around her like clay. She felt a cold tingling inside her. It began in the small of her back, raced up her spine, and exploded throughout her entire body.

Suddenly everything began to go numb. She became very still, almost lifeless in the dark, but she could feel her heart pounding. Soon that started to fade. Then the crypt door shut and she felt nothing at all.

33
DAWN MINUS
TWENTY MINUTES

CONRAD, STILL LASHED TO THE COLUMN, could feel the walls of the silo throb as the powerful thrusters of the Solar Bark began to hum. The greasy air from inside the ship now seeped out and smothered Conrad. He could also feel it heating up. The sunken shrine's open roof revealed the sky had turned overcast. Then the silo doors parted wider and loose rocks and debris began to fall.

Conrad closed his eyes as the dust came down. Blinking them open, he gazed out over the cavernous launch bay. For a moment, with all the smoke and confusion, Conrad couldn't see the starship and feared she was gone. Then a curtain of smoke parted and he glimpsed the unreal image of the Solar Bark shimmering behind the smoke. He could also see an AK-47 lying on the ground, apparently dropped by one of Zawas's soldiers in the panic of their retreat. But the machine gun was more than ten yards away, useless to him in his present predicament.

The air started to taste smoky. His eyes began to

burn, his nose tingled in the grimy air. He struggled against the column, coughing on the smoke. With or without the Secret of First Time, he realized, the Scepter of Osiris was his only shot to reset the star chamber in P4 and stop the earth-crust displacement. And it was on board the starship. Somehow he had to break free and retrieve the scepter before the Solar Bark took off and fried him alive.

The thought of fire reminded him of the Zippo lighter Yeats had given him. He still had it in his breast pocket. If only he could figure out a way to get it into his hand, he could burn off the ropes. Conrad dropped his chin to his chest and pulled out his sunglasses with his teeth. He then slowly dug into his breast pocket with the glasses and attempted to lift the lighter. After a couple of minutes he gave up, his neck aching, but another jolt from the Solar Bark's engines drove him to give it one more try.

This time it worked. He was able to scoop the lighter into one of the glasses' lenses. Now with the glasses hanging from his mouth, the lighter balanced precariously, he decided to turn his head to the left and slip the extended goggle under the collar of his jacket and over his shoulder. If he could just reach the armpit of his sleeve . . .

The lighter slipped down his sleeve and with a few shakes landed in the palm of his hand. With some dexterity he flicked it on. The flame burned his hand and he cursed, almost dropping the lighter on the spot.

For a moment he froze, trying to figure out some way of burning the ropes off without inflicting third-degree burns on his wrists and hands. Finally, he concluded there was no way around it. He took a deep breath, clenched his teeth, and flicked the lighter. The flame stabbed his wrist as he worked on the ropes. Everything inside him wanted to drop the lighter but he forced himself to grip it tighter. Soon tears were streaming from his eyes. But he focused on the Solar Bark and the goal at hand.

The smell of his own charred flesh on the back of his hand—like burnt rubber—made him reel with nausea. Unable to bear it any longer, he felt the lighter slip from his fingers and heard it clank on the stone floor. The understanding sank in that he had lost his best chance for escape. Worse, he realized the smell of rubber had been the band of his wristwatch, which he had burned off.

Conrad groaned. With nothing left to lose, he attempted to pull his wrists apart. He felt the charred rope give a little before the sensation of it sliding across his wrists reached his brain and he shouted in agony.

One last time he pulled his hands apart, giving it all he had. His scorched, tender wrists strained at the ends of the rough ropes until finally the toasted strands began to shred, and suddenly his hands broke free.

Conrad lurched forward and stared at the rings around his trembling hands. He then tore two strips of cloth from his uniform and tied them around his wrists. He grabbed the AK-47 off the ground and ran wildly through the dust toward the Solar Bark.

He entered the rotunda and reached the outer door to the ship that he had found with Yeats earlier. It was closed tight, throbbing with energy that encompassed the entire giant obelisk. He placed his hand on the square pad.

The platform carrying Conrad emerged into the cool cryogenics level a minute later. Directly overhead he could see the hatch that led into the ship's command module. The circle of lights told him that Yeats was up there with the obelisk.

He looked to his left down the corridor that led to the Osiris chamber and to his right down the corridor that ended with the Isis chamber. He turned right.

At the end of the dark tunnel was an eerie blue light. As he approached the cryocrypt door, Conrad could see that it was closed and that the grooves carved into its metallic surface were glowing. In an instant he knew "Isis" was inside. Yeats had frozen Serena.

"Damn you, Yeats," he growled and struck the door with the butt of the AK-47.

He examined the square pad next to the door. He placed his hand on it and heard a high-pitched hum. The lights behind the grooves suddenly grew brighter, glowing with such intensity he had to shade his eyes and step back in the corridor. Then just as quickly the brightness faded to a dull glow, flickered like the last embers of a fire burning out, and finally went black.

Oh, God, Conrad thought. What have I done?

He struck the thick door, colder than ever, with his hands. He tried in vain to move it. But he knew it was futile. He gave up and let his body slide down the door to the floor when he felt it vibrate. The door was moving! He jumped to his feet and watched as the cryocrypt cracked open, an icy mist flowing out into the corridor. He didn't wait for it to clear before he plunged in to search for Serena.

She was in the crypt, her translucent skin almost blue when he grabbed her and carried her out over his shoulder into the corridor. He set her on the floor and began to massage her arms and legs. She was barely breathing.

Oh, God, he prayed under his breath. Don't let her die. "Come on, baby, come on," he repeated. "You can do it."

Slowly the color came back to her cheeks and her breathing became deeper and more rhythmic. When she opened her eyes, Conrad was shocked by their empty, lifeless quality.

"Serena, it's me, Conrad," he said. "Do you know where you are?"

She moaned. He brought his ears to her lips. "If you're Conrad Yeats, then this must be hell."

"Thank God." He breathed a huge sigh of relief. "You're OK."

She struggled to sit up and get her bearings. "Yeats?"

"Up in the capsule," he told her. "But he's going to come down before the launch to put himself into the Osiris cryocrypt. When he does, I'll be waiting for him."

"And me?"

"While he's with me, you go up into the capsule and get the scepter. Whatever happens to me, you've got to stop this ship from launching and get back to P4. Understood?"

She rubbed her temples. "So you really think we can stop the displacement?"

"I don't know, but we have to try," he said when the circle of lights above the central platform flashed.

"He's coming down," Conrad said. "I've got to take my position. You wait until he's well along the other corridor before you go up."

She nodded.

Conrad ran down the corridor toward the Osiris cryocrypt. By the time he got to the central shaft, the platform was on its way down with Yeats. Conrad ran through the mist into the open Osiris crypt and waited for Yeats.

Breathing hard, back against the wall, he felt something along his shoulder and turned to see the alien harness. The last thing he needed was to accidentally lock himself in the cryocrypt for the better part of eternity. Then he heard the chamber door open.

Conrad blinked his eyes and saw Yeats's figure in the mist. Conrad raised his AK-47 and stepped forward. "Mission aborted, Yeats."

"Is that you, son?" he said. "I'm impressed. I knew you'd join us."

"Give me the obelisk and Serena."

Conrad could see Yeats's eyes quickly take in the bandages on his wrists and note his unsteady grip on the AK-47. He couldn't believe he was pointing a gun at his father. Even if Yeats wasn't his biological father, and even if he hated him more often than not, Yeats was the only father Conrad had ever known.

"You're not going to use that on me, son."

"I'm not?"

"Kill me and you kill any chance of fulfilling your lifelong quest," Yeats said. "Only by lifting off in this new obelisk—the starship—and taking it to its intended journey will you ever discover your true origins."

"And what about my fellow man?"

"You're not a man, and it's too late to save Earth. The human race hasn't proved itself worthy, and the Secret of First Time can only be found at the end of the Solar Bark's celestial journey. You want to know it as much as I do. Hell, it's probably been programmed into your genetic code."

"Don't bet on it." Conrad pointed the AK-47 at him. "Remove your sidearm. Slowly. Two fingers."

Yeats unfastened the leather strap on his belt and carefully removed the Glock 9 mm pistol from its holster.

"On the floor."

Yeats placed the gun on the floor and lifted his hands up.

"Step back."

Yeats managed a smile as Conrad kicked the Glock away. "You and I are more alike than you care to admit."

"You're dreaming, Yeats." Conrad could tell Yeats was stalling for time, hoping to let the Solar Bark launch into its self-directed trajectory. But Conrad was waiting for Serena, hoping she'd hurry down with the Scepter of Osiris.

"I too am curious about a lot of things," Yeats said. "Not just the origins of human civilization but the universe itself. Ever wonder just why I wanted to go to Mars in the first place?"

"To plant your flag on the planet and be the first man to piss in red dirt."

"Comparative planetology, the scientists call it." Yeats seemed to grow more confident as he assessed that Conrad wasn't really going to shoot him. "They'd like to study the history of the solar system and the evolution of the planets by comparing evidence found on Earth, the Moon, and Mars. When we explore other worlds, we really explore ourselves and learn more accurately how we fit in."

Conrad said nothing, only watched in fascination as Yeats's worn face lit up with an almost spiritual inner light.

"For centuries we were guided by the ideas of the Egyptian astronomer Ptolemy, who taught that Earth was the center of everything," Yeats went on. "Then Galileo set us straight and we learned the sun is the local center about which we and the other planets revolve. But psychologically we still cling to the Ptolemaic view. Why not? As long as we stay here on Earth, we're the de facto center of everything that matters. You don't have to go to the Moon to understand this matter of watching Earth from afar. Space isn't about some technological achievement but about the human spirit and our contribution to universal purpose. Space is a metaphor for expansiveness, opportunity, and freedom."

Conrad raised his weapon again at Yeats's chest. "I must have missed the pancake breakfast with the Boy Scouts where you delivered that bullshit speech."

Yeats held his gaze, undeterred. "You want to know where this ends as much as I do."

A voice from behind Yeats said, "It ends right here, General."

Yeats spun around to see Serena, who was holding the

Scepter of Osiris in her hand. Conrad could see Yeats's back stiffen in rage.

Conrad said, "Now you know the cryocrypts work, Yeats. So you won't mind stepping into this one for the time being." Conrad gestured toward the Osiris chamber.

"I think you should drop your weapon, son."

Conrad did a double take. Yeats had slipped his hand behind his back and produced a small pistol. Conrad never saw it coming. Neither did Serena.

Yeats smiled. "Be prepared, the Boy Scouts say."

Serena said, "Shoot him, Conrad."

Conrad took a step forward, but Yeats dug the snubby barrel of the pistol into Serena's temple. "Stay right where you are."

Conrad took another step closer.

Yeats yanked Serena's long black hair until she cried out in pain. "Now or never, son."

Conrad took a third step.

"I said drop it!" Yeats yanked Serena's hair even harder. Conrad knew he could snap her neck in a second if he wanted to.

"Don't listen to him, Conrad," Serena strained to say. "You know he's going to kill you."

But all it took for Conrad was another look into her frightened eyes to convince him that he could take no chances. He lowered his weapon.

"Good boy," Yeats said. "Now drop it."

Conrad dropped his AK-47 on the floor of the fore-aft passageway, where it clanked. He could see tears roll down Serena's face as their eyes locked.

"You're hopeless, Conrad," she whispered.

34
DAWN MINUS
FIFTEEN MINUTES

CONRAD WATCHED YEATS pick up the AK-47 from the floor. They were only a few feet apart now and Conrad could see a manic look in Yeats's eyes that he hadn't detected from a distance. The man looked like an animal trapped in a snare, willing to bite his own leg off to get free.

"I knew you couldn't kill me," he said, keeping a tight hold on Serena, who struggled in his grip. "And I sure as hell don't want to kill you. But I will if I have to."

"Get your claws off her, Yeats."

"As soon as you're good and frozen, son. Maybe when we get to wherever we're going and thaw out, you'll come to your senses."

Conrad said, "You're going to have to kill me before you freeze me, Dad."

Conrad dove for the gun, and it exploded, the bullet plowing into his shoulder and spinning him to the floor. Dazed, he clutched his shoulder and saw blood pumping out between his fingers. He then looked up to see Yeats step forward to finish him off.

"I'll say hello to Osiris for you."

Yeats was about to knock him out with the butt of his gun when Conrad rolled back on his other shoulder and kicked Yeats in the chest with both feet.

The blow drove Yeats back into the pointed end of the Scepter of Osiris Serena was holding and she screamed. Yeats hit it with such force that he cried out in agony.

Dropping his gun, Yeats staggered for a few seconds before Conrad body slammed him into the cryogenic chamber. He shut the door as a blast of subzero mist blew out.

Suddenly all was quiet, save for the low hum of the ship's power surging through the consoles, walls, and floors.

Conrad struggled to stand in the shaft of light when Serena ran over and embraced him. Then she must have felt the warmth of his shoulder.

"You're a bloody mess," she told him.

"You just figured that out?"

She ripped off a strip of cloth from his sleeve and wrapped it around his upper arm and tied it tight, aware of his stare. "And now you've got everything you ever wanted. Maybe we really should walk off into the sunset together."

Conrad saw the bloody Scepter of Osiris on the floor. Picking up the scepter, Conrad realized she was right. All he had to do was let the Solar Bark take them to its preprogrammed destination and he'd finally discover the Secret of First Time.

He stared at her in disbelief. "Do you hear what you're saying?"

"I'm saying we don't know if this ECD is a global extinction event," she said. "Maybe humanity survives, or maybe we go the way of the dinosaur. But the only way to ensure the survival of our species is for you and me to proceed on course."

Conrad looked into her pleading eyes. She didn't want to go along for him, he realized, but rather for humanity. And she was willing to give up everything she held dear to do so.

"You'd have us condemn the world to hell?" he said.

"No, Conrad. We could create a new Eden on another world."

As he considered this insane idea, the ship started to rumble. He put a finger to her cheek and wiped away a tear. "You know we have to go back."

She knew, and she didn't resist as they silently rode the platform down to the base of the Solar Bark.

When they finally surfaced several hundred yards from the silo, the ground rumbled more violently than ever. He had barely pulled Serena out of the tunnel when a geyser of fire shot into the air, hurling them across the ground.

When he looked up he saw a dozen other geysers erupt in a ring around the silo as the Solar Bark lifted out of its crater and climbed into the sky. Conrad watched the starship carrying his father, dead or alive, disappear into the heavens.

"I hope to God you know what you're doing, Conrad." Serena ripped a torn lace from her boot and tied the burnt ends of her hair back. "Because that was the last flight off this rock."

35
DAWN MINUS TWO MINUTES

STANDING IN P4's STAR CHAMBER, tears flowing down her cheeks, Serena watched the geodesic ceiling spin. The noise of the grinding, whirling dome was deafening, and she couldn't hear what Conrad was saying. He was standing by the altar, motioning her to come over.

"Put the scepter in the stand," he shouted.

She looked at the Scepter of Osiris in her hands and once again read the inscription to herself: *Only he who stands before the Shining Ones in the time and place of the most worthy can remove the Scepter of Osiris without tearing Heaven and Earth apart.* Was there ever such a "most worthy" moment in human history? Or was the Hebrew prophet Isaiah right when he said human acts of righteousness were like "filthy rags" before the holiness of God?

"Yeats was right, Conrad," she said as she felt her heart sinking. "The Atlanteans were too advanced for our level of thinking. We can't win."

"I thought we agreed that the gods of Egypt were defeated once before," Conrad said. He started talking faster, his voice rising. "Well, just when was that?"

Serena paused. "During the Exodus, when Moses led the Israelites out of Egypt."

"Exactly," Conrad said. "It was one of those cosmic events that changes cultural history, like a colliding meteorite changes natural history. If no Exodus, then no epiphany at Sinai. And if no Sinai, then no Moses, Jesus Christ, or Mohammed. Osiris and Isis would reign supreme, pyramids would dot Manhattan's skyline, and we'd be drinking fermented barley water instead of cafe lattes."

Serena felt her blood pumping. Conrad was onto something.

"The question is," Conrad continued, eyes gleaming as if on the verge of a great discovery, "what was the straw that broke Pharaoh's back and led him to release the Israelites?"

"Passover," Serena said. "When the God of the Israelites struck down the firstborn of every Egyptian but 'passed over' the houses of those Israelite slaves who coated their doorposts with the blood of a lamb."

"OK," said Conrad. "Now if only there was a way to be more inclusive and extend the Passover to all races."

But there was, she suddenly realized, and blurted out, "The Lamb of God!"

"Jesus Christ, you're right!"

Conrad's hands flew as he began to reset the stars on the dome of the chamber to re-create the skies over Jerusalem.

Suddenly the entire chamber seemed to turn upside down. But it was an optical illusion, she realized, as the heavens of the Northern Hemisphere suddenly flipped places with the Southern Hemisphere.

"OK, we've got a place on earth," Conrad said. "We need a year."

That was harder, Serena thought. "Tradition says Jesus died when he was about thirty-three, which would place the crucifixion between A.D. 30 and 33."

"You've got to do better than that." Conrad looked impatient. "Give me a year."

Serena fought the panic inside. The Christian calendar was based on faulty calculations made by a sixth-century monk—Dionysius Exiguus. Latin for "Dennis the Short." Appropriate, considering that Dionysius's estimates for the date of Christ's birth fell short by several years. Church scholars now placed the Nativity no later than the year King Herod died—4 B.C.

"A.D. 29," she finally said. "Try A.D. 29."

Conrad adjusted the scepter in its altar, and the dome overhead spun around. The rumble was deafening. "I need a date," he shouted. "And I need it now."

Serena nodded. The Catholic Church celebrated Easter at a different time each spring. But the Eastern Orthodox Church kept the historical date with astronomical precision. The Council of Nicaea in A.D. 325 decreed Easter must be celebrated on the Sunday after the first full moon of the vernal equinox, but always after the Jewish Passover, in order to maintain the biblical sequence of events of the Crucifixion and Resurrection.

She shouted, "Friday after the first full moon of the vernal equinox."

"Friday?" There was doubt in his eyes. "Not Sunday?"

"Friday." She was firm. "The resurrection was a demonstration of victory over death. But the most noble time had to be when Jesus was dying on the cross for the sins of humanity and forgave his enemies."

"OK," he said. "I need the hour."

"Scripture says it was the ninth hour," she said.

He looked at her funny. "Huh?"

"Three o'clock."

Conrad nodded, made the final setting and stepped back. "Say a prayer, Sister Serghetti."

The geodesic dome spun round and locked into place, re-creating the skies over Jerusalem circa A.D. 29 at the ninth hour of daylight on the fifth day after the first full moon of the vernal equinox.

"But now a righteousness from heaven, apart from the law, is revealed," she prayed under her breath, repeating the words of St. Paul to the Romans.

A sharp jolt rocked the chamber and she jumped back as the floor split open and the altar containing the scepter dropped down a shaft and disappeared. Before she could peer over the ledge, the shaft closed up into a cartouche bearing the symbol of Osiris. And she could hear something like the peal of thunder rumble below.

Suddenly it was eerily quiet. Serena could hear someone sobbing. It sounded like a young girl. She felt a tear roll down her cheek and realized it was her. For some reason she felt clean inside, as if all her worries and fears and guilt had been washed away.

"You did it," she said, embracing Conrad. "Thank God."

"How about when we get out of here?" he said when a deep, disturbing rumble echoed all around, inside and out.

Serena grew very still. "What's happening, Conrad?"

"I think we're about to be buried under two miles of ice."

36
DAWN

ZAWAS AND HIS MEN were watching the Solar Bark disappear into the sky from their camp on the promontory of the Temple of the Water Bearer when the first big shock wave hit. Tents began to collapse, and Zawas panicked as he watched his only working Z-9A jet helicopter skid across the helipad to the ledge.

"Secure the chopper!" he shouted, and five Egyptians raced to tie it down.

No matter what may befall the rest of the world, Zawas told himself, no matter how many coastline cities should be swallowed up by the sea, there was no safer place on earth than where his team was established at that very moment. For should it take a day or a week, once the earth-crust displacement had run its violent course, the ground on which they were standing would be the center of the new world.

This is what he kept telling himself as his thoughts drifted to his extended family back in Cairo, most living in substandard "luxury" high-rise apartments that were bound to crumble in any major quake.

The air suddenly felt very warm, and the shocks grew more violent.

They were becoming so jarring, in fact, that he began to reconsider his strategy of encamping inside the Temple of the Water Bearer and wondered if an open area away from any monuments or shrines would be more prudent.

Zawas stepped inside his chamber off the promontory, found the Sonchis map on his desk, and rolled it up inside the nun's green thermos along with the American blueprints to the Solar Bark.

Another shock nearly threw Zawas from his chair. He gripped his desk to steady himself. But it too began to move. He screwed the outer shell of the thermos into place and threw it in his pack before the shouts of his men brought him outside. What he saw made him shrink back in terror.

The sky seemed to be falling.

Zawas grabbed a pair of binoculars and scanned the mountains of ice that formed a ring around the city. And then it hit him: the sky wasn't falling. Rather, it was the cliffs of ice surrounding the city that were falling.

An avalanche of ice from all sides was about to bury them all.

"Into the chopper!" Zawas shouted, waving his men in as he climbed inside the Z-9A and started the motor in a frantic bid to get airborne before impact. The blades started to move but then sputtered. The chopper was designed by the French but built under special license by the Chinese, who had supplied the Egyptians with several models. "Damn those infidels in Beijing!"

He tried to get the blades moving again while a dozen Egyptians piled inside. As the pilot took the controls, Zawas adjusted his binoculars to make a quick estimate of how much time they had until impact.

A wall of ice jumped into focus, and it was on course to slam the chopper and crumple them all into a bloody pulp of twisted metal and flesh. Zawas felt his heart stop beating as the foaming avalanche swept under the temple and began to rise toward the promontory. Then he could feel the chopper being lifted up toward the sky.

Inside P4's star chamber, Serena felt hot as she climbed up the southern shaft using the line Conrad had taken with him when he first surveyed the city. But when she looked back, Conrad was still in the chamber below, trying to pull himself up with one hand, the other dangling uselessly to the side in the bloody tourniquet. She could see water bubbling around his ankles and began to panic.

"Conrad!" she shouted.

She braced her boots against the sides of the shaft and stretched out her hand to grasp his right arm. She pulled with a grunt but felt his hand slip away and heard a splash.

"Use this," he shouted, waving what looked like a long scarlet bandanna. It was his tourniquet. He had untied it.

She wrapped one corner around her wrist and lowered her arm so Conrad could wrap the other around his wrist. She pulled so hard she could feel her back spasm in pain, and she cried out as she pulled harder until he finally climbed up in the shaft.

"Thanks," he said, breathing hard. "Now let's go."

Serena looked up the shaft at the square of blue sky. "Why bother?" she said, out of breath. "There's nothing out there. No radio, no way to signal anybody."

"It's our only shot," he said. "The subterranean geothermal vent is powering down. The last blast of heat it's giving off is probably melting everything around us, pumping the water through its hydraulic system. But the water is about to turn to ice. Everything's going to freeze."

Serena understood. "The girl in the ice. That's going to be us."

"Not if I can help it. Take this." He gave her the bloody tourniquet strip. "Use it like a flag. Now move! I'll be right behind you."

Reluctantly, she took the bloody rag and made her way up the shaft, aware of Conrad falling behind. Occasionally she'd call back and hear him reply, but each time the echo grew fainter.

Finally, she reached the square of the shaft, her fingers turning cold as they clawed the edge. The wind was howling, and the temperature was dropping just as suddenly as it had risen. She pulled herself up to look out and beheld a fantastic sight that took her breath away.

The entire bowl of ice surrounding the city was crumbling, the melting snow turning into a huge lake that was drowning the city a mile below. Already only the tops of the taller temples and obelisks were visible. And the waterline was rising against the pyramid below. It would be only minutes before it reached her.

"No, God, please," she said and looked back to Conrad.

But he was gone.

Filled with panic, she screamed, "Conrad!"

There was no answer.

She peered down the darkened shaft and saw something flicker. It was water, rising her way. And there was no sign of Conrad.

Conrad, unable to hold on any longer, slipped down the shaft into P4's star chamber, which was filled to the ceiling with water. Desperate for air, he clawed at the stone ceiling in the dark to find a shaft opening again. But all he felt was the water closing in on him.

Then a powerful suction from below grabbed his legs and pulled him down the pyramid's Great Gallery into some sort of pipe. Unable to hold his breath any longer, he let go and felt the water fill his lungs.

He was sinking into blackness when his body slammed against a stone grating. The water suddenly washed over him and receded down the drain.

Soaked and gasping for breath, he put his hands on the grating and pushed himself up. Then he ran wildly down the tunnel, trying to get his bearings, knowing he was totally lost. He was confused and more than a little worried about Serena. His body ached all over as he slogged through the water, which was ankle deep and getting deeper. Then he heard a rumble from behind.

He didn't need to turn around to know what was coming. He simply braced his body and took a deep breath.

A wall of water slammed into him and swept him down a smaller tunnel. He gulped in some water as he was sucked in, tumbling over and over beneath the current.

Conrad held on as long as he could but felt his consciousness slowly slipping away. Unable to cling to anything, he let go. A blackness overwhelmed him and he felt himself whooshing through a tunnel.

Suddenly he was pushed into daylight and thrown almost fifty feet into the air by a geyser of water blasting out of the drain. He landed with a heavy thud on the trembling ground, the wind and water knocked out of him.

Unable to move for a few minutes, he was shaken by the earth tremors and deafening rumble of the ice mountains tumbling down into the city valley.

A trickle of water ran past his ear, and he realized there was no place to hide: above or below ground, anything under an altitude of two miles from the subglacial surface was about to be deluged and frozen. With dread he recalled the people in the ice he had seen during the descent to P4 and decided he did not want to be one of them.

Somehow he managed to get on all fours and crawl through the rising water. Within a few paces he could feel the temperature dropping as the winds whipped. He shivered in the cold, damp air.

He slowed down for a second when he saw a body floating his way, bloated and blue. As it passed by, Conrad recognized the face of Colonel O'Dell from Ice Base Orion. The expression of horror on the corpse's face motivated Conrad to pick up his pace.

The water was up to his knees now, and the bowl of mountains around the city was beginning to collapse like a tin can under the tremendous pressure. His shoulder hurt more than ever, the stabs of pain unbearable. He applied more pressure with his other hand as he rose to his feet and staggered. Then he saw a flash of color through the water.

It was a smashed red Hagglunds, a relic from Ice Base Orion. It was useless for travel, but the forward cab might provide a cocoon of shelter and life support.

Suddenly the ground pitched violently and Conrad was thrown facedown. He looked up to see a fifty-foot wall of water and ice thundering down on him. His jaw dropped in surrender at the spectacle. There was simply no place to hide from such a force of nature, and he knew then it was time for him to die. But he thought of Serena and with one last push reached up to the door of the Hagglunds and twisted the black handle until the hatch opened.

Then the water came. First a few droplets on his head. Then a spray.

He hoisted himself inside and barely managed to snap the seat belt in place and shut the door before the wall slammed into the Hagglunds and it was lost in a cauldron of churning water and ice.

37
DAWN PLUS ONE HOUR

SERENA LOOKED OUT ACROSS the stormy skies from inside the mouth of the southern star shaft near the top of P4. Whiteout conditions threatened, the clouds over the ice deserts in the distance were heavy with snow, and bolts of lightning flashed on the distant horizon.

Then she heard a familiar whirring noise overhead and looked up in stunned disbelief to see a U.S. military Black Hawk helicopter drifting across the stormy sky. She waved frantically.

A rope ladder dropped down like something out of a dream, and she took a firm hold. She glanced back down the dark shaft and saw something shiny. She hesitated and looked closer. It was water, coming up like a geyser. She tugged the rope ladder and was lifted away as a spray of water shot into the air, barely missing the chopper.

An American airman grabbed her shoulders and dragged her into the Black Hawk. She could see from the faces of the crew that they were as shocked to see Mother Earth as she was to see them. Almost as shocked as they were to survey the ruins below. Their commanding officer introduced himself as Admiral Warren and shouted to the pilot over the roar of the helicopter and waters outside.

"Take us out!" Warren ordered.

"No," Serena said, her teeth chattering. "We have to find Conrad, Doctor Conrad Yeats. He's still down there."

Warren stared at her. "You mean General Griffin Yeats?"

"No, I mean his son."

Warren looked at the pilot who shook his head. "Believe me, no one's down there now."

The Black Hawk began to pull away.

"No!" Serena tried to climb in front and grab the controls. But four airmen restrained her and shoved her back against the medical supplies. She tried to get up, but all energy left her. Then the medic stabbed a needle in her arm.

"Calm down, Sister, you've been through a lot," Warren said as he wrapped a navy jacket around her shivering body. She felt dizzy and light-headed.

She brushed back wet strands of hair from her face and looked out the window. A whirlpool of water had nearly swallowed the city. Only the peak of P4 stabbed out from the murky deep. She had often imagined as a child what it must have been like when the Red Sea parted for the children of Israel to pass through and later came together again to drown all of Pharaoh's horses and chariots. Now the picture was all too clear.

She prayed to God that Conrad was safe but knew better. In her delirium, she could picture herself searching for him. Then, through the sheets of ice, Conrad would be spotted stumbling across the plain, miraculously having survived. He would emerge from the mist whiter than snow, his eyebrows and hair white, almost glowing, like he had come forth from the shiny veils of the holiest of shrines. The Americans would be forced to land the chopper. She would run to Conrad and embrace him. He would return with her to the awaiting chopper, his past buried behind him. They would hold each other tightly as snowflakes fell around them like stars.

But there was no Conrad, she realized bitterly. And God didn't always answer her prayers the way she liked. As the chopper lifted off and away, she looked down to see the flattened tip of P4 barely showing above the water. It was as if they were flying over the Southern Ocean now. Not a trace of the city below—or Conrad. It was all gone, swept clean as if it had never been there.

Warren started shouting something again. She couldn't pick up much of what he said under the whine of the blades and howl of the winds. Then she looked up to see him hanging out the open doorway. The Black Hawk swung toward whatever he was pointing at.

Serena was on her feet in an instant, clinging to Warren, peering out. There was a lone figure atop P4. The man who waved frantically was in a U.N. uniform.

"That's him!" she said with as much force as she could muster.

"Get lower!" Warren ordered the pilot, who was struggling against the wind gusts.

Serena grabbed Warren's binoculars as the Black Hawk started down. When they were no more than thirty feet away, she could see the man look up. With dismay she realized that the face she was looking at wasn't Conrad's at all. It belonged to one of the Egyptians, and his arm came up holding a machine gun.

"Admiral, pull back!" she said.

"We got him, don't worry," Warren said, and Serena looked back to see two marksmen with rifles trained on the man. "I want him alive."

Serena felt a pop of air brush past her ear and looked down to see a bullet catch the Egyptian in the leg and send him down with a splash.

Warren nodded approvingly. "Move in."

As soon as the chopper came in, however, the Egyptian rose from the water and started shooting wildly into the air.

Warren, standing in the open door, took a bullet in the throat and fell back against Serena, dead. She struggled to push his heavy body off her and called for help. But when she looked over her shoulder, she saw one of the Americans, also hit, falling backward. As he went down, his machine gun raked the cockpit with bullets. Serena heard the pilot cry out.

The Black Hawk lurched forward, and Serena grabbed at a strut for support. Then the chopper lifted violently, and she was thrown out through the open door. She felt herself falling through space. Then she splashed onto the top of P4.

She rolled onto her back and looked up. The Black Hawk bucked twenty or thirty feet up in the air, veered sharply to the left, and exploded in a great ball of fire. Burning debris scattered like shrapnel, destroying any hopes she had for escape.

Soaked to the bone and waist-deep in water, she stood

up and faced the wounded Egyptian. The lone remnant of Zawas's army, blood spurting from his leg, pointed his unsteady AK-47 at her.

She didn't bother to put her hands up as he approached her with a desperate expression on his face. Or was he looking at something over her shoulder?

She turned to see another military chopper sweep in, this one with U.N. markings. Its heavy machine guns exploded and bullets kicked up water along the P4 summit, hitting the Egyptian and driving him backward over the edge and into the water.

Serena looked up as the chopper circled overhead. A ladder was lowered for her. She grabbed the first rung and started climbing. When she reached the top a strong hand helped her in. She looked up to see the face of Colonel Zawas. In his right hand was an automatic pistol and it was pointed at her.

She was numb with shock as Zawas smiled, the wind blowing his cap off.

"You do not disappoint, Doctor Serghetti." He held up her green thermos. "Now that I have the Sonchis map there is nothing to stop me from returning one day to complete that which I've begun. History, as I've mentioned, is written by the victors."

Maybe, she thought, but a quick glance told her it was just Zawas and the pilot aboard. "Tell me, Colonel, did you twist the thermos shut clockwise or counterclockwise?"

"Clockwise." Zawas eyed her dubiously. "Why do you ask?"

She smiled and said, "Oh, nothing."

Zawas's confidence began to waver. He lowered his gun to untwist the thermos. As he did, Serena tried to kick the gun out of his hand. She missed the gun but hit his arm and the gun went off. The chopper veered up, throwing Zawas off balance, but not before he put two more bullets through the window in his efforts to kill her.

Serena looked at the pilot and saw that he had been hit. She jumped in front, shoved the man aside, and grabbed the controls. She looked over her shoulder in time to see an angry Zawas rise to his feet.

"Colonel!" she screamed. "Do you know how to fly a helicopter?"

Zawas frowned. "Of course, woman."

"So do I."

She banked sharply and watched Zawas tumble out the door. He dropped like a stone, his arms windmilling until he hit the surface of the churning water and disappeared.

She took a deep breath and steadied the chopper. A quick scan of the instruments told her she might, if she was lucky, have enough fuel to make it within radio range of McMurdo and land on more solid ice. But she couldn't make herself proceed without looking back. She scanned the ice below, fighting back the tears. The city was gone and her fuel gauges were dropping.

As she hovered in the gusty skies over the hardening ice, she prayed for the soul of Conrad Yeats. Then she turned the chopper in the direction of McMurdo Station on the Ross Ice Shelf and flew away.

38
DAWN: THE DAY AFTER

AT 0600 HOURS ZULU, Major General Lawrence Baylander, a hard-nosed New Zealander, led his UNA-COM weapons inspection convoy of Hagglunds around a fissure and crossed into the target zone.

The area had been wind-whipped, and any evidence of American nuclear testing would not be visual. Dosimeter readings, thermal scans, and seismic surveys would be necessary to detect any radiation, buried facilities, and the like. Even then they would have to drill for subglacial core samples, he thought. If only they had more time.

But Baylander had already pushed the search and rescue team too far, he realized, and supplies and thus time were running low. He had already concluded they'd have to abandon the tractors and fly back once air support arrived. Worst of all, international politics and funding being what they were, he knew there would be no returning to this wasteland. About the only thing he would get out of this frozen hell was the grim satisfaction that the U.N. would stick the Americans with the tab.

He could feel his opportunity to nail the Americans

slipping away. Exhausted and irritated, he was about to radio back to base to tell them that his team was ready to turn around when the convoy found the way blocked.

A red Hagglunds tractor, half protruding from the ice, had apparently sunk into a fissure, its wafer treads locked. It was still upright, slightly skewed. The forward cab was smashed.

Baylander swore and radioed the convoy to brake to a halt. Pausing just long enough to square up his custom-made polyplastic snowshoes, he decided to keep his engine running. He yanked his cab door open, jumped down, and started across the waist-deep snow in long, slow strides.

He surveyed the wreck grimly and circled it once. Something behind the cracked, fogged-up windshield caught his attention and he leaned over for a closer look. There was a figure inside, curled up in a fetal position. A frozen corpse. If it was an American, he had his proof. Baylander straightened and ran over to the cabin door.

He knew the handle would be useless, but he tried anyway. It was frozen solid. He then took his metal staff and smashed the side window and carefully crawled in.

The man was lying across the leather seats. Baylander turned him over. The pasty white face had once belonged to a relatively young, handsome man. For a long minute Baylander stared down at the ghostly apparition, then bent down to listen for shallow breathing. There was none.

Baylander proceeded to unbutton the corpse's coat to discover a UNACOM uniform underneath. Bloody hell, he thought. He must be one of ours, from the first team. He could find no identification.

He studied the body to determine a time of death. It must not have been too long, he decided, maybe twenty-four hours, because the corpse was only now turning a dull shade of blue. Remarkable, considering how long it had been there. The cabin must have provided enough of a shield from the elements to enable the inspector to have survived far longer than he expected. Baylander suspected the man's last hours were an unforgiving mix of semiconsciousness, delirium, and the slow shutdown of vital organs. It must have been an altogether unpleasant way to go.

Baylander removed his thick gloves and put two fingers on the carotid artery. To his astonishment he could detect the faintest rhythm of a pulse.

39
DAWN: DAY TWO

CONRAD YEATS AWOKE the next afternoon in a private room inside the main infirmary at McMurdo Station. He lay still for a long time, becoming slowly aware that his hands were swathed in bandages and one shoulder was in a sling. His head, meanwhile, pounded like a drum. He found a buzzer and pushed it with a bandaged hand, but the navy nurse who came told him to lie quietly.

So he lay and, piece by piece, recollected the events of the previous day until the middle of the morning. Along the way he drew a picture by gripping a pen between his bandaged hands. After that he dozed off again. When he woke, a woman was sitting by his bed. She smiled.

He stared at her. "Just like the hospital rooms in the old days—a bed and a sister," he said. He tried to smile, but it hurt. His voice was not much stronger than a whisper. "How long have you been here?"

"Only a few minutes," she said, her smile warming him.

But Conrad knew she was lying. He had awakened in the middle of the night and seen her sleeping in that chair. At the time he thought he was dreaming. "You're alive."

He reached for her hand, and she touched his bandage. "So are you, Conrad."

"And the rest of the world?"

"Everything's fine." A tear sparkled on her cheek. "Thanks to you."

"What about Yeats?"

She seemed to stiffen. "Past Pluto by now, I should imagine."

"You think what he said about me was crazy?" Conrad searched her eyes.

"No more than a lost city under the ice cap."

Conrad paused. "Does that mean yes it's crazy or no it's true?"

"There is no city, Conrad," she said. "The whole affair's over. Complete. Finished. Do you understand?"

"Not quite," he told her. "I've made one hell of a discovery, Serena. Look at this."

He showed her the rough sketch he had made of the Solar Bark.

Serena frowned. She looked so beautiful.

"Don't tell me I made that up, Serena," he said.

"No, you didn't, Conrad," she said. "I've seen it before. The original blueprints for the Washington Monument looked exactly like this about two hundred years ago, including the now-missing rotunda at the base."

Conrad stared at his drawing and realized that Serena was right. Suddenly he decided he would have to get back to Washington. There was his father's estate, naturally, and tying up loose ends. Maybe some of those loose ends included files from his father's office at DARPA.

A new journey was beginning to form inside Conrad's head, but apparently Serena didn't like what she was seeing.

"Listen, Conrad," she told him gently, almost seductively. "You're a great archaeologist, but a lousy amateur in every other way. You're going to publish nothing. You're going to produce nothing. For one thing, you've got nothing to produce. No Scepter of Osiris. Nothing. The only memento of our great escapade is the Sonchis map, and it's going back to Rome with me, where it belongs."

Conrad glanced over at his nightstand. "Where's my camera?"

"What camera?"

He grew still. "What about us?"

"There is no us. There can't be. Don't you see?" There was pain in her eyes. "You have no story to tell. You have no evidence. The city is gone. All that remains is your personal word. If you insist on talking, nobody will believe you except some of Zawas's friends in the Middle East, and they'll come after you. You were the victim of your own lunatic ambitions. You're lucky to be alive."

"And you?"

"I'm director of the Australian Antarctic Preservation Society and an adviser to the United Nations Antarctica Commission investigating breaches to the environmental protocols of the International Antarctic Treaty," she said.

"You're all that?"

"It was my team that found you in the ice," she went on. "Since you're the only eyewitness to alleged events, any information you can recall would be deeply appreciated. I'll include it in my report to the General Assembly."

"They picked you to write the report?" Conrad managed a weak laugh. Of course, he realized. Who else had the international standing or passion concerning the preservation of this great white virgin continent?

Serena stood up to leave. She looked down at him, eyes tender but her body stiff with resolve. "Oh, lucky man." She leaned over and kissed him on the cheek. "God's angels were watching over you."

"Please, don't leave." He really meant it. He was afraid he'd never see her again.

She turned, hand on the doorknob. "Take a word of advice from Mother Earth, Conrad." She spoke bravely, but he could tell she was fighting back tears. "Go back to the States, bang some more coeds, and stick to university lectures and cheap tourist haunts. Forget about everything you think you saw here. Forget about me."

"Like hell I will," he said as she closed the door.

He stared into space for what felt like an eternity, thinking about Serena. Then a nurse entered and the spell was broken. "There's a phone call for you," she said. "Oh, and the doctor said it's OK for you to drink coffee if you'd like. It took me forever to find that thermos you wanted."

"Sentimental value," he said as the nurse placed the green thermos on the nightstand. "It was kind of Doctor

Serghetti to keep it for me. I hope you replaced it as I requested."

"I packed her one just like it with your little gift inside," she said. "I'll come back and pour your coffee for you in a couple of minutes."

"Thanks," he said as she left.

He looked thoughtfully at the coffee thermos, then awkwardly picked up the phone with his mitts for hands.

It was Mercedes, his *Ancient Riddles of the Universe* producer in Los Angeles, laughing on the line. Everything about their last encounter in Nazca was forgiven and forgotten. "I just saw the wires on the Internet," she said. "What happened down there? Are you all right?"

Conrad cradled the phone on his good shoulder. Somehow he felt strangely content. "I'm fine, Mercedes."

"Awesome. When are you going to be mobile?"

The door was cracked open and Conrad could see a couple of U.S. Navy MPs posted outside. "Give me a couple of days. Why?"

"The sweeps are over and the networks are looking for filler. We've cooked up a special that's right up your alley. How does Luxor sound?"

Conrad sighed. "Been there, done that."

"Picture yourself standing among the ruins of a slave city," Mercedes said. "You're revealing to the world how the Exodus is true. We've even got a Nineteenth Dynasty Egyptian statuette of Ramses II to prove it. You'll get twice the usual fee. Just make sure you patch things up with the Egyptians. When can you start?"

Conrad thought. "Next month," he told her. "I have to stop over in Washington first."

"Awesome. By the way, this Antarctica thing. Is there a story?"

"No, Mercedes," said Conrad slowly. "No story."

the pope said. "This is a trust. This is a gift. And if I were you, I would accept it. For the one who follows me may not be as accommodating to you as I have been."

Serena understood, but hesitated. To officially declare herself a bride of Christ again would permanently keep her from Conrad and cut off any possibility of them ever consummating their relationship.

The pope seemed to sense her inner conflict. "You love Doctor Yeats," he said.

"Yes, I do," she replied, shocked to hear the words come out of her mouth.

"Then surely you must know he is in greater danger now than ever."

Serena nodded. Somehow she had sensed this ever since leaving Antarctica.

The pope said, "You will need all the resources of Heaven and Earth to protect him."

"Protect Conrad?" she said. "From what?"

"All in good time, Sister Serghetti, all in good time. Right now, we have more pressing duties."

What could be so much more pressing? she wondered when the pope showed her the front page of the *International Herald-Tribune*.

"Four nuns were raped and murdered in Sri Lanka by Hindu nationalists with ties to the government," he told her. "The crimes against Muslims have now turned against Christians once again. You must go there first thing in the morning and do what you do best, plead our case with the world watching."

"But it is the morning, Your Holiness."

"Yes, you must be tired. Rest a few hours."

Serena nodded. The concerns of the real world were too overwhelming, so overwhelming that they crowded out even thoughts of a lost civilization buried under the ice. There were larger battles to consider, she realized, battles against hate, poverty, and disease.

"I will go as you request," she told him, pausing for a moment. "First I will go to Sri Lanka to document the crimes. Then I will go to Washington, D.C., and press this issue with the American Congress before I take it up with the United Nations."

"Very well."

She let Benito drive her to her apartment overlooking the Piazza del Popolo. It was a plain room, nothing more than a bed and nightstand. But she felt better back in her own world, the one in which she first took her vows.

Next to the French doors that framed a pale moon was a crucifix on the wall. She knelt before the crucifix in the early morning light. As she looked up at the figure of Christ, she confessed to God her arrogance in thinking that she knew more about suffering and loss than he did, and she thanked him for his provision for humanity's sin in Jesus.

Then she stepped out onto the balcony and looked across the piazza at the Egyptian obelisk brought to Rome by Augustus two thousand years ago.

The monument reminded her of another obelisk, one buried in a pyramid under two miles of ice in Antarctica. And she wondered: was it really Christ's redeeming work on the cross that broke the curse of the ancient "sons of God" and saved the world? Or was it the selfless act of a godless man like Conrad, who sacrificed his life's obsession and returned the obelisk to the star chamber? In the end, she concluded that the latter could not have happened without the former.

As she listened to the cheerful sounds of traffic in a city that never slept, she reached into her pocket and removed the lock of hair she had cut from his head. In time, if she could ever let it leave her grasp, it would be analyzed.

For now she simply prayed for the immortal soul of Conrad Yeats, whoever he was, and for the forgiveness of her own, knowing in her heart of hearts that, one way or another, they would meet again.